CW01523200

THE WIFE COACH

A NOVEL

MELISSA HILL

Fully revised and updated edition, 2022.
Originally published as 'All Because of You' by Random House, UK.
© Little Blue Books, 2022.

The right of Melissa Hill to be identified as the Author of the Work has
been asserted by her in accordance with the Copyright, Designs and
Patents Act 1988.

All rights reserved. No part of this publication may be reproduced, stored
in a retrieval system, or transmitted, in any form or by any means without
the prior written permission of the author. You must not circulate this book
in any format.

All characters in this publication are fictitious and any resemblance to real
persons, living or dead is purely coincidental.

NOTE

This book was written, produced and edited in the UK, where some spelling, grammar and word usage will vary from US English.

PROLOGUE

So this was how real love felt, she thought, her body humming with joy as she lay back and closed her eyes. This was what she'd waited all this time for.

He was what she'd waited for.

And it was just as wonderful as she'd imagined.

She turned in the darkness and watched him sleeping peacefully alongside her – watched the way his long eyelashes looked strangely feminine against such a masculine face. He was beautiful, she mused, gently stroking his cheek.

And after tonight, he was hers at last.

She still couldn't believe that it had happened, that he'd conceded that she was the one for him.

OK, so he hadn't uttered those exact words, but he'd said them in other ways... She sighed as she recalled the softness of his skin against hers.

But what would happen to them now? Her initial euphoria was slowly being replaced by creeping trepidation to say nothing of gnawing guilt. There would be problems to overcome certainly and people might get hurt, but this was meant to be, wasn't it? *They* were meant to be.

And that was all that mattered. They couldn't help how they felt about one another. And even though it was supposed to be wrong, it had all felt so right. Yes there was some stuff to sort out, but whatever came next they'd face that together.

Just then, the sleeping figure beside her stirred and opened his eyes.

"Hey there," she smiled, leaning forward to kiss him. "You nodded off."

Although she had dozed a little herself, there had been no question of her falling asleep – not after such an amazing night and certainly not here. There was way too much to think about.

But instead of returning her affection, he quickly sat up and stared wildly around as if trying to remember where he was.

"What's going on? What are you ...?" Running a hand through his hair, he turned to look at her, taking in her (and his own) still-dishevelled state. "Oh hell."

This was inevitable, she told herself calmly. It was only natural he'd be somewhat taken aback. After all, she'd already spent time thinking about the implications while he'd slept things off.

But catching sight of his expression, her heart sank. It wasn't just disorientation she realised, gathering her clothing protectively around her – he was already having second thoughts.

Oh no, please don't. Please don't ruin this ...

"What is it?" she asked, longing to touch him, but sensing that she shouldn't.

"What is it?" he repeated, his voice shaking. "What do you think? We didn't ... we weren't careful. How could we have been so stupid?"

She gulped. She was aware of that too and cognisant of how crazy they'd been in continuing regardless. But she'd been dizzy – not just on alcohol – but on emotion too, so at the time everything else just seemed unimportant.

He was different now - jumpy, irritable even.

"It'll be OK - honestly," she soothed, trying to convince herself as much as he.

"Even so ..." His tone was now considerably calmer and gentler - more like the real him. "I'm sure we both know that all of this was a mistake – a stupid mistake."

She didn't know how she found the strength to nod, never mind speak. "A ... mistake?"

"Of course you know I care for you, but this should never have happened. We ... I really should have known better." Then he stood up and ran a hand through his dark hair. "You have to know that I don't make a habit of this sort of thing, I've never ... well, we were both reckless and if anyone were to find out – "

"It's OK," she told him quietly. "No one will find out."

Relief crossed his face and he reached across and pecked her chastely on the cheek, while her heart broke a little. How could he be like this? So cold and distant - utterly different from before.

"Thank you." He turned away and began gathering his things. "I appreciate that. And please don't think badly of me. Like I said, I don't make a habit of this and the last thing I'd want is to ..."

"It's fine." She tried not to let her disappointment - not to mention utter humiliation - show.

How could he shift so suddenly from the wonderful guy she knew to this ... aloof and detached one?

"Hey I'm sorry if I sounded a bit ... off there," he added, as if reading her thoughts. "This was great – it's just ... you know," he shrugged, "obviously it shouldn't have happened – and especially not like this. But please don't think badly of me. *You're* great and the last thing I want to do is hurt you."

"You haven't," she said trying now to harden her heart and pretend that she wasn't really hearing this. "You're right – it should never have happened and I'm as much to blame as you." She shook her head. "And I feel guilty too." She did feel some guilt, but her overpowering emotion right then was regret.

Regret that the perfect night with whom she'd thought was the perfect man, had turned out like this.

ONE

"Before you ask, no, I haven't."

"You haven't what?"

"I haven't lost any weight since the last time I was here." The stance was resistant - almost hostile - Tara noted. "I know I should have but – "

"Mary wasn't achieving fitness your primary goal the last time you were here?"

"Well, yes but ... I haven't done it," she replied quickly. "I know I should join a gym or something but ..."

Lots of 'buts' and 'shoulds' in this conversation...

"You spoke about joining a gym last time we met, didn't you?" Tara said, trying to keep her tone non-judgmental.

"I really didn't have the time," Mary replied defensively.

She immediately changed tack. "OK, besides the gym, what other everyday things could you do to increase your fitness levels. Simple things that don't take up too much time."

Mary shrugged. "I suppose I could use the stairs at work instead of the lift."

"Good." Tara nodded approvingly. "What else?"

"Em . . . I could walk to the corner shop when I need milk or a newspaper instead of taking the car?"

"Very good. Any other forms of exercise that you used to like doing, or would possibly do if you had more time?"

After a beat her client replied, "I suppose I like swimming. I was in the pool every day during our last holiday in Spain so I should do it at home too. That's a form of exercise, isn't it?"

Mary's use of the expression 'should' yet again put her on alert. She wouldn't get results if she had to force herself to achieve them, and it was up to Tara to ensure she didn't frame it that way. "OK, what would you need to do to enjoy swimming at home here in Ireland?" she asked her, using a slight inflection on 'enjoy'.

"I'm not sure really."

"Perhaps you could arrange to go with a friend, or a work colleague, even?"

Mary didn't look too thrilled about the prospect.

Tara put down her pen and looked her client directly in the eye. "Mary, on a scale of one to ten - ten being fully committed to becoming fitter - where are you?"

The other woman sighed and looked away. "About five or six."

Tara's tone immediately became firmer. "Then, do *right now*, what you need to take your commitment to preventing heart disease to ten."

Mary looked up, a little taken aback at this. She thought

for a moment before answering. "Well, now that you mention the reason I'm doing this, it's ten, definitely ten."

"So on a scale of one to ten, how committed are you to becoming healthy?"

"Definitely ten."

"So, if your commitment to becoming healthy is ten, what is your commitment to taking the stairs instead of the lift? Or walking instead of driving to the shop?"

"Ten." Mary was speaking with much more conviction now, exactly the response that Tara wanted.

"Great," she enthused, before asking casually, "And on the subject of swimming, how committed are you?"

Mary took a deep breath. "I suppose about eight or nine."

"And how are you going to ensure that you enjoy swimming here instead of just on holiday?"

"Well, I've always thought I might like to try an aqua-aerobics class or something like that."

"Why aqua-aerobics?"

"My friend Sinéad goes, and she enjoys it. I suppose I could go along with her."

"Would going with Sinéad help you keep to your commitment to increasing your fitness levels?"

Mary nodded, now at last getting the idea. "Yes, it would."

"So on a scale of one to ten, how committed are you to joining Sinéad at aqua-aerobics class?"

"Ten," Mary replied proudly.

"Are you sure?"

"Yes."

"And what do you need to do today to ensure that you attend the next class?"

"I need to call Sinéad and arrange it."

"What time will you call?"

"Well, she gets back from the school run around four."

"So you're committed to ringing Sinéad this afternoon between four and five o'clock to arrange the aqua-aerobics class, yes?"

"Definitely yes."

"Great. I look forward to hearing all about it at our next session." Tara was feeling a little drained by the repetitive (and rather patronising) process of getting her client committed to attaining fitness. But she'd achieved it (for the moment at least) and that after all, was what any life coach worth her salt wanted.

Mary was a good three stone overweight and if she wasn't careful, heading toward chronic obesity. Having tried every fad diet under the sun she'd eventually sought out Tara's help.

From the outset, Tara was always careful to distinguish between 'becoming healthy' which had positive connotations, and 'losing weight' which had negative ones and (as every woman who'd ever tried to lose a few pounds knew) naturally fostered mental resistance. The only way her clients could achieve their goals was to feel that responsibility for success was within themselves.

So today, at least she'd helped get Mary back on track.

Her client stood and picked up her jacket. "I'll see you when you get back, then. Enjoy your holiday." Then she added, winking, "I'd say it'll be relief to get away from us whingers for a while."

"Don't be silly, I love my job," Tara replied good-humouredly as she saw Mary out the door of her office. "Like I told you that very first day, I'm in show business and —"

"I know," Mary repeated, grinning, "you *show* people how to achieve the life they want."

Tara waved goodbye to her final appointment for the evening, then closed the door of her office and went into her home.

Although 'office' was a bit of an overstatement given it was actually the converted front room of her house (yet another overstatement as the place was rented – there wasn't a hope of her and Glenn being able to afford exorbitant Dublin rates).

But the room was quiet, restful and its homely qualities seemed to put clients at ease. People often mentioned that they felt as though they'd just popped over to a friend's house for a cup of tea and a chat, which was exactly the cosy atmosphere Tara had been aiming for, rather than the stuffy and sometimes overwhelming surroundings often associated with counselling or therapy.

Unlike psychology or psychiatry, coaching helped with issues of self-esteem and inability to achieve desired goals. And these days it seemed there was no shortage of dissatisfied individuals seeking assistance in finding what they really wanted out of life. Plus a burgeoning succession of singletons or not-so-happy couples wanting to avail of relationship advice too.

These days, the dating element of the consultancy was in so much demand that new clients could be waiting up weeks for an appointment.

After spending three solid years building the business to such a level (with darling Glenn supporting her from the sidelines) she felt that this year they were justified in taking a well-earned break. And were heading off for a ten-night vacation in Sharm El Sheikh.

"Egypt, though?" Glenn moaned when Tara had initially announced she'd booked their first trip abroad in years. "Does this mean you'll be dragging me around creepy mummies and ancient tombs?"

"Maybe, but it also means that we'll be sunning ourselves under blue skies and in thirty-five-degree sun," Tara had explained. And when she'd pointed out the glorious five-star hotel she'd chosen, there hadn't been another word out of him.

They both really needed this holiday. Glenn had been working like a demon too; in fact, he'd had to beg for the time off himself.

Having changed out of the formal skirt and blouse she wore for seeing clients into more comfortable sweats, Tara went back downstairs and into the kitchen.

She found Glenn sitting at the counter eating takeaway pizza and looking so utterly handsome that her heart skipped a beat. Jet-black hair, liquid brown eyes and naturally sallow skin, he was the kind of guy that always turned heads and not for the first time, she couldn't quite get her head around the fact that he was actually hers.

"I thought you were making dinner?" she said, referring acidly to the pizza. Although she loved it, she knew it wouldn't do her bikini-body any good to be munching on cheese and pepperoni stodge.

"I did – well, Four Star Pizza did," he replied, shrugging. "I didn't have time to make anything else. I'm due at work in an hour." Glenn had recently begun working overtime in the run up to their holiday.

She looked at the clock. It was almost six and she'd promised her mum she'd be there by seven. Blast it – she didn't really have time to make anything else either – the Friday evening traffic was bound to be crazy.

"Just don't make a habit of it, OK?" she said, picking up a slice of pizza and taking a huge satisfying bite. "Otherwise, we'll both end up looking like the Michelin Man."

"No worries. From now on, I solemnly swear to make the boring chicken and vegetable stuff we usually have."

"It's not boring, Glenn, it's *healthy* and you could do with keeping an eye on what you eat now and again," she said, conscious that she was still in coaching mode. "That Red Bull rubbish you drink is not good for you either. It's full of caffeine."

"Tools of the trade," he replied, mouth open as he ate and she elbowed him.

"Were you brought up or dragged up?" Tara teased. His job as a Systems Analyst necessitated working long hours in front of a screen, so he relied on caffeine to keep him alert.

"You finished for the day then?" he asked, eyeing her casual clothes.

"Finished for two long weeks you mean," she replied with a self-satisfied sigh. "I can't wait for this break, I really can't. A blissful fortnight of sunshine."

"Hmm, it remains to be seen how blissful it'll be." He was still convinced he'd be roped into discovering the more 'cultural' side of Egypt. "Knowing you, we mightn't even get a chance to relax."

"Believe me, we'll be doing lots of relaxing. And I'm determined to make the most of being off-duty too. But speaking of duty," she looked up again at the clock, "I'd better get a move on. I told Mum I'd be there by seven." She grabbed a napkin and began to wipe her sticky fingers.

"Oh, I forgot you were heading home for the night," Glenn said, scooping up another slice. "Say hi to them all for me."

"I will." Then catching sight of a pile of recycling by the back door, she sighed. "Damn. I meant to drop all that off to the centre today," she said, eyeing the tidily bound newspapers, crushed aluminium cans and washed glass bottles. "I'll hardly have time to do it now and the stuff is really piling up."

"I'll look after it. Although I still can't understand why you don't just throw the whole lot in the wheelie bin and be done with it."

Tara fixed him with a look. "Because unlike you, I want to do all I can to help the environment – while we're here it's the very least we can do and – "

"I know, I know," he interjected wearily, having heard the same argument many times before. "It's the least we can do and future generations will thank us for it. And how will they do that incidentally? Send us a postcard or something?"

When she didn't seem to find this funny, he raised his hands in the air in a gesture of defeat. "OK, OK, I said I'd do it, didn't I? Anything to make you happy."

"Anything to stop me nagging you maybe," Tara said

with a grin. "And you might as well get rid of that pizza box while you're at it – don't forget to clean it off first though."

Leaving him in peace, she went to check her appearance in the hallway mirror and wiped a very obvious splodge of tomato sauce from her face. Then quickly applied a coat of lipstick before running a brush through her fair hair.

Going back into the kitchen she gave Glenn – who had another huge slice of pizza in his mouth mid-bite – a quick kiss on the cheek before picking up her stuff. "See you tomorrow night, sweetheart – don't work too hard."

"I won't ... oh and let me know what the gang think of the car," he shouted to her retreating back. "I bet that'll get a reaction."

Tara grimaced as she closed the front door behind her. She'd forgotten that her parents hadn't yet seen the new car.

Well, it would get a reaction all right, she thought as she reversed out of the driveway and drove off in the direction of her hometown, though hardly the one that Glenn anticipated.

TWO

She smiled to herself as she drove along the dual carriage-way, enjoying the feel of the wind on her face.

Despite the late hour, the sun was still shining, the sky was blue; everything was so perfect, you'd think whoever was in charge of the weather had given her this fabulous evening on purpose.

Tara always looked forward to returning home to Lake-view, the small, picturesque tourist village some twenty miles outside of Dublin, and again she wondered if she and Glenn should think seriously about moving there permanently.

But he loved living in Dublin and with the majority of her clientele to be found in the capital, it wouldn't be practical just yet. But certainly something to think about for the future.

Approaching a set of traffic lights on red further down the road, Tara eased off on the accelerator. Typical – once you got stopped at the first set, you got stopped at them all she groaned, tapping her nails against the steering wheel impatiently. Then vaguely sensing she was being watched, she looked to her left and spotted the driver of the car alongside flash her an appreciative smile.

She supposed she should be used to the attention by now, the sporty Renault soft-top turning heads wherever they went – much to Glenn's delight – but Tara always felt like such a poser in this thing. Why on earth she had let him talk her into buying it she'd never know.

She eventually spied the turn-off for her parent's place, situated in a small mews not far from Main Street and made her way tentatively along the road, hoping no one she knew would see her driving this pretentious car.

It was bad enough that her career choice was something her mother couldn't quite get to grips with.

"Surely people don't need to be told by you how to live their lives?" Isobel commented, when Tara had first set up the consultancy. She had long since given up trying to convince her mother that there were lots of people who needed direction in their lives, or needed somebody objective to help them get to grips with things like time management, relationship issues and – more often than not – boost their self-confidence.

"It's perfect for you!" her best friend Liz had enthused, when Tara originally broached the idea. "You have natural empathy and a terrific ability to see things objectively – not to mention a lot of common sense about things – well, your love life aside," she added sardonically.

Tara ignored the jibe. For as long as she'd known her friend, Liz had wanted marriage and babies and happy families. While she on the other hand, had no interest whatsoever in marriage, especially when she and Glenn had always been perfectly happy just the two of them.

While she spent most of her time trying to help people decide what it was they wanted from life and how to get it, despite what Liz thought, she herself didn't have that problem.

Reaching her parent's house, Tara rang the doorbell and cast a nostalgic glance around her dad's well-tended garden. Her parents had lived in the same housing estate since she was born. Thinking of her and Glenn's rented place in Dublin and their polite but rather detached neighbours, she felt a brief nostalgia.

Most of the neighbouring families had lived here just as long as her parents and knew each other well. It was nice to know that there was someone you could trust with a set of spare keys, or someone to call in to for a chat whenever you felt a bit lonely.

Tara had nobody like that in Dublin now, not since Liz had moved here with her husband Eric (who was a childhood friend of Tara's, and also from here) and their young son. And single-handedly running a one-to-one life-coaching consultancy wasn't exactly conducive to gossipy chats.

Now, Tara smiled warmly when her mother opened the door.

"I thought you'd be here earlier," Isobel grunted by way of greeting, her face impassive as she regarded her eldest daughter. "Too busy telling people how to live their lives, I suppose."

"Hi, Mum." Ignoring the jibe, she stepped forward and

gave her mother an enthusiastic hug. "I thought I'd be earlier too, but the traffic was heavy."

"Is Glenn not with you?" her mother asked, looking behind Tara and then her eyes widened as her gaze rested on the car. "Is that ... *thing* yours?"

She shrugged. "Yep. Glenn's been on about getting one for ages. As long as it's got four wheels and a steering wheel, I couldn't care less."

"I see. A bit ... fancy, isn't it?"

"It's just a car, Mum. And no, Glenn's not with me. He had to work extra hours to get time off for the holiday."

"Right. Well, it's probably just as well he isn't," Isobel replied cryptically as she closed the door behind them but Tara hardly heard her.

"The garden looks great – and I can't believe how much the clematis has spread since last year ..." She rambled happily on through the hallway and out back to the kitchen. Then she stopped short.

Her younger sister Emma was sitting at the kitchen table alongside their dad, her face solemn and mournful. And instantly Tara knew that something was up.

A few days back, Isobel had briefly mentioned something over the phone about Emma being a bit off form.

"What's wrong with her?" Tara had asked before adding silently – *this time.*

"Ah, she's very down in the dumps," Isobel replied. "She's been going around with a face on her like a wet week."

Emma was three years younger and, in more ways than one, the baby of the family. Probably got a bee in her bonnet over some guy she was seeing, and had come home for attention and sympathy.

Which of course, she'd get from Isobel in spades. Emma was always experiencing some kind of drama and if it wasn't trouble with a man, or one of her friends, it was trouble with work.

"Hey sis – how are things?"

"Hi," Emma responded with one of her trademark mournful looks – the one that implied the world was conspiring against her.

"Maybe you could use your life-coaching skills on your sister," her mother said, her voice tinged with annoyance. "After what she's just told us, she certainly needs them."

"What do you mean?" Tara looked curiously at Emma.

"I'm three months pregnant," her sister replied in a small voice.

Yikes.

"I told them just before you arrived." Emma glanced away, refusing to look any of them in the eye.

"But ... how?" Tara replied in bewilderment. "I mean ... I didn't know you were seeing anyone or – "

"Neither did we," her mother interjected, her voice laden with disapproval.

"I'm not ... I wasn't seeing anyone," Emma confirmed quietly. "It was ... an accident."

"An accident? You mean a one-night stand?" Tara persisted, while her dad, Bill looked away.

"Er, I'd better go back out to the garden." Feeling awkward with the conversation and the direction it was taking, he stood up. "I'll be back in later," he told Isobel who remained stony-faced as he went out and closed the door behind him.

Emma nodded, her huge blue eyes filling with tears.

"Oh, Emma ..." Her heart instantly going out to her sister, Tara took a seat alongside her at the table.

"I know I should have been more careful, and I didn't mean for it to happen," her sister said, her eyes shining with tears. "Believe me, it was the last thing I expected – "

This was awful. Though in her thirties at least Emma was old enough to cope.

"So, have you told the father?"

She shook her head vehemently. "No, and I'm not planning to."

"What? What do mean you're not planning to tell him?" Isobel's eyes flashed with annoyance. "Why *wouldn't* you tell him?"

This was a shock for every parent, but perhaps even more for their mother. Coming from a small community like this, Isobel's initial concern would be for what the neighbours might say.

"It's complicated, Mum," Emma replied, her face going even paler and Tara wondered why she looked so uncomfortable.

"Complicated? What could be complicated about it? Call me old-fashioned but the two of you were there, so the two of you should be responsible. Or is it that you don't even know who he is?"

Tara sighed inwardly. Isobel could be unnecessarily vindictive when upset. Though not usually where Emma was concerned.

"It'll be OK," Tara interjected softly, hoping to diffuse the situation. "I'm sure everything will be OK."

"It certainly *will* be," Isobel remarked, her tone brooking no nonsense. "As long as the lad in question whoever he is, admits his responsibility and stands by you."

"That's not going to happen, Mum," Emma stated, her chin lifting in determination. "The father will have nothing to do with it."

"Now, it's like this –" Isobel warned.

"Mum, like I said before, it's complicated," Emma's voice was raised. "I didn't want this to happen and I certainly don't need you making me feel any worse than I do already, OK?"

For a little while, the three sat in the sun-filled kitchen, each lost in her own thoughts; Tara deciding that you didn't need to be a life coach to figure out that something was very wrong here and that Emma wasn't giving them the entire picture.

Granted, if she didn't know the guy that well, fair enough, but didn't she realise how difficult this was going to be without help, financial or otherwise?

"You're certain you don't want to tell him?" Tara asked gently. "It'll be tough bringing up a child on your own, you know and – "

"I'm sure," Emma replied firmly, looking her straight in the eye. "I don't want to tell him and before you ask, I'm not going to tell you either. This is all my own fault – I did something stupid and now I'm paying the price."

THREE

Liz McGrath had just put her eighteen-month-old son down for a nap when she heard the familiar cacophony of agitated barks signalling the arrival of her latest houseguest.

She ran her fingers through her cropped dark hair and briefly wiped the front of her top. Dried strawberry yoghurt on a blue cotton T-shirt was not a good look, and while she'd normally never greet a customer looking so bedraggled, today she'd had no time to change.

Still this particular guest wouldn't care less, she thought, smiling. In fact, there was a really good chance that he'd be thrilled to see her covered in goo – tasty, slimy goo that he would only be too delighted to lick off.

Bruno was like that.

"Hello!" Liz waved a greeting at the woman coming through her front gateway and her heart lifted at the sight of one of her favourite customers, who at that very moment was straining on his leash excitedly. "Hey Bruno," She bent down and tickled him behind the ears and the German Shepherd responded by licking her chin enthusiastically.

"Will you stop that?" His owner, a stern woman in her early fifties quickly jerked him back.

Liz had been looking after Bruno since he was a three-month-old puppy, yet she'd never quite been able to take to Jill Walsh (unlike her skittish, adorable pet who in fairness was extremely well-cared for).

Still, in this business, it didn't matter what you thought of the owners – the most important thing was what they in turn thought of *you*. And with previous 'guests' returning on a regular basis since she'd first opened her kennels business six months back, Liz was very well liked amongst the cat and dog owners in the region. In fact, most of her customers were not from the village but the bigger town nearby.

"Oh he's grand, Mrs Walsh aren't you, Bruno?" Liz stood and wiped her hands on her jeans, before taking the leash as was their routine. Some dog owners liked to see their pets settled in their accommodation before leaving, whereas others like Jill preferred to just drop and go.

"I'll be back on the twenty-fifth," she told Liz, her tone businesslike. "But I'll give you a call before I come to collect him."

"That's no problem – one of us will be here anyway."

They had been living here almost a year now and, although she was a Dublin girl by birth, Liz was loving it, especially since the move out of the city had given her the freedom (and space) to do so.

But what she was enjoying most was finally having a family of her own. Growing up, she had always been shunted from family to family, her own parents having died when she was twelve years old.

While she adored her brothers, and now as an adult could truly appreciate the sacrifice their respective wives had made in taking her in, all the chopping and changing meant that Liz had always been on the periphery of their families, and had never truly been part of any of them.

So for as long as she could remember, it had always been her dream to have a family and home that she could call her own. Now here, with Eric, baby Toby and their lovely (albeit still-dilapidated) home, complete with dogs Ben and Jerry, the dream had finally come true.

Course the best thing about the business meant that Liz could be a working mum with the all the benefits of a stay-at-home one too. It had taken a while to get into a routine, and was getting trickier as Toby got older and was starting to walk a little, but so far it was working out OK.

It would be even better if maybe Eric could find work in the village instead of having to commute to and from Dublin, but she was sure that would happen in time.

Not long after she'd settled Bruno into his lodgings, Liz had another visitor – the approaching car again setting off a chorus of yaps and barks from the dogs, while the cats just yawned, pretending to be bored.

All this recent activity had in the meantime woken Toby, and by the time Tara appeared on her doorstep, it was an excited but weary Liz who came to greet her at the front door.

"Yikes, sorry," said Tara, taking in the toddler's red-rimmed eyes and mussed-up hair. "Was he asleep?"

"For about all of ten minutes," Liz replied, rolling her eyes. "But don't worry about it – he doesn't stay down for long these days, and I've just taken another dog in so ..."

She shrugged, then beckoned her inside the small cottage. "Great to see you. And I *love* the new car – when did you get that? Come in for a cuppa first, and afterwards we'll go out for a good look." Going through to the kitchen, she set Toby down on the floor amongst his toys, hoping that watching *SpongeBob SquarePants* on TV would keep him occupied for a little while.

"Mmm, I'm still not too sure about it," Tara said, taking a seat at the kitchen table. "It's more Glenn's choice than mine."

"Eric's eyes will pop out of his head when he sees it. He's in bed sleeping off the night-shift by the way."

"Pity – it seems like ages since I've seen you both," Tara replied automatically lowering her voice so as not to be responsible for waking yet another occupant.

The two had been friends for a long time, having worked side by side in the same Dublin telesales company, and Liz was really looking forward to a good natter. In fact, it had been Tara who'd first introduced her to her old friend and fellow native, Eric. And since they'd moved away from city, they didn't see one another as often as they'd like.

"So how come you couldn't come over last night?" Liz queried, throwing an eye towards Toby. "Are your Mum and Dad OK?"

"They're fine but ..." Tara hesitated. "I probably shouldn't be telling you this," she bit her lip, "but no doubt you'll find out soon enough anyway. Especially in this town."

"Telling me what?" Liz put two mugs of coffee on the table and took a seat beside her.

"Emma's pregnant."

Liz winced.

"I know," Tara picked up a Jaffa Cake.

"But she's not seeing anyone, is she?"

"She's not seeing anyone – and she's not saying who the father is either."

"What does your mother think? I'll bet she isn't too happy about it."

"That's an understatement."

"I can imagine. But hey, Emma's old enough to – "

"Old enough to know better? You'd think so."

"That's not what I was going to say. I meant she's not a teenager. It's not as hard for people these days, is it?"

Tara nodded. "I know, but it still won't be easy. I know Mum will help, but she's getting on herself now and wouldn't be able to handle a young baby. Not to mention that she shouldn't have to."

"I'm sure it'll all be fine – and I'm sure she knows you'll do your best to help too."

Tara sighed. "I suppose I'm just a little ... disappointed – considering. And then all this fuss about who the father is ..."

"She really won't say?"

"She's adamant about it."

There had never been any great love lost between Liz and Emma, mostly stemming from the fact that the 'oul wagon and her own husband had once been an item.

Despite herself Liz was curious, very curious as to why Emma was being so reticent. It certainly wasn't the girl she knew; if anything she'd have thought Emma would be only too eager to boast to all and sundry about her mystery guy.

So why all the fuss about the father? Liz wondered.

And why had this entire scenario sent an inexplicable shiver up her spine...

LATER THAT EVENING as she prepared dinner, Liz found herself still pondering the news.

Toby gave a loud wail, temporarily putting a stop to his mother's musings and she whirled around, wondering what the problem was this time.

Since starting to stand up on his own, her son had become a handful, and lately was getting himself into to all sorts of trouble. The other day, he'd almost pulled a bookcase down on top of him while trying to climb it. These days, she had only had to turn her back and he was into cupboards, pulling down curtains and grabbing at everything he set his sights on.

"Oh, Toby!" This time, it seemed, her son had had a run-in with a drum of baby powder and had emptied the contents on top of his head and shoulders, and all over much of her newly polished kitchen floor. Blast it. She was sure she'd put that out of sight.

"What are you up to now, you divil..." As if on cue, Eric walked in and promptly swept his errant son into his arms, getting the front of his T-shirt covered in talc.

"I don't know how he does it," Liz said, shaking her head in exasperation as she went to clean up. "One minute he's playing quietly under the kitchen table, the next he's on the way to causing World War Three."

"Ah, he's just trying to make sense of the place, aren't you, Tobes?" His dark hair still wet from his shower, Eric kissed him on the head. Seeing father and son together like that – both so alike – made her stomach give a little flip.

Four years on, and still Eric McGrath had the power to make Liz go weak at the knees. Back then, when she'd first met him, she had been powerless to resist his lively green eyes, hearty laugh and infectious lust for life.

He hadn't changed much, and was still a very attractive guy – possessing the same lean build and chiselled good looks as when they first met.

Liz, on the other hand, had put on a few pounds over the years, especially after the pregnancy. And these days with the kennels business, Eric was coming home to find his wife in a pair of wellies and baggy jeans instead of the short dresses and sexy heels she used to wear before they married.

Now he was expertly manoeuvring Toby into his high-chair, laughing and cooing as if this was all a great adventure.

Typical, she thought smiling as Eric patiently brushed the powder out of his hair and clothes – like a raging bull for most of the day and then as soon as Daddy appears ...

"So how are things?" Eric asked, once Toby had quietened and they were eating dinner. "How's Eminem getting on? Has he settled down yet?"

One of the dogs they had staying with them – a fabulous St Bernard burdened with the rapper moniker – was a first-time boarder and finding it difficult.

"He's much better today," Liz replied. "He's stopped pacing and I think he and Bruno took a bit of a shine to one another, actually."

"Bruno – back again? Your woman takes a lot of holidays, doesn't she?"

"I don't know that Jill does – she never says a word about where she's going. For all we know, she could be travelling with work. But speaking of holidays, Tara was saying earlier that she and Glenn are heading to –"

"Oh Tara was over?"

"She popped in for an hour this afternoon. She was home visiting the folks before she and Glenn head off to Egypt next week. Lucky things."

"I haven't seen either of them in ages."

"Well, she's so busy hasn't been home in ages. She's really made a go of that life coaching business, fair play to her."

Eric wrinkled his nose. "A load of old codswallop if you ask me. Surely people have more cop-on than to pay good money for someone to tell them what any eejit could. But that's city people for you – more money than sense."

Liz gave him a withering look. "Well, she's obviously good at what she does if she can afford trendy sports cars and luxury holidays." She went on to tell him all about Tara's new motor - a million miles from her own ancient embattled Peugeot.

"Maybe we should think about doing a spot of coaching ourselves then," Eric suggested. "We could get the house done up properly, and sort out all the village oddballs at the same time. Hold on – forget kennels, what about *dog* coaching? I know a few mutts who badly need help in finding their way in life. John Kavanagh's useless bloodhound for one."

"Stop," Liz laughed.

Eric had been working additional shifts at the security company to raise the extra cash for redecorating (or in truth, *restoring*) the house. So, while the old tumbledown cottage was without doubt their dream home, it hadn't fulfilled its true potential as yet.

She had hoped that the kennels would generate some additional income so that Eric didn't have to work so many long hours in Dublin. When they moved here originally, the plan had been for him to look for work in the village but so far he'd had no luck.

"So anything else strange with Tara?" he asked, taking a forkful of pasta.

"Well, now that you say it . . ." Liz paused slightly, "apparently Emma is pregnant."

His fork stopped halfway to his mouth. "Oh? I didn't know she was seeing anyone."

And how would you? Liz wondered.

"Well, that's the thing – apparently she wasn't ... seeing anyone." She was a little disconcerted by Eric's reaction and worse, his interest.

"So who's the lucky dad then?"

"Who knows," she replied shrugging. "According to Tara, she reckons she can go it alone."

"Right."

"Seems she got involved with someone she shouldn't have – hence all the mystery."

"Uh - huh."

"But Tara also says that Emma can be a bit overdramatic at times so it could very well be a big deal over nothing. She might just have got caught out by a one-night stand."

Eric nodded. "Could be."

She stood up and began to clear the table. "Course I feel sorry for anyone having to deal with something like that, but ... " Liz shrugged as she went to the sink, "as they say, she's made her bed and now the poor girl has to lie in it."

Liz sounded nonchalant but as she rinsed off dinner plates, she couldn't help but notice how strangely silent her husband had become, and just how hard her own heart was beating in her chest.

FOUR

Natalie Webb was having a very bad morning. "What do you mean he's at it again?" she cried down the phone. "Bloody hell, can't he keep it in his pants for more than two minutes?"

She locked eyes with the cabbie in his rear-view mirror and he quickly glanced away. Natalie knew he was straining to hear every word. He'd have been straining even more if he realised who she was discussing – not some errant boyfriend but England soccer star, Michael Sharpe.

Sharpe by name, *not* so sharp by nature, she mused, staring out the window at the London traffic, incensed that the player had landed them in it - *again*.

She cursed the day Blue Moon PR had agreed to take him on as a client. If it wasn't lap-dancers and soccer groupies, it was drunken bust-ups with his team-mates. And the closer he was getting to the end of his career, the more reckless he seemed to become.

"The *Sun*'s planning to break the story this week," Natalie's assistant informed her. "Apparently they've got photos of Michael and this girl coming out of the nightclub together last Saturday night and – "

"What?! How many times have we warned him?" Natalie shook her head, trying to think straight. Their client list made up a mix of high-profile sportspeople, singers and TV stars, the kind of stuff on which the UK media preyed and thrived.

Natalie and her colleagues were on permanent alert, ready and waiting to skilfully control their client's profile by putting out fires. But they'd need to employ a full-time fire brigade to handle Michael Sharpe ...

"Right." Glancing surreptitiously at the cab driver, who now seemed to have lost interest, she spoke low into the phone. "Tell him I want him and the missus at the ceremony," she said, knowing that Dani would understand she was referring to the Player of the Year Awards on Saturday night. It didn't matter that he wasn't up for nomination – she wanted them there anyway, on the red carpet, posing lovingly for the cameras and acting the happily married couple. "Send her over –" she hesitated, glancing again at the driver, aware that the tabloids would lap up an inside story from a London cabbie, "something spectacular . . ."

"Something that'll really wow the cameras."

"Exactly. In the meantime, see if we can come to some agreement with ... um ... the *others* about his latest indiscretion." She glanced again at the driver who seemed to be concentrating on the heavy traffic.

"OK, I'll talk to Michael and see about getting his wife a designer dress, but with the weight she's packed on recently, it might be difficult," Dani said dryly. "Do you think you'll be back to the office later?"

Natalie sighed. "I hope so. Depends on how long this lunch takes, really."

"Nab them while they're young and innocent, eh?" Dani joked, referring to the prospective client she was on her way to meet.

"Savour it while it lasts you mean," she replied, before ringing off and replacing her mobile in her bag.

HOURS LATER, Natalie arrived back at Blue Moon HQ and the MD accosted her on her way up to her office.

"Well," Jack Moon queried, his curiosity almost palpable, "how'd we do?"

Despite her optimism, she was non-committal. "Well, it's not official, but I got the handshake...."

"Oh, well done you," he replied effusively. "Securing someone like Jordan is a massive coup for us, Nat. I knew I could rely on you."

"No problem."

"Did I hear you correctly?" Danni squealed as Natalie approached her desk. "Did you just tell Jack that we're representing *Jordan King*?"

"Yep," she replied proudly. "His dad was a tough nut to crack but I think I nailed it in the end."

They wouldn't officially be representing Arsenal FC's latest teenage wunderkind until contracts were signed, but things were definitely looking good.

"Oh, I can't wait to tell Lee! He's such a fan and – "

"Don't go shouting about it to your hubby too soon – not until we get the signature," Natalie warned.

"Oh, all right." She slumped glumly back in her seat. "So what's he like?"

"Nice kid actually – little bit naïve, but that's probably a good thing. Makes a nice change from the usual prima donnas. Any calls while I was out?"

Danni grinned wickedly. "Plenty, now that you ask." She flicked through a list of messages. "Dean Phillips wants to know if you can arrange tickets for The Murderers concert on Saturday night, *Heat* magazine want to know if Melanie Adams is ready to talk about her divorce, Ken Forde wants to go over publicity plans for Blast's new single and – "

"OK, OK, just give me the bloody list," Natalie said, groaning. She still had to try and sweet-talk the *Sun* over the Michael Sharpe scandal, never mind arranging concert tickets for a fussy tech MD, interviews for a soap star, and media appearances for a teenage boy band.

But that was the job and despite her exasperation, she loved every second of it and in any normal day would approach each task with gusto. But not today.

Today – or more accurately – *tonight* could very well be the most important night of Natalie's thirty-odd years, and as the evening drew ever closer it was difficult to concentrate on anything else.

"Just one more thing," Danni added, her voice dropping to a whisper. "The clinic phoned to confirm your next appointment for ..." she trailed off and cast a furtive glance around the office, "you know."

"For my lipo?" Natalie finished out loud. She didn't care if the entire world knew she was having treatment – everyone over twenty-five was at it anyway. Natalie dealt with excess flab as she did with most things in life: if you didn't like it, do something about it. Not for her the furtive sneaking in and out of clinics for lipo or botox. How different was it than going to the gym? The end result was the same so what was the big bloody deal? "Great, I'll phone them later. Did you manage to speak to Michael?"

"Yeah."

"So how did he react to my suggestion about the awards ceremony?"

"He said he'll do it because he trusts you, but if the press start giving Clara a hard time about anything, he'll deck them."

"Wonderful. Pity he doesn't think more about his wife's feelings when he's screwing bimbos," Natalie replied tersely. "And tell him if he even *thinks* about going off on a cameraman again, I'll ..." She shook her head and went towards her office. "On second thoughts, don't bother, I'll give him a call myself."

"Sure." Danni was only too happy to offload the troublesome soccer player to someone who knew exactly how to handle him. "But don't forget to call Ken, OK? He was insistent."

Insistent, insistent, Natalie echoed inwardly – they were all bloody insistent, weren't they? Retreating into the sanctuary of her third-floor office with its relaxing views over the Thames, she sat down and slipped off her heels.

"Mark?"

"Well, hello there!" the big-shot concert promoter replied. "How's London's sexiest PR queen?"

She grinned. "You sure know how to flatter a girl. But

hey, any chance you could get me a couple of tickets for The Murderers gig next weekend?"

"Sure, no problem. I didn't know you were a fan."

"I am but they're not for me, unfortunately. Thanks for that, – I owe you one."

"Anytime, Nat. But with all the tight spots you've got me out of over the last few years you know damn well you owe me sod all."

She glanced guiltily at the rest of her telephone messages. Damn it, they'd have to wait until tomorrow – as would her emails. Normally, she wouldn't dream of leaving a clients or contact waiting overnight, but today, she couldn't help it. She just wasn't in the right frame of mind. Nah, for once, she'd have to give over some of her precious time to her personal life. Hopefully, it would be worth it.

Picking up her Balenciaga bag and D&G trench, Natalie left her office and went back out front to Danni.

Her colleague looked at the clock, mock surprise written all over her face. "What's this? Leaving for home *before* eight o'clock on a weekday?"

Natalie winked. "I've got a date tonight, remember? A very important date."

"Oh, I totally forgot. Your anniversary?"

"Yep. Hence the lipo and yesterday's spray tan."

Danni sat back, a dreamy look on her face. "So where is Mr Wonderful taking you tonight, then?"

Natalie grinned. "As if I'd discuss our bedroom antics with you."

"Oh, you know what I mean!" Her assistant reddened. "What have you got planned? Are you two going somewhere nice?"

"I don't know yet," Natalie told her truthfully. "I think he's planning to surprise me." *Hopefully not just with the location.*

"You lucky thing," Danni sighed. "For our last anniversary Lee and I sat in with a takeaway. He wouldn't go out because Arsenal were playing, and the only celebrations that night were for the ball hitting the back of the net."

Natalie said nothing. Danni and Lee had married earlier this year and clearly adored one another, and in truth she would have given her right arm to be in that position of cosy coupledom

But if all went well tonight, it mightn't be as far away as she thought.

"Well, have a great night, and you can tell me how it all went tomorrow," Danni said, shaking her head despondently. "Make me even more jealous that you managed to land a dreamboat like Steve, while I ended up with a yob like Lee."

FIVE

Outside the office building, Natalie tried in vain for fifteen minutes to hail a cab. Damnit, today of all days she'd hoped she wouldn't have to take the Tube.

Tottering along on her heels, she made her way down the street to the nearest underground station, trying to remember the last time she'd travelled this way.

Since she usually left the office late, there was never any problem getting a cab and she wasn't usually in that much of a rush to get home.

But this evening, the dreaded Tube would have to do, despite the fact that the dead air in the tunnels always seemed to tire her out.

And Natalie wanted to be fully alert tonight – especially if tonight turned out to be *the* night. It had to be, didn't it? They got on fantastically well, were madly in love, and the sex was just amazing ...

He'd ask her tonight, she was almost certain of it. He'd been a bit coy and evasive lately, which was a huge hint.

Her boyfriend's confidence and single-mindedness

were some of the traits that had made her fall for him in the first place.

They'd met at one of the many social events she attended in the course of her work and had been introduced by mutual friends. That night, she couldn't take her eyes off this tall, handsome and self-assured hunk who, with his broad chest and closely cropped blonde hair, seemed the embodiment of potent masculinity, and who unfortunately also seemed hell-bent on resisting her charms.

It had taken a while (and a few glasses of Veuve Clicquot) for Natalie to break him down and interest him enough to ask her out, but break him down she did, and the two had been together ever since.

Hopefully after tonight they'd be together for good, she thought, feeling the distinctive warm blast of air that signalled the imminent appearance of the next train to the platform. Soon after, she boarded the train and squashed into the carriage with what seemed like half the population of the city, trying her utmost to ignore the sweaty stench emanating from the person brushing up alongside her.

Her flat wasn't far from Central London, just a few stations away. Eventually reaching her destination, she practically raced out of the carriage and away up the stairs towards the exit.

Seven p.m. Hee would be picking her up at eight. Despite their intense relationship, the two hadn't yet moved in together, although this was because of Steve's necessity to be near the airport for all the travelling he tended to do with work.

Natalie, on the other hand, preferred the city on her

doorstep, though she knew this couldn't last forever, particularly if they were to get married.

No doubt he'd want to move somewhere sensible and affordable, whereas she would give anything for a pied-à-terre in Belgravia. Well, a girl could dream.

Reaching her flat, she flung her bag and coat on the sofa and headed directly for the shower. One thing at a time, she thought, massaging shower-gel onto her bronzed skin – bronzed courtesy of the good people at Sun FX. If tonight Steve produced a ring like she was certain he would, they could think about the practicalities some other time.

Half an hour later, she was fully made up and dressed to impress in a strapless raw silk Ben de Lisi, the raspberry colour of the dress setting off her dark eyes and glossy hair, now styled with seductive flicks à la Kelly Brook.

An hour later she was still waiting, the flicks drooping in tandem with Natalie spirits.

Where the hell was he? He'd assured her he'd pick her up at eight before heading out to this surprise destination, which she hoped was a suitably romantic spot for a marriage proposal. She'd tried his phone, which was switched to messages, and sent him a text enquiring about his whereabouts.

At about nine thirty, when she was just about to give up and change into a pair of comfy pyjamas, ignoring the La Perla ensemble she'd bought especially for the occasion, the love of her life appeared.

"I'm so sorry," he said, when she threw the door open, hands on her hips and the expression on her face leaving him in no doubt that he was in the doghouse. "Something came up at work, and I couldn't get away."

"You couldn't get away for long enough to call?"

"Don't be like that, babe," he soothed, lightly caressing her bare arm, "You know how these things can go."

Almost immediately her resolve softened. She could hold a conversation with someone as charismatic as Bill Clinton without batting an eyelid, but when it came to this man she was a piece of limp lettuce.

In a way, it was what she loved most about Steve. He was unpredictable, could be very unreliable and yet totally addictive.

"You could have let me know," she went on, her tone softening.

"I know and I was going to, but I didn't think things would go on this late. If I had known I wouldn't got caught up in it. Especially when you look so good," he pulled her into his arms, "so good that I don't know if I want to go out at all." He began to gently nuzzle her neck.

"But what about your surprise?"

"My what?"

"Your surprise," she reminded him. "You told me you were bringing me somewhere special for our anniversary, but you wouldn't say where."

"For our what?" Suddenly, Steve released her from his arms and drew back.

"Our anniversary," she said. "We've been together six months."

He gulped. "Em, right."

By his tone, Natalie knew he'd forgotten all about it. He hadn't planned any surprise at all, never mind a bloody proposal.

"I'm sorry, I erm ... thought we were just going out for a bite to eat . . . I didn't realise it was that important."

Obviously not, Natalie thought, disappointment flooding through her as he went through to the living room. So maybe she'd jumped the gun a bit with the proposal thing. But she was so sure she'd read the signs.

She and Steve adored one another, and he was always telling her how wonderful she was – particularly in bed, where they tended to spend most of their time.

So why wasn't she wonderful enough to marry? Sod it. Natalie followed him into the room, yet again cursing herself inwardly for wanting it so much – and admittedly so soon.

Maybe it wasn't that long after all – not long enough for Steve anyway. Six bloody weeks had been enough for Natalie to know she wanted to marry him.

Despite her exciting career and lively social life, lately she'd been thinking a lot about settling down and starting a family. She'd been living, working and partying in London for years and at this stage was beginning to tire of it all. While she adored her work, there had to be more to life than working eight to eight and schmoozing the city's self-important glitterati.

Natalie had been ready to settle down and get married for some time, and the fact that her best friend, Freya had recently beaten her to it merely made her want it all the more. Plus the fact that every woman she knew – Danni included – seemed to be settling down.

Having decided that it was too late to go out to dinner, Steve had since settled himself comfortably in front of the TV. "You don't mind, do you?"

"No, I don't mind," Natalie replied, slumping down on the sofa alongside him, her silk Ben de Lisi decidedly wrinkled from all the sitting around. "I'm up early tomorrow morning anyway. I've got a lot of work to catch up on."

The comment was intended as a jibe but sure enough, he didn't seem to notice. Steve was like that sometimes, Natalie thought wryly, the little barbs and remarks that could be so effective at work making no impression whatsoever on her easy-going boyfriend.

But Steve wasn't work, was he? And Natalie couldn't just dream up a fast-fix solution to this particular problem.

Her gaze drifted idly towards the TV programme Steve was watching, some holiday show.

He yawned. "I'd kill for something like that," he said, nodding at the screen.

And just like that it hit her. *A holiday?* Perfect.

She and Steve hadn't been spending enough time together lately – a trip to some fabulous destination would surely convince him once and for all that she was the one for him.

She sighed. A week in blissful sunshine at a gorgeous resort, being waited on hand and foot, doing nothing but eating and drinking and ... well.

By the time she was finished with him, Steve wouldn't be able to remember what life had been like without her.

SIX

"Mᴜᴍ, can you speak up a little? The line is terrible," Tara urged, pressing her phone closer to her ear.

But no amount of bad lines could obscure her mother's disapproving sniff on the other end.

"It isn't any wonder it's a bad line, Tara," she replied tetchily, "and you all the way out there in the desert." Isobel, who had never travelled outside of Ireland, couldn't understand the attraction people had for gadding off on fancy holidays. "How's Glenn?" she added, yelling and nearly taking the ear off her daughter in the process. Evidently she felt that her voice needed to carry all those thousands of miles in order for Tara to hear her. "Are the two of you drinking enough water? Or do you have to get it at one of those mirage things?"

Tara bit back a laugh. "Mum, I told you – Egypt isn't all desert," she said, her own voice echoing back on the line. "We're staying on the coast in an amazing resort by the sea. Glenn's out snorkelling as we speak."

They were finally in Egypt and Glenn was in his

element. He was a decent swimmer but since they hadn't taken too many holidays abroad, he hadn't tried snorkelling until now. And you could get no better introduction than the crystal clear waters of the Red Sea.

Even from the jetty Tara had - as a non-swimmer - been able to enjoy the magnificent marine life of the Egyptian Sinai Peninsula by peeking into the turquoise waters and watching a host of colourful tropical fish swim lazily amidst the coral.

They were staying in a spectacular and sinfully luxurious five-star resort overlooking the reef, and since their arrival, Glenn had thrown himself with gusto into the variety of water sports available, leaving Tara relaxing poolside.

Now sitting on her hotel balcony, overlooking the peninsula's beautiful coastline, Tara once more tried to reassure her mother that she and Glenn weren't at risk of severe dehydration.

"We're having a wonderful time," she told Isobel. "I'm taking lots of photographs to show you and Dad. How is he by the way? And Emma?"

"Your father's fine and sends his love!" her mother yelled back, but in the next instant her voice lowered and her tone changed. "As for Emma, I suppose it's getting to her that you're off sunning yourself in Egypt not a bother on you, while she's going through all this hardship on her own."

Tara gritted her teeth. What did they expect her to do – cancel her holiday just because Emma was pregnant?

"Well, I'll have another chat with her when we get back," she said, trying to keep the frustration out of her voice. "Tell everyone I said hello, and we'll see you all again soon."

"How long will ye be there again?"

Not long enough, she stopped herself from saying. "Ten days in all, Mum – we've another week to go yet."

"OK then, well … enjoy yourselves!" Isobel yelled once more before ringing off.

Dressed in the soft squishy towelling robe and satin slippers the hotel provided, Tara stood up from the patio chair, switched off her phone and went into the bedroom.

Today she would be breakfasting alone. Although, blast it, she thought, gazing out at the brilliant blue sky, it was such a beautiful morning she might just skip breakfast altogether and head straight for the pool.

Tara generally enjoyed a good lie-in instead of running around at all hours for a spot by the pool. She didn't care where she ended up – as long as it was under this glorious sky. But as the resort was busy, sun-loungers could be difficult to get unless you were up out of bed with the sun.

Though that morning she was lucky. When she reached the first of the hotel's three cascading pools, she spied a couple of vacant sun-loungers right alongside the water and, although it was unlikely Glenn would need it, Tara threw a spare towel on it anyway. He'd have to emerge from the depths of the sea sometime, and she had no intention of sharing hers.

While she'd thought the luxurious Arabic-style architecture was impressive, the pool area was truly magnificent – a veritable aqua-oasis, with three cascading pools surrounded by waterfalls, whirlpools and tiny grottos; all bordered by a variety of exotic palms and abundant pink and purple bougainvillea.

Yep, Tara thought, as she put on her sunglasses and lay back languidly on her sun-lounger, a relaxing morning here would be just perfect.

She'd been lying there about an hour, deeply engrossed in the book she was reading when Glenn returned from snorkelling, his skin still wet and brown eyes shining.

"Guess what?" he said, grinning from ear to ear. "They run PADI courses here."

Tara couldn't help but smile. "And?"

"And I've always wanted to try scuba diving – you know that."

She shook her head indulgently. Glenn was an out-and-out water baby, and she had known it was only a matter of time before he realised that scuba courses were part of the hotel's facilities. In fact, it was partly the reason she'd chosen this hotel in the first place; it would make the pain of dragging him off to Cairo to see the pyramids next week that bit easier.

"So try it then."

His eyes lit up. "Are you sure? I've had a look at the course and it seems pretty intense – it'll take a couple of days at least."

"I know that, don't worry about it."

"You're absolutely sure you don't mind me leaving you on your own again? Like I said, it could be a few days."

"Of course not," she assured him. "I'm fine here. You go and enjoy yourself."

He bent down and gave her a quick kiss on the cheek –

his delight almost palpable. "You're the best, you know that?"

She smiled, delighted. "I know."

Once again, she wished that she'd learned how to swim as a child, like he had. It was like learning to drive; the older you became, the more fear you seemed to have. And given that Tara wasn't the best driver in the first place, she wasn't about to throw caution to the winds when it came to swimming.

So let Glenn get his scuba lessons; she was perfectly fine where she was. She'd stocked up on books at the airport and was looking forward to getting through them. It had been years since she'd had the time to sit and read purely for pleasure, so she was going to make the most of it.

As Glenn once again took off toward the beach, she picked up her book, repositioned her sunglasses, and settled down again to some serious relaxation.

But before she could manage to read a sentence, she was interrupted once again. "Excuse me – is this bed free?"

Tara looked up to see a bikini-clad and stunningly attractive girl with glossy dark-brown hair smiling hopefully at her.

"Is it free?" she repeated. "Or are you holding it for somebody?"

Tara felt guilty. It wasn't fair of her to keep this for Glenn when it was unlikely he'd be using it.

And even if he did return later, Tara was sure he wouldn't mind her giving it away. Certainly not to this stunner, she thought wryly, with her huge almond-shaped eyes, full lips and even fuller bosom.

Tara's chest was as flat as day-old champagne and

industrial strength padded bikinis couldn't do a thing to change that. By comparison, this girl looked like she belonged in a lingerie advert.

"Yes it's free," she said warmly, moving Glenn's things out of the way. "But just the one, I'm afraid."

"You're a doll, thank you," the girl replied in a pronounced English accent. She sat down gratefully on the lounger. "One is all I need."

Tara smiled and resumed her reading but as the other girl settled herself alongside her, she couldn't help notice how remarkably clear and tanned the English girl's skin appeared in comparison to her own.

Not to mention how glamorous and confident she seemed, dressed in a fabulous red bikini that displayed her perfect curves and remarkably smooth, cellulite-free thighs to perfection – she guessed they were both around the same age and while Tara was riddled with it, this other girl's skin was baby-smooth.

She had to be a model or something, she thought enviously, as the girl began applying sunscreen in a sensuous manner that would make Hugh Hefner blush. Now she hoped Glenn *did* stay away for the afternoon. He'd be frothing at the mouth ...

"So sorry to interrupt again," the girl said, startling Tara out of her envious reverie, "but would you mind spraying some sunscreen across my shoulders? The UV is so high I don't want to take any chances –"

"Of course not." Tara swung her legs off the lounger and took the bottle.

"Thanks. Normally I'd get my boyfriend to do it, but because I'm on my own here –"

"On your own – at the resort?" She couldn't conceive of the fact that this gorgeous creature was on holiday without a man equally as attractive. She knew some people liked to travel alone but ...

The girl sighed and piled her shiny chestnut hair on the top of her head before turning her back. "He was supposed to come with me but then he cancelled at the last minute – while I was on my way to Heathrow, can you believe it? 'I have to work, Natalie,' he says. 'Something important's come up and I just can't get away,'" she mimicked exaggeratedly as Tara sprayed sunscreen onto her shoulders. "Our very first trip together, and he has to work."

"That's unfortunate." The job complete, Tara handed her back the bottle and the two resettled themselves on their respective sun-loungers, Natalie lying on her stomach and exposing her newly protected back to the sun.

"Tell me about it," she said rolling her eyes while chattily continuing to fill Tara in. "But I decided to come anyway. I haven't had a break in yonks, and work has been crazy so I figured why waste the opportunity?" She giggled. "Although I suppose there are some compensations. With Steve not here, at least I can just lounge around with no make-up, and not have to worry about trying to look effortlessly perfect."

"Now I don't think you'd have to try too hard," Tara chuckled, having already decided that despite her intimidating beauty, she already liked this girl.

And it seemed they had a thing or two in common. Like Tara, she evidently had a hectic work life since it was also her first holiday in ages and each had pretty much been abandoned by the men in their lives.

"So thanks a bunch for the lounger," the girl went on. "I've only just arrived, and it's so busy I really thought I'd have to spend the day in my room – not that that's too much of a problem – have you seen the size of the jacuzzi bath? Oh, I'm Natalie by the way." She offered Tara a perfectly manicured hand.

"Tara – nice to meet you," she replied, trying to hide her own nail-bitten paw. "And yes, the bath is huge, although I haven't tried it yet – despite the fact that we flew in on Wednesday."

"From Ireland?"

"The accent is obviously a giveaway."

"Oh I love the Irish accent," Natalie declared, sitting up. "I worked with a girl from Dublin yonks ago, and we all adored the funny little expressions she always used – 'Jaysus' and 'Almighty' and all that."

Tara bit back a smile. "I'm from Dublin too."

"Really? How fabulous! I've never been, but I've heard it's marvellous fun. Great shopping, apparently. But I expect you probably have much the same stores we have in London."

She nodded. "What about you? You mentioned London – is that where you're from?"

"Yep. Well, I was born in Hertfordshire, then moved when I was eighteen. I've hardly left the place since. Which I suppose, is part of the reason I needed this holiday."

"And how long are you here for?"

"Just a week unfortunately. But this place is so fabulous, I could easily stay for a year – you?"

"Ten days, and I know what you mean. It's amazing, isn't it?"

"So are you here with your husband then?"

"I'm not married but –"

"Me neither," Natalie groaned, shaking her pretty head from side to side. "Something I had *really* hoped to get to work on changing this week," she muttered under her breath.

Tara said nothing, even though she was sorely tempted to pry some more. Naturally curious and she supposed, because of her profession, she was naturally intrigued by other people's lives and what made them tick.

Plus she was full of admiration for Natalie travelling on her own, especially to such a far-flung destination. Despite herself she couldn't help but compare this self-assurance with Emma's annoying listlessness. At times, her sister could be so lethargic that going as far as corner shop on her own was an ordeal, let alone to the Middle East.

The two lay side by side in companionable silence for a while, Tara becoming nicely engrossed in her book and Natalie just as engrossed in her sunbathing until before they knew it, it was lunchtime.

"Do you fancy getting a bite to eat?" Tara asked, nodding in the direction of the pool snack bar. "They do great sandwiches and pizza." While she had anticipated having to do everything alone for the day, it might be nice to have some company.

"I'd love to," Natalie grinned, getting up and wrapping herself in an indecently short sarong that made the most of those fabulous legs. "In fact, while we're at it," she added with a wink, "we could always try something from the cocktail bar too."

"I'd love a cocktail, but it'll be a virgin one for me."

"Oh, you don't drink?"

"Nope." She had to laugh at Natalie's shocked expression. "Not exactly living up to the drunken Irish stereotype, am I."

The other girl blanched. "Goodness no. I mean – that's not what I mean and – oh, I'm frightfully sorry – I really should just quit while I'm ahead." The poor thing looked embarrassed and Tara felt for her. "I'm really sorry. I hope I haven't made you uncomfortable."

"Don't be silly. I'm not an alcoholic or anything," Tara told her easily, as they sat down at a vacant table. She picked up the menu. "I'm just not mad about alcohol. I got drunk once in my life and believe me, once was enough."

"Bad hangover?"

"Something like that."

"Oh I know where you're coming from. Although unfortunately, it's never stopped me going back for more. But I do love a cocktail on holiday – so you don't mind if I ...?" she trailed off apologetically.

"Of course not." Tara insisted. "Work away."

It was funny really she thought, how people reacted to her teetotal ways. Most seemed to automatically assume Tara was an alcoholic, and found it hard to come to terms with the fact that she just didn't like drinking alcohol. And for a someone who associated the Irish with being rip-roaring drunks, no doubt it was doubly confusing.

"A Mai-Tai, and a chicken sandwich," Natalie told the Egyptian waiter, who was busily trying to avoid looking at her magnificent bosom, his culture totally at odds with all this Western exhibitionism. But refreshingly, Tara thought, the girl seemed totally unaware of the effect she was having.

"And I'll have the virgin Poco Loco and a pizza," she told him, throwing her usual healthy eating habits out the window. To hell with it, she was on holiday.

"Well," Tara's new friend smiled, when the waiter had taken both their orders and left, "thanks to you this trip mightn't turn out to be such a disaster after all."

SEVEN

Later that evening, Natalie sat alone in the hotel, still unable to believe that she'd come to this amazing resort all alone. It was such a pity that Steve hadn't been able to make it.

Such a pity because he'd sounded so eager when she'd first mentioned the idea.

"Sounds good," he'd said. "I could do with a break. We're in the middle of a huge deal at the moment, and it's been hard going. After all this, I'd jump at the chance to get away."

As a property developer, he didn't have to keep nine to five office hours and (unlike Natalie) could easily get away at the drop of a hat. This had been the main reason she'd been so confident about booking at such short notice.

"I'll let you know when would be a good time for me, and we'll talk about it then, OK?" he told her.

Natalie gulped. It was obviously not the time to tell him that she'd already arranged the entire thing - first class flights, five-star resort - lock stock and barrel.

But she'd been certain that Steve would be fine with it in the end. After all, what man *wouldn't* want to be whisked away on a last-minute exotic trip? Guys loved an assertive woman, didn't they?

So later that week, she'd phoned Steve and excitedly left a message on his answering machine, informing him that she'd booked them a fabulous trip to Egypt, and they'd be leaving first thing Saturday morning.

And after that particular week, she sorely needed a holiday herself.

Michael Sharpe had been involved in yet another punch-up - this time with a teammate right on the soccer pitch in full view of fifty thousand or so spectators.

By the weekend, Natalie had been feeling the effects of a full week's troubleshooting and was only too ready for a relaxing week off.

However, with all the hullabaloo, she hadn't managed to get Steve on the phone and instead, messaged the details of their flight and planned to meet him at the airport.

He was trying to get this property deal sewn up before they went, so better to just let him get the job done and then they could both enjoy their time away. On her way to Heathrow in the cab on Saturday morning, she'd sent him another text telling him she'd meet him outside WH Smiths in Terminal 2.

Almost immediately he phoned.

"Natalie, I can't fly out today," he cried, sounding flustered. "What on earth made you think I could?"

"But we're leaving this morning. You knew that."

"I did *not* know that! As far as I was concerned it was just an idea. When I got these texts telling me we were flying out this weekend, I didn't know what to make of it. To be honest, I thought you were having me on."

"But –"

"Natalie, are you out of your mind? What made you think I could just drop everything and take off at such short notice? I have a business to run."

He sounded very upset, considerably more upset than the situation merited. He was the one leaving *her* stranded, after all.

"Nat, this is coming across a little bit weird ... a little bit *heavy*, to be honest. And the thing is – "

"The thing is what?"

"I don't like being railroaded."

Sensing that she'd crossed an invisible line, her heart began to race. "We obviously just got our wires crossed," she said quickly. "I really thought you were fine about this trip, so I went ahead and booked it. Obviously I was wrong."

"Yes, you were."

This was followed by an uncomfortable silence, and Natalie wanted to kick herself. Why oh why had she pushed it – why had she been so impulsive?

When Steve eventually spoke again, his voice had softened. "But hey, why don't you go along without me? You said yourself you need a break."

The idea of going on holiday alone quite frankly, sounded a little sad but unlike Steve she *could* get away. Jordan King had since signed with the agency and her boss, Jack was so pleased about that he'd have let her fly to the moon if she wanted to.

"Honestly, you should go," Steve insisted. "And I'll pay you back for my ticket."

"Don't be silly. It was my fault for booking without consulting you properly." It *had* been rather rash of her. But he'd seemed so enthusiastic about the idea ...

"Even so, there is no point in letting a perfectly good holiday go to waste," Steve went on, his tone now sounding rather ...impatient.

So Natalie decided that she would go. If anything it proved that she was an exciting unpredictable woman, confident and assertive, no? She bid Steve a regretful goodbye over the phone and promised to call him when she got to the resort.

"I'll be very busy," he replied, his voice sounding tense yet again. "So it mightn't be that easy to reach me."

"Well, don't work too hard," she said, her voice breaking with emotion, as they said their goodbyes. "I'll miss you."

"Yeah, me too," Steve said, ringing off. He was obviously very stressed by this deal she decided, putting her phone back in her bag.

Never mind, she'd speak to him again soon. In the meantime, she'd just have to try and get through this week on her own.

EIGHT

HAVING SPENT an enjoyable afternoon sunbathing and chitchatting with Natalie by the pool, Tara got ready to go out to dinner.

Glenn – who'd finally returned to the room a good hour after Tara had finished sunbathing – was still wildly enthusiastic about his scuba-diving lessons, but weary after the initial preparation.

"First, I had to swim a couple of hundred metres, then the instructor got me to tread water for a full ten minutes, which was hard going on the calves I can tell you," he told her as they made their way to the resort's Bedouin-themed dining area.

Situated outdoors on the uppermost level of the building and overlooking the bay, the Souk consisted of a variety of five different restaurants, some offering traditional Lebanese and Middle Eastern *mezzeh*, curried and spiced meals, hummus and *aish* – a type of Egyptian flatbread.

Another specialised in mouth-watering Mediterranean

food reflecting the traditional cooking of Spain, Provence, Italy and Greece, while the chefs at the Oriental kitchen prepared seafood, noodles and rice dishes judiciously seasoned with soya sauce, oyster sauce, rice wine, sesame oil and lemongrass.

Guests could, on any given evening, choose from a range of dishes from any of the five kitchens, meaning there was no shortage of variety and little chance of anyone getting bored. The balmy outdoor setting and fragrant mosaic of herbs and spices in the air, set against the background of traditional music and rhythmical drumbeat, made for an exotic and enjoyable Arabian experience.

Glenn wasted no time in finding them a vacant table overlooking the tip of Naama Bay, the bright lights of the town twinkling brightly against the darkness. However, he was less interested in the view, and more in getting a waiter's attention.

"I'm starving," he told her. "I think I'll try something from all five places tonight."

"Won't all that extra weight affect your buoyancy?" she teased, studying the drinks menu.

"Dunno, but all that training sure makes me hungry," he replied, before trying to smother a yawn. "Not to mention exhausted."

"Are you sure you wouldn't rather wait and do the scuba course some other time?" she asked, concerned. "Sounds like you won't have much time to relax."

According to him, the course was to take place on three consecutive days and in order to successfully achieve his PADI diving qualification, along with the training, he'd also have to complete two open-water dives – a punishing schedule.

"Nah, I'm not bothered about relaxing anyway," he assured her. "I'd much rather be doing something interesting. And I've been dying to do this for years, so I wouldn't dream of giving up now."

No, Tara thought fondly, he wouldn't. Back home (when he wasn't stuck in front of a screen) Glenn was always off rock-climbing, orienteering or other adventure activities. So it was no surprise that he wasn't concerned about missing out on relaxation. She still had to broach the subject of their day-trip to the pyramids the following week though.

No point in fretting about it now, she thought, looking around for a waiter who would put the tired and hungry soul out of his misery.

As she did, she caught sight of Natalie being led to a table not far from their own. This evening, she looked even more beautiful, dressed in a stunning jade satin dress that flattered her curves and accentuated her dusky colouring. By comparison Tara was struck by how drab she must look in her boring khaki linen trousers and black halter-top.

She wasn't usually insecure about her looks, at least not in the way Liz could be sometimes, but she didn't think there was a woman alive who wouldn't be intimidated by Natalie.

Tara had really enjoyed their chat earlier over lunch. There was something very liberating about chatting to someone you hardly knew, and who knew absolutely nothing about you. They'd exchanged snippets of each other's lives, Tara telling her all about her and Glenn, and hearing about Natalie's glamorous London lifestyle in return.

They'd then spent a comfortable afternoon sunbathing and dipping in and out of the pool. Well, Tara had 'dipped', Natalie, a confident and elegant swimmer, had *glided*.

Now, in the restaurant, she tried to catch her attention.

"Who are you waving at?" Glenn asked, turning round in his seat. Predictably, his eyes nearly popped out of his head when he spied the stunning creature walking towards them.

"The girl I met at the pool earlier. She's lovely and she's on her own, so be nice."

"Hello there!" Natalie waved as she approached and the two women embraced. "And you must be Glenn," she greeted enthusiastically. "I've heard all about you. How are the scuba lessons going?"

He couldn't have looked any more shell-shocked than if Kim Kardashian had walked up and kissed him on the lips. Despite herself, Tara had to laugh.

"Uh ...great to meet you," he mumbled, unsure where to look since Natalie's dress was daringly low-cut.

"You'll join us, won't you?" Tara urged.

"Oh, no, I couldn't impose – "

"Don't be silly," she assured her, "we'd love you the company, wouldn't we, Glenn?"

He nodded dumbly.

"Well, if you're sure ..." Natalie smiled at the waiter, who quickly went to fetch another place setting. "I must admit I didn't relish the thought of having dinner on my own. But I feel awful about intruding on your holiday -

again. Please don't feel like you have to take pity on me because I've been abandoned."

"Abandoned?" Glenn enquired.

"Natalie's boyfriend was supposed to come on holiday with her," Tara informed him, stressing the word 'boyfriend' out of divilment, though she knew there was precious little to worry about. Even if he did take a shine to her (and what man wouldn't?), someone like Natalie was *way* out of Glenn's league. "But he had to cancel at the last minute."

The three of them chatted easily over dinner, and once again Tara marvelled at how down-to-earth and lovely the other girl was. Then, when the plates were cleared away, she suggested the three head off for drinks.

"We could go to the piano bar. It's really relaxing on the terrace with the music drifting along the air and out over the water."

"Sounds perfect." Natalie looked uncertainly at Glenn. "Again, if you don't mind my tagging along –"

"No, you two work away actually," he replied, stifling a yawn. "I might hit the hay early tonight if that's OK. I'm whacked after all that swimming, and I've an eight o'clock start in the morning."

"You go ahead, love," Tara soothed, and shot a mischievous wink at Natalie. "We'll be grand without you."

"Sounds punishing," Natalie commented.

"Worth it though. I can't wait to get my PADI cert. Problem is, when I do, I'll only have time to get in a couple more open-water dives before we head home."

Tara seized the moment. "Don't forget that we need to fit in a trip to Cairo next week too."

As expected, he wasn't receptive. "Ah, we don't have to do that as well, do we?"

"You know I've always wanted to see the pyramids, Glenn." Tara was equally petulant. "And it wouldn't kill you to spend even *one* day with me on this holiday."

"But it's such a long trip up – I'll be shattered after all my training..."

He was right: the day trip to Cairo had a four a.m. start and it would be nearly bedtime by the time they got back. She bit her lip. It was annoying, but maybe it was a bit too much to ask.

"Well, I'd love to see them too," Natalie piped up. "But I wouldn't dream of going all that way by myself. Anyway, these things are never much fun on your own, so if you don't mind my tagging along, I'd be happy to come too. That is, if Glenn doesn't mind."

He didn't mind at all. "That's a great idea – you should definitely go together," he said, quickly seizing the opportunity. "At least then you get to go with someone who'll actually enjoy it. Me, I couldn't give a toss about pyramids and museums and the like. I'd much rather get a few more dives in."

Granted, it would be more fun going on an excursion with someone who actually wanted to be there, and even though they'd only known each other a few hours, Natalie had already proven to be great company.

Still, she felt guilty about leaving Glenn at the resort on his own. "You wouldn't mind my flying up there without you?" she asked.

He laughed. "Believe me, I wouldn't mind at all!"

"Thanks a million," she replied, a little stung.

"You know what I mean. This way is much better for all concerned. I can get another dive in, and you can go and visit the pyramids with someone who appreciates them."

"And doesn't have a face like a wet week," Tara teased.

He was sheepish. "True enough, but it's not my fault that ancient mummies don't float my boat."

"OK then, great," Tara looked at Natalie. "We could book for next Wednesday, say?"

"Sounds good to me."

True to his word, Glenn headed straight for bed, leaving the two women alone at the dinner table.

"He's *gorgeous*," Natalie enthused, when he was out of earshot.

"You think so?" Tara was secretly proud.

"Absolutely – those amazing brown eyes! And he's quite muscular too, isn't he? Those arms."

"Well, no disrespect, but he's strictly off limits..."

"Oh goodness, I didn't mean that! I just meant it, you know, as a compliment."

"I know – I was just kidding," Tara replied, although the idea that a woman like Natalie found Glenn attractive *was* a little unsettling.

Having decided to skip dessert, the two retired to the bar and settled in for another cosy chat. Over a couple of champagne cocktails, Natalie told Tara some more about Steve.

"We have a wonderful relationship and I really feel that he's the one. I just wish he'd get round to popping the question. It was our anniversary last week and I'd sort of hoped that it might happen then. And if not, at least on this holiday."

"So how long have you two been together?"

Natalie took a sip from her drink. "Six months."

"Six ... months?" Tara couldn't keep the surprise out of her tone.

"Yes, I know it doesn't sound like long. But we're in love, and time is moving on – especially for me." She rolled her eyes. " If it doesn't happen soon, it never will."

"Why do you say that?"

She shrugged. "The fact that I'm almost forty."

Tara's eyes widened with disbelief. *Forty?* That was it, once she got back home she was going on a *serious* diet...

"Well, thirty-two," Natalie admitted then, much to Tara's relief. "But the point is I'm not getting any younger. This year alone I've watched my assistant and *three* of my best friends get married and they're all younger than me."

"Do you feel that age alone is a good basis for wanting to get married?" Tara said, automatically switching to coaching mode and kicking herself for doing so. "I'm sorry, ignore me," she added quickly, shaking her head. "I'm a Life Coach by profession, and sometimes I can't help myself."

But Natalie didn't bat an eyelid. "A Life Coach? How fabulous! My assistant Danni sees one in Bloomsbury that she's always raving about. I keep promising to try one myself some time, but work's been so crazy lately, I just don't have the time."

Tara grinned. Many Irish people (like her own mother) were horrified by the very notion, thinking her some kind of unscrupulous quack, which was the main reason she hadn't mentioned her profession to Natalie before now. "I love it, but like I said, sometimes can't help slipping into work mode."

"Don't worry, I'm the same. I work in PR and size up every person I meet as a potentially useful contact. But now I understand why I find you so easy to talk to."

Natalie did seem happy to have someone to confide in, and confessed quite candidly her deep need - almost to the point of obsession - with finding a husband.

"I know it's not fashionable to say it, and most women I know would kill me for even *thinking* it, but it's what I want. I want to be married, I want to be somebody's wife."

"I don't think that's so terrible."

"I'm just so bloody *tired* of all the empty socialising and arse-licking," she went on, as if Tara hadn't replied. "London's a big city and while it's wonderful, it can get lonely sometimes. Now, don't get me wrong, I wouldn't dream of living anywhere else and most of the time it's great fun, but sometimes I feel like there has to be more to life than parties at Claridges and media launches in Soho."

Tara hid a smile. Parties at Claridges sounded pretty amazing to her. But no matter who you were and what you did, somehow the grass always seemed greener elsewhere didn't it? She'd seen it time and time again in her line of work.

"I feel like such an idiot for thinking this way," Natalie continued. "As though I'm betraying the sisterhood. We're all supposed to be independent, women-of-the-world types who don't need men, aren't we? According to the magazines, in a few years' time we'll all be so self-sufficient we'll have no need for them at all. But deep down I really don't feel that way. I want to be a wife. I want to be Steve's wife."

Tara's heart went out to her, this beautiful, successful and self-assured woman who on the face of it, was the *Cosmo* female ideal incarnate.

"Don't beat yourself up. My best friend Liz was exactly the same, and since she got married I don't think I've ever seen her happier. And there's certainly no shame in wanting to be happy. I certainly never thought any less of her for admitting that she wanted the big white wedding, even though I didn't necessarily feel the same way – and still don't."

"You don't want to get married?"

"Not particularly. I'm perfectly happy the way I am. I adore Glenn and the life we have together. We're very happy – well, most of the time," she added, smiling fondly, "and that's enough for me."

"But don't you think that might change sometime in the future? That you might want something more?" Natalie persisted, her eyes widening. "Oh, I'm sorry, now I'm being nosy, aren't I? Just tell me to sod off and mind my own business."

"No, it's fine." Tara sat forward, not at all bothered by the question. "But it's funny; you sound like Liz, the friend I was talking about just now. Like I said, she's been married for years, is blissfully happy and for the life of her can't understand why I'm a million miles away from following suit. But in all honesty, I love my life the way it is and I've never had any interest in getting married."

"Why not? Don't you want the fairytale and the big white dress and all the trimmings?" Natalie's face took on a faraway expression. "Personally I can't wait and I'd give *anything* to walk up the aisle."

"You're certain that's what you want?" Tara asked and Natalie nodded dreamily.

"And what about Steve – what do you think he wants?"

"Hopefully the same thing," Natalie replied grimly. "If not, I'm in a spot of bloody bother, aren't I?"

NINE

LIZ STRAPPED Toby into his buggy and took the short walk down the hill from her house to the centre of the village.

Although the weather was chilly, the sky was a glorious blue and as she crossed the low stone bridge over the lake, she thought the large body of water after which the village was named had never looked so impressive.

As she and Toby walked along, most of the villagers she passed gave her friendly but distant smiles.

"Liz, hello!"

She looked up to see Colm, one of Eric and Tara's childhood friends, waving at her from across the road. He was standing outside the popular village café he worked in, which had an enviable position right at the edge of the lake on the corner where Main Street began. He was also one of the few people in the village that Liz had got to know properly since the move from Dublin.

"Hey," She waved back, nipping quickly across the road to talk to him.

"Hello there, little lad," he greeted bending down to

Toby, having paused in his task of cleaning the cafe's glass frontage. "Gosh, he's gorgeous. Who would have thought an ugly bastard like Eric would produce a cutie like that?"

"Wash out your mouth, or I'll set my dogs on you," Liz laughed, and he feigned terror.

"Hmm you didn't threaten to set your husband on me all the same – he must still be as much of a wimp as ever," he grinned. "How is Eric anyway? I haven't seen you two around in a while."

Liz grimaced. "We haven't been around in a while, unfortunately. And he's fine, working like a maniac lately – he's hardly ever at home." She rolled her eyes. "I'm beginning to think he has a mistress on the go."

"Well if he does, he's an idiot," Colm replied a little more earnestly than the remark necessitated. She'd been joking after all.

"So are you coming inside for a cuppa? I'm trying out a new recipe involving sinful amounts of cream and mascarpone – and I'd love a guinea pig."

Judging by his slim and perfectly toned physique, Colm obviously didn't try out too many of his creations on himself or if he did, was conscientious enough to work the excess off.

"Don't tempt me – not this early in the morning," Liz replied, groaning. "But I might call back later. I've a bit of shopping to do first and then I'm popping up to Eric's mum. I think she may have forgotten what Toby looks like at this stage."

"How *is* the old bag?" he said, rolling his eyes. "I haven't seen her in donkey's years myself – but of course, she wouldn't *dream* of coming into a place like this.

Heavens no," he mimicked exaggeratedly. "After all, who knows *where* the chef's hands have been!"

Liz smiled. Old Irish prejudice died hard.

According to Eric, Colm had recently begun a serious relationship with a guy living locally and while she hadn't yet met the boyfriend, she was pleased for him.

Living in a small, close-knit community like this couldn't be easy, but at the same time it was impossible not to love Colm. Outgoing and gregarious, his gossipy mannerisms always made her laugh, yet he wasn't over-the-top camp.

"Tara was telling me she and Glenn met you in the pub last time the two of them were home," Liz said, her thoughts segueing to her friend.

"Yes, she looked stunning as usual," he said. "Such great taste. You know, I still can't figure out how a girl from this dive ended up being so goddamn *fabulous*. She really knows how to make the most of herself, doesn't she?"

"I hear you..." Liz grimaced, suddenly aware of her own dowdy jeans and boring T-shirt.

"Although, I have to hand it to you, Liz, you've smartened Eric up quite a bit yourself. Honestly, when we were teenagers, we were all bewildered as to where that boy got his clothes – especially those reindeer jumpers he loved so much."

Liz giggled. "Reindeer jumpers?"

"You mean you've never seen the pictures?" Colm's eyes widened dramatically. "I must hunt them out and show you sometime. Eric used to wear this *horrific* brown jumper with patterned reindeer prancing gaily all over the front of it. Can you imagine? Talk about ironic!" He winked conspiratorially. "Anyway, I'd better get back inside – I see another horde gathering."

Deciding she'd better not keep him any longer, Liz bade Colm a quick goodbye, having promised to return soon for a cuppa and another chat, and continued along.

Within the next half hour, she'd done most of her shopping and was inelegantly trying to stow her vegetables at the back of Toby's pushchair, when she looked up and came face to face with another local resident - this one not such a welcome face.

"Emma..." Liz blurted in surprise, her face suffused with colour – not just in surprise, but from her exertions in stowing away the heavy groceries.

"Oh, hello."

Tara's sister was typically off-hand and more maddeningly, looked stunning dressed in a pretty floral skirt and stylish white top that showed off her tanned shoulders.

Blast it, Liz thought, why hadn't she made more of an effort? Baggy jeans and a sweatshirt that had seen better days were barely suitable for slobbing around at home, let alone going shopping.

But Toby had been narky that morning and Liz had a couple of dogs changing over before she left, so really she had been lucky to get out of the house at all.

But trust Eric's ex to look like she'd stepped out of the pages of *Vogue*, all pretty and feminine and glowing with health while *she* looked like something from *Down-and-Out Weekly*.

Then Liz recalled *why* Emma was glowing.

"Tara tells me you're moving back home," she said, trying to inject some warmth into her tone. Granted over the years, neither had made any bones of their dislike for one another, but Liz saw no reason not to be polite, if not exactly friendly. They would never be bosom buddies but ...

"Did she?" For a brief moment, Emma looked surprised and a bit wrong-footed. "I didn't realise my personal life was up for public discussion."

Liz gritted her teeth. Right. If the girl wanted to play silly buggers, then to hell with being polite.

"I was just making small-talk. Good luck to you." She went to push the buggy away.

"Will Eric be at home this weekend?" Emma enquired pointedly. "I haven't seen him around in a while."

"Of course, where else would he be?"

"Oh, I don't know. He seems to be spending a *lot* of time in Dublin. I bumped into him once or twice up there and we had a few drinks. Good fun actually."

Despite herself, Liz's heart began to pound. "Did you really?" she asked, trying to sound nonchalant.

"Yes, just like old times actually," Emma replied jauntily, before walking away in the other direction, leaving Liz staring bamboozled at her pert backside.

Her hands gripped the buggy so tightly her knuckles almost broke through skin. What the hell was that all about?

Granted, Eric *had* been spending a lot of time in Dublin lately but he was working ... wasn't he?

She took a deep breath and shook her head, trying to get a grip, trying to contain the jealousy and suspicion that had bubbled up within.

What on earth was wrong with her? Why did the mere

sight of Emma Harrington turn her into a jealous wreck? It had been years since those two had been an item – way before she and Eric even met, she reassured herself, as her heartbeat began to slow a little and her stomach stopped spinning. And as far as she knew, Eric had barely even spoken to Emma since.

As far as she knew ...

Despite herself, the words planted themselves in Liz's brain. *"I bumped into him once or twice – we had a few drinks."*

Had Eric and Emma been meeting up when he stayed over in the city?

And if they did, wasn't it strange that her husband hadn't mentioned it...

EMMA WALKED FURTHER ALONG, a mischievous grin plastered across her face. OK, so she shouldn't have said anything to Eric's wife, but she couldn't help it.

For some reason that goody-two-shoes friend of Tara's had always got up her nose, and she couldn't resist.

That had certainly wiped the smug smile off her silly little face. The slip of the tongue had been worth it, just to see her stupefied reaction.

Well, she'd lit the fuse, now all she had to do was sit back and watch the fireworks.

TEN

ERIC RETURNED from work that evening bustling with energy, and all throughout dinner raved enthusiastically about the extra hours he'd secured.

"Which means an extra few quid to spend on the house, love," he told his wife, gleefully rubbing his hands together, not noticing her sombre mood.

"Or maybe just blow it on your nights out on the town," Liz replied bitterly.

"What?" he asked, frowning. "What are you talking about?"

She lifted her chin and continued feeding Toby at his high-chair. "From what I hear, you've been having the life of Riley, while I'm stuck here with Toby and the dogs."

Eric set down his fork. "Liz, I don't know what – "

"I'm only telling you what I heard. I bumped into Emma Harrington today who wasted no time in telling me what a wonderful social life you seem to lead."

Immediately he coloured. Why did he look so guilty? she thought, her senses tingling afresh.

"Liz, what's going on?"

Unable to stop herself, she sniffed defiantly. She knew she was acting childish and setting up a conversation that could only end in trouble. Still she couldn't help it.

"You tell me," she snapped. "All I know is that some stranger seems to know a lot more about your exploits in Dublin than I do."

He frowned. "I still don't understand what you're getting at. OK, if I did bump into Emma. So what?"

Liz didn't reply; she just sat there, defiant.

"Liz, I'm not in the mood for this," Eric warned. "If you've got something to say, then just come right out and say it. What's on your mind?"

Just then, Toby let out an anguished cry, evidently unused to his mum and dad speaking to one another like this.

Liz wasn't used to it either and despite her sense of grievance, realised that she was sounding like a nag. But Emma's comments earlier had really unnerved her, and she was determined to demand some kind of explanation.

It seemed Eric was in no mood to oblige. "Look, it's obvious you're in some snit, but whatever *is* wrong with you, don't go taking it out on me." With that, he got up and walked out of the kitchen, Toby still wailing in his wake.

Her mind racing, Liz got up to tend to her son and tried desperately to get a grip on her whirling thoughts and emotions. Why was he angry when *she* was the one who should be feeling hard done by? When *she* was the one who sat alone on weeknights while he lived it up in the capital?

It had been mostly his idea to move down here in the

first place after all. "It'll be better for the baby, and all the space is perfect for setting up your kennels," he'd told her enthusiastically.

And yes, village life had indeed been better for Toby, and setting up the kennels had been a dream come true for Liz, but if living in Lakeview was so wonderful, why did it seem that Eric was lately finding more reasons to stay away?

Her son's cries eventually abating, she slumped back down at the kitchen table. What was wrong with her? Why did she feel so insecure all of a sudden? For the most part, she'd never really felt anything other than secure and happy when it came to Eric.

Except when it came to Emma Harrington.

The idea of the two of them together just wouldn't go away – however hard she tried. It probably didn't help that she had never been able to communicate her concerns. Tara was her best friend but Liz couldn't exactly voice her feelings about her own sister, could she?

Liz took a deep breath and made an effort to think rationally.

There was nothing between Emma and Eric – nothing. So what if she had met him on a night out in Dublin? It wasn't that big a city, and there was always a chance they could bump into one another.

And just because they'd bumped into one another didn't mean they'd gone off and had a raging affair, did it?

Oh, she'd drive herself crazy if she kept thinking like this. How had a simple comment from a girl who was known for her deviousness, and who Liz didn't like in the first place, sent her into convulsions of suspicion?

She guessed it was all the mysteriousness surrounding Emma's pregnancy.

Tara had been puzzled by her sister's out of the blue pregnancy. And they'd both mooted the likelihood of a clandestine affair.

But there was no reason, no reason at all, for Liz to think that such an affair could involve her own husband.

Was there?

Getting up from the table, she reached for a tissue and quickly wiped her eyes and nose. She had to snap out of this. She was being hysterical, over-emotional – completely unreasonable.

"Love, what's the matter?" Eric reappeared in the doorway, concern written all over his handsome face. "Why are you crying?"

"I don't know," Liz answered truthfully, her thoughts scattered all over. "I don't know why I went off on you like that and I'm sorry. I just ... I suppose I just find it hard sometimes when you're away from us and supposed to be working."

"But I *am* working, love – and working very hard." He moved across the room and put a comforting arm around her shoulders. "I thought we'd agreed that I'd put in the extra hours for a bit, so we can afford to get the extension built."

She sniffed. "I know – and I'm sorry, but for some reason I'm having images of you living it up in pubs and . . . " She shook her head. "I'm sorry. I'm just being silly."

"Yes, you are," Eric agreed firmly, before adding tenderly. "So are we friends again?"

"Of course we are," she replied, resting her head against his chest and hugging him close.

Eric was her husband, the love of her life, the father of her son, and the man she really should know better than to doubt.

Blast Emma Harrington. As far as Liz was concerned, if she never saw the girl again for as long as she lived, she'd be happy.

ELEVEN

BACK HOME IN LONDON, Natalie unpacked her luggage and flung various items of clothing into the laundry basket.

Despite the fact that she'd arrived at Heathrow a good two hours ago, she hadn't yet heard from Steve.

It was strange because she'd had visions of him waiting for her in the Arrivals area, all handsome and smiling and ready to whisk her into his arms and off her feet, like something from a rom-com.

But she'd scanned the crowds a couple of times and there'd been no sign.

Despite herself, she was beginning to worry. All throughout the trip she hadn't heard from him. Despite a few texts asking how he was and if he was missing her, but he hadn't replied.

And of course she'd checked her voice messages too, and there was nothing either, just a series of calls from the office and a few from her mum, who'd obviously forgotten she was away. Or had she even told her? She couldn't remember. These days she was so caught up in work (or indeed Steve) that she'd barely had the time. Oh well, she'd call her later.

Now, she smiled as she unpacked her favourite Cavalli sheath dress, the one she'd been wearing the first night she'd met Tara and Glenn.

She was so lucky to have met those two; the holiday could have been a disaster otherwise. Well, lucky to have met Tara anyway – after the first day or so she hadn't seen that much of Glenn.

They were a good pair who obviously adored one another, though oddly they didn't seem to have that much in common – she with her pyramids, he with his water sports.

But Natalie envied the fact that Tara would never be lonely with Glenn around – the two seemed so easy together and seemed to enjoy a great relationship.

The fact that she had no interest in settling down and getting married was a refreshing perspective, but also a little frustrating for someone like Natalie who would give *anything* to settle down.

Unlike her, Tara had someone to come home to every evening. She didn't know what it was like to return to an empty flat after a hard day's work and have nothing but four walls to complain to.

Having unpacked and sorted her clothes, Natalie padded barefoot out to the kitchen and rummaged around in the drawers for a takeaway menu.

Although, she thought, there was indeed something nice about being able to slob around in comfortable sweats, something she couldn't do if she was living with Steve.

He'd never seen her without make-up. Even when he

stayed the night she made sure she removed her face only after sex, and since he usually snoozed on the following day, she usually had the war paint applied well before he surfaced.

She picked up her phone to order dinner and having placed the order, once again checked her messages. Nothing.

Not a single reply to the messages she'd sent him while away. Granted, she'd only sent – what – one or two brief texts and ... damn she realised, horrified, as she scrolled through the thread, make that eleven or twelve ... no, *thirteen*. How on earth had she managed that?

All those late-night drinks with Tara had obviously loosened her fingers, because most of these were very definitely tipsy-texts. Yikes. Steve would think she'd gone barmy. She'd better call him now and apologise and –

As if on cue, and much to her delight his name appeared onscreen. Actually, now that she thought about it, maybe it wasn't possible to reach her through the network in Egypt so that was why she hadn't heard from him.

Excitedly she clicked onto the message. With any luck she might see him tonight. OK, so she was dog-tired and if he called round the frumpy sweats would definitely have to go but ...

Please stop stalking me.

Puzzled, Natalie stared at the words. *Stalking?* What was he on about? Then she smiled and rolled her eyes. This was obviously one of his little jokes. Still grinning, she hit the 'call' button and waited. He could be a howl sometimes. But at least now she knew he was in a good mood and –

"Yes?"

Hearing him pick up on the other end, she beamed. "Hey babe, just back – "

"Sorry, but I really don't have time for this now," the object of her affection interjected shortly. "Can't you just leave me alone?"

She blinked. "Steve, it's me, Natalie."

"I know bloody well who it is – unfortunately," he groaned. "Look Nat, I thought I made this clear."

"Made *what* clear?"

"Hey we had a few dates and it was great but –"

Her heart began to thump. "But what?"

"But, that's it. We're not really suited, you and me. I thought you understood that."

"Understood what?"

He took a deep breath. "Look, you're great and it's been fun but – "

Her eyes widened in disbelief as she sensed what was coming, "But what?" she repeated timidly.

"I just don't think this is going anywhere." On his side, she heard another phone ring in the background, and guessed he must still be at the office.

"Don't be so silly," she said, trying to keep her voice light, "of course it's going somewhere. You have no idea how much I missed you while I was away and – "

"Yeah, I do actually – I have all the sodding texts to prove it."

"Right, well, I can explain those." She gave a little laugh. "I'd had one or two too many so – "

"Natalie, I really don't have time to discuss this," he said impatiently. "As I said, I just don't think we're suited."

Of course they were suited! She and Steve were great

together – perfect together. How could he say that they weren't?

"But – but what about our trip?" she spluttered. "If we 'weren't suited' as you say, why did you so readily agree to come on holiday with me?"

"What? I didn't agree to anything. It was all your idea and you had it all arranged before you even asked me!" Steve sounded mightily put out. "Talk about railroading somebody."

"Well, you could have let me know that you didn't want to go instead of letting me down at the last minute," she said, irked that he saw things in such a way. "I paid a fortune for that resort."

Steve seemed to be struggling to hold his temper.

"Natalie, I told you at the time that I would let you know if and when I had time to take a holiday, and that we would discuss it. But you didn't listen. You just went right ahead and booked it anyway. Man, we barely know one another. In all my life I don't think I've ever met a bird so pushy."

Her heart sank. "We barely know one another? Steve, we've had sex at least a hundred times."

"Yeah, well ..." He paused for a minute, as if trying to choose the right words. "Look, Nat, as far as I'm concerned it was just that – sex. Maybe you thought it meant something more but ..."

She couldn't remember ever feeling so low. *Just sex?* What about love and companionship and all the things she thought they'd shared? How could it've been 'just sex'?

"We weren't a couple, Nat. I wasn't looking for a relationship. I thought you knew that – especially when I told you I wasn't keen on that holiday, and I'd blown you ... I mean, hadn't seen you that much beforehand."

"But I thought that was because you were busy with work. You *told* me you were busy with work. And I was busy too, so I thought the trip would be a good opportunity for us both to kick back, and ..." Natalie couldn't finish the rest of the sentence. She'd thought he'd be thrilled at the idea, delighted that she'd gone to such effort just for him. But obviously she'd been wrong.

"Nat – it's not going to work, OK?" Steve interjected, his voice softening somewhat. "You're a great girl, but I'm just not ready for a relationship with – with *anyone* at the moment. There's too much going on in my life right now."

"Like what? Maybe I can help," she replied eagerly, heartened by his change in tone. She could help him through whatever was going wrong in his life at the moment. That was what supportive girlfriends did, didn't they? They could put their passionate romance aside and she'd just concentrate on being Steve's confidante, his shoulder to cry on, his rock of strength –

"I don't need any help," he hissed. "Look, can't you bloody just take the hint? I don't know where you got the idea that this was something serious. Yes, we had some good times together but – "

"*Some* good times together! Steve, we were –"

"Ah, Natalie, please just ... leave me alone, will you? If I'd known you'd turn out to be some psycho bunny-boiler, I'd have run a mile."

She - a bunny-boiler? *Psycho* bunny-boiler?

"But how could I possibly crowd you when I hardly ever see you?"

"I'm sorry, you're a nice girl, Nat, but it's just not meant to be. See you round."

With that, he rang off, leaving her staring dumbly at the handset for what seemed like an age.

What had happened to the grand homecoming she'd anticipated? The big love affair she'd described to Tara in Egypt?

Had this really happened? Had Steve – the love of her life, the man she was supposed to marry – had he just ... dumped her?

She was eventually snapped out of her reverie by the ringing of the intercom. For a brief second, she wondered if it was Steve at the front door, if he had been playing an elaborate (and admittedly cruel) joke on her.

But no, it was the delivery guy with her takeaway.

Wishing that she'd ordered a fattening and more comforting dish like fried rice and crispy duck, instead of anaemic low-fat chow mein, Natalie went out and dazedly paid the delivery guy.

Her appetite by then having completely deserted her, she went back inside and threw the whole lot in the bin.

She was just no good at this, was she?

For all her achievements, her business savvy and professional expertise, when it came to matters of the heart, Natalie didn't have the first idea.

TWELVE

"So how's everything?" Tara asked her mother. It was her first visit home since her return from Egypt, having been up to her eyes with work after the ten-day break.

"Everything is the same as it always is," Isobel replied with a put-upon sigh.

"And Emma? How is she now?"

Her sister was in bed, apparently 'worn out from her pregnancy'. "She's finding it very hard. And sure why wouldn't she - doing it all on her own."

Tara smarted. "Mum, don't you think all this secrecy about the dad is a little bit foolish? Fair enough if she doesn't want to tell him, but why not us?" Not to mention that it was also starting to smack of attention-seeking.

"Well, it's her own business, isn't it? And who's to say that telling him will make things any better? He could be an awful layabout for all we know."

That was true, Tara thought, a little guilty that she hadn't considered that perhaps Emma was being secretive about the dad simply because she wanted nothing to do with him.

"Well, yes, of course it's her own business, but by refusing to ask him for help, she's making things hard on you and Dad too. It's hardly fair at her age that she should be moving back home and expecting you to look after her."

Isobel smiled. "She was always a home bird," she replied fondly.

Tara said nothing. Having got over the initial surprise, Isobel had now resumed normal service and was back to feeling sorry for – and needlessly indulging – her youngest.

Of course, Tara couldn't blame their mum for wanting to help Emma out in her hour of need, but still she felt annoyed at her sister for blatantly exploiting her parents' generosity. Still, those two always had a close relationship, and she knew Isobel would go to the ends of the earth to keep Emma happy.

"I'm sure she has her reasons," her mother went on, "but to be truthful, I'm wondering lately if she might have been in contact with him. She's going out in the evenings a lot these days, and doesn't say where."

"Oh?"

"And when she comes back she's usually in much better form."

"I wonder is it anyone from around here then?" Tara wondered out loud. They'd all assumed the father was some guy she'd been seeing in Dublin during her short stint living there.

But perhaps not.

With that, Emma appeared at the doorway and they

looked up guiltily, both wondering if she'd overheard them talking about her.

"Emma, pet." Isobel cried, getting up. "Did you manage to get any sleep?"

Her daughter gave a deep sigh in reply. "Actually, I was just about to drop off when I heard Tara come in." This sounded innocent, but she knew her sister well enough to understand the deliberate dig. "Did you have a nice holiday?" she asked and again there was an edge to her tone.

"It was great, thanks. Sorry I haven't been to see you before now. Work has been manic."

"Oh, that's OK – I'm sure you've got much more important things to be doing than worrying about me," her sister replied mournfully.

"Sit down there and take the weight off your feet, pet," Isobel urged, going over to the sink and filling the kettle. "Would you like a cup of tea?"

Tara marvelled at the way she fussed over her. Fair enough, she'd been sickly as a child and this had always given Isobel reason to worry, but by the way her mother carried on, you'd swear Emma was still a helpless baby.

It hurt too that her mother had never exactly fallen over herself to do the same for Tara, but the Harrington family dynamic was ever thus, and at this stage in their lives it was hardly going to change.

"I was just telling Tara all about Dave McNamara getting engaged," Isobel said and, confused, Tara's head snapped up. When she flashed her a pointed stare she realised that their mother was trying to give Emma the impression that she and Tara had been partaking in a bit of local gossip rather than discussing her.

"Yes," she replied after a beat, deciding to play along, despite the fact that this was the first she'd heard of the aforementioned engagement. But perhaps this time her mother was right; Emma seemed in bad enough form as it was. "That's a bit of a surprise, isn't it?"

"I suppose so," Emma replied sourly.

"He's about the same age as you, isn't he Tara?" Isobel persisted as she stood waiting for the kettle to boil.

"Yes – we were in the same class at school." She grinned. "It's funny – he used to have a bit of a crush on me, actually."

"He had a crush on *everyone*, Tara," Emma said testily, spots of colour appearing on both cheeks.

"Right – I take it he tried it on with you too?" she laughed, but inside she was a little miffed by her reaction to what had only been a joke. Her little sister also seemed to really enjoy cutting Tara down to size. "Well, he hasn't changed much over the years apparently."

Again Emma rolled her eyes – Dave McNamara and his antics evidently the last thing on her mind.

"So really - how have you been?" Tara asked, changing the subject. "Morning sickness any better these days?"

"Morning sickness?" Emma grumbled. "It lasts all bloody day."

"There's been no let-up at all, sure there hasn't?" Isobel added, putting a mug of tea in front of her youngest. "She's been terribly misfortunate altogether. I never really suffered with that kind of thing when I was carrying ye, thank the Lord."

Hearing this, Tara quickly admonished herself for being so unfeeling about her sister's plight.

Still, try as she might, she just couldn't help but feel that Emma was keeping them all in the dark for a very good reason. And if as she suspected, her sister had been messing around with someone she shouldn't have, then it was very difficult indeed to feel sorry for her.

She'd always been the same growing up – only keen on the boys who weren't openly interested in her. Was it the challenge, the thrill of the chase?

Tara couldn't understand it. Then again, she'd never been able to truly understand Emma anyway; the way her sister was so determined to feel continually hard done by, and quick to manipulate.

The two of them truly were chalk and cheese.

THIRTEEN

Despite her determination not to let Emma's comments get to her, Liz discovered that this was far more difficult than she'd thought.

One evening, shortly after he and Liz had finished dinner, Eric announced that he was thinking of going out for a bit.

"I thought I might give Colm a ring – see if he fancies a few pints in The Bridge," he said. "You don't mind, do you? I haven't seen him in ages."

"Of course I don't mind," Liz had replied easily. It was Eric's first Friday night off in ages and even though she was a little stung that he'd chosen to spend it elsewhere, she didn't blame him. And after their argument about his socialising in Dublin, she wasn't about to start behaving like a shrew. "He was only saying the same thing the other day, actually."

"I'm sure I won't be too late – Colm won't drink too many pints – you know how these lads don't like to let themselves go."

Liz smiled inwardly. Despite his apparent open-mindedness, Eric nearly always referred to his friend's sexuality in a joking manner. Typical macho Irishman, she thought affectionately as he went off to get ready.

But her affection turned out to be very short-lived.

Eric was in the shower, his deep baritone singing voice filling the house and causing Toby to look around in wonder, trying to figure out what the awful noise was.

Liz was in the bedroom, putting away some newly laundered clothing when Eric's phone beeped from the bed. She picked up the handset and nonchalantly checked the screen, suspecting that it must be Colm replying to his friend's invitation. But when she saw the name that appeared, Liz's blood went cold.

The phone still in her hand, she slumped heavily down on the bed. Why was Emma Harrington messaging her husband?

And *was* it Colm he was planning to meet tonight? Her hand shaking, she dropped the phone on the bedcovers. As much as she wanted to, she couldn't bring herself to read the message. That was crossing a line.

But hadn't Eric crossed a line by corresponding with his ex-girlfriend behind Liz's back?

It was obvious they had been in contact before. Emma's name was stored in Eric's contacts. So what the hell was going on?

A couple of feet away, the water stopped.

Feeling like an interloper, she quickly dropped the laundry on the bed and exited the room.

OK, she thought, trying to get a grip on herself as she

went back into the kitchen. It might be nothing – it might *mean* nothing.

Soon, Eric reappeared in the kitchen, clean-shaven and nicely dressed in jeans and a blue button-down shirt. A bit too nicely dressed for a visit to the local? Liz wondered.

"I think I heard your phone go off while you were in the shower," she said, trying to keep her voice steady.

"Did it?" Eric went back into the bedroom and soon after reappeared in the kitchen with the phone in his hand. "It's from Emma Harrington," he said, his tone a little too wary for Liz's liking, although she couldn't help but be heartened by the fact that he'd told the truth.

"Emma? Why would she be texting you?"

He shrugged. "She said something before about maybe having a tip for me about a job . . . "

"Oh, where?"

"Well, it's just a blank message so it's obviously a mistake."

Liz knew he was lying. His face had turned bright red and he couldn't bring himself to look directly at her.

"Right." Her insides burned as she tried to think of a response. A blank message? What planet did he think she was from?

"Anyway, I'd better head away," he said, apparently satisfied that he'd come up with a convincing explanation. "Colm said he'd be there around half past."

"Right," Liz replied, her brain scrambling. As far as she knew her husband hadn't yet phoned Colm about this unplanned night out, so she wasn't sure how Eric knew what time he would be there.

Deep down, she knew all too well that her husband of three years wasn't meeting his childhood friend.

At least not the one he'd told her he was.

FOURTEEN

THE SECLUDED LAKESIDE area had always been a favourite for amorous young locals, and although it felt very different these days, for Eric there was still something calming and peaceful about the area.

"I think Liz saw your name come up on my phone earlier," he said tentatively. "It looks bad."

"I'm sorry. I just wanted to let you know I'd be late, and to be honest I didn't think for a second that she'd check your messages. Isn't that an invasion of privacy?"

"I didn't say she did, I said I *thought* she might have seen the name," he replied testily. "I don't think she did, but I had to admit that it was you, just to be on the safe side."

Emma's eyes widened. "And what explanation did you give?"

He shrugged. "I said the message was blank, so it must have been a mistake."

She shook her head. "She's going to suspect something you know. I really think you should just tell her."

"How can I?"

"She's your wife. At this stage, she deserves to know. And she's going to find out sooner or later."

"Yeah, but I still don't know how I feel about it myself yet ... so I don't want to have to deal with her feelings too. I know that sounds awful, as if I don't care. But right now, I really don't think I could cope with that on top of everything else."

"You can't let it drag on forever, though."

"I know," he replied, his head heavy. "My head is just so messed up at the moment. I don't want to hurt her ..."

"People will get hurt whatever you do. And the more time we spend just talking, the worse it'll be in the end – especially if she already suspects something."

"I know, I know ..." His voice trailed off and for a long moment the two remained silent, lost in their own thoughts.

Eventually, he spoke again. "So what about yourself?" he asked. "How are you feeling now ... about everything?"

She sighed. "It's hard when everyone is so curious. It all seems so furtive and I know Tara thinks I'm doing it on purpose. Still, nobody knows – well, nobody except you anyway."

"How did the two of us ever get ourselves into such a mess, Em?" he said, shaking his head, addressing her as he used to when they were growing up.

"We're some pair all right." She managed a dry laugh. "Tara's trying her utmost to wrangle it out of me. Having these long chats about how tough it'll be for me on my own."

"Are you going to confide in her? Maybe you should - Tara of all people knows ..."

"Yeah, yeah Tara knows everything," Emma interjected dismissively. "You sound like my mother."

"I hope not. But maybe it's no harm to look at it with an adult eye all the same. It's too easy to fall back into our old ways growing up."

"Hence the problem." She snorted. "Well, at least the sex was good, *that* was an eye-opener, let me tell you..."

He smiled self-consciously, a little taken aback that she could be so candid about the whole thing. But that was Emma – tough as old boots.

Then he looked at his watch, and his tone grew serious. "I'd better be heading back. I told Liz I was meeting Colm for a few drinks ..."

"Right," she replied, a clear trace of annoyance in her tone this time. "Where are you going? The Bridge?" It had always been their pub of choice when they were younger. "Wish I could tag along. Any excuse to get out of that house."

"Your parents still giving you trouble?"

"Well, not exactly – my mother is all over me at the moment and it's really doing my head in." Then she sighed deeply. "It's my own fault for coming home. I suppose. Maybe I should have stayed in Dublin, moved in with Tara or something." She giggled. "I'd say she'd love that – little sis moving in and disrupting her perfect life."

He could hear the bitterness in her voice but said nothing, because in a way he could understand why Emma felt hard done by in comparison.

Tara was a go-getter, someone who had made a great success of her life, with her nice career, nice car and plenty of money. Unlike her little sister who now had to contemplate an altogether more bleak future as a thirty-something single mother living under her parent's roof.

"Does Colm know anything?"

"Nah – not the kind of thing you discuss with him, really," Eric said, shaking his head slowly. "And of course he knows Liz so ..."

She looked thoughtful. "I don't think she likes me very much. I met her on Main Street the other day and she wasn't happy when I mentioned I'd met you in town."

"I know – she told me." His tone was disapproving. "And to be honest, you put me in a bit of a spot with that."

"It just came out in conversation," she said quickly. "I didn't mean to cause trouble or anything." She sighed. "Are you sure you don't want to tell her? It would make it so much easier for both of –"

"Not yet. I don't have to heart to shatter her illusions about me. Not just yet."

"As long as you're sure. And in the meantime, know that I'm here whenever you need me."

"Thanks. I don't know what I'd do without you. You're the only one who understands."

FIFTEEN

STEVE HAD DUMPED HER, but Natalie was beginning to get over it. What else could she do?

Granted in the interim, she had sent him one or two late-night texts, tentatively suggesting that they talk but had given up when he'd eventually replied: *Leave me alone, you psycho bitch!*

So that was that. Another love lost, another dream shattered.

Since then, she did what any normal broken-hearted girl would do and threw herself into her work even more.

Jordan King, her latest recruit, was taking up much of her time as she and Danni worked strenuously on keeping his profile squeaky clean, while Michael Sharpe, the regular thorn in Natalie's side, oddly seemed to be behaving himself.

So work was going smoothly as ever while Natalie's personal life went from bad to worse. And this time, it seemed she no longer even had Freya to help her get over it.

Her best friend had since moved to a fabulous stately

pile miles away in Richmond; way too far for Natalie to pop over and cry on her shoulder like she used to when she lived in the city. She'd called Freya the night after Steve dumped her – hoping for some much-needed sympathy.

"I always thought he was a prick anyway," her friend stated. "You deserve much better."

"But I really thought he was the *one.*"

"Oh, for goodness' sake, Nat – you barely knew the guy. And you'll find someone else – you always do."

Natalie was taken aback by her friend's irritable reaction. She'd hoped that Freya might suggest coming over for the night, so the two could sit in and spent the night scoffing chocolates and bawling over *Sleepless in Seattle,* the way they used to before she met boring old Simon.

"That's easy for you to say. You're engaged, and happy and – "

"Pregnant," Freya finished dryly.

"What?"

"I'm pregnant. And before you ask, no – it wasn't planned. It very definitely wasn't planned."

"Oh." Natalie didn't know what to think. Freya was not the maternal type. She'd even go as far to say that her best friend hated kids, hated being in same room as them, breathing the same air ...

So her first reaction to this news was amazement. Though her second was pure and unadulterated jealousy. Freya was getting married with a baby on the way. She was living Natalie's dream.

"I didn't know what to say either when the doctor confirmed it," Freya said when Natalie remained silent. "I've been on the Pill forever and me and Si aren't exactly at it like the newlyweds we're soon supposed to be. But it's happened and he's thrilled, and it's the end of my life as I know it. And of course now we have to postpone the wedding until after it's born, which is obviously a total bore."

She sounded so hard and dismissive about the whole thing that Natalie wanted to throttle her. How could she be so callous? Did she not realise that she had the perfect house, the perfect man – the perfect life? As it was, Natalie couldn't even find herself a decent prospect, let alone a boyfriend, and lately was reduced to making eyes at homeless men on the bloody Tube.

"Well ... congratulations," she said tentatively, while at the same time bracing herself for an onslaught of abusive outrage. 'What do you mean congratulations?' she could imagine Freya wailing, 'This is my worst bloody nightmare!'

But instead her friend replied simply. "Thanks – I suppose. But sorry, Nat, I really can't chat for much longer. Si's parents are coming over for dinner this evening and – "

"That's OK. I'd better go too." *Back to my sad, lonely and pathetic existence*, she added inwardly. "Talk to you soon."

"No problem, darling. And don't worry too much about that idiot. Plenty of fish in the sea and all that."

Natalie smiled tightly. *That idiot was the man I was hoping to marry.* "Of course. See you soon."

She'd been so sure Freya would understand, had been certain that her friend would be only too happy to help her get over the humiliation– like they'd done for one another all throughout their friendship. And her other close friends were all either happily married, engaged or long-term attached.

No point in phoning them either; no doubt they were just as uninterested as Freya was about the ups and downs of her pathetic love life.

OK, so she had only been with Steve for a few months. That didn't mean her relationship was any less worthy than theirs, did it? Although, evidently, in Happily-Married Land, it did. Natalie's disastrous love life was a million miles away from her friends' cosy coupledom and happy domesticity.

Now despite herself, as she and Danni grabbed a cab and drove in the direction of Kensington, she was looking forward to the launch of Purple Grapefruit, the latest in a long line of ultra-trendy London clubs.

While a rival PR firm was handling the account, invites had been issued to Blue Moon, their rivals evidently hoping that some of the company's more prolific clients – England international Michael Sharpe, actress Jennifer Cox, or the much-photographed glamour model Cassandra – might make an appearance. Cassandra would be there, Natalie knew; the model (and her humongous breasts) never lost an opportunity to be photographed for the tabloids, earning herself a fat fee in return. The girl was a nightmare to work with, but despite her trashy image was a very shrewd busi-nesswoman, determined to use her ...erm ... *assets* to the best of her ability.

Reaching the venue, Natalie got out of the cab, adjusted her Pucci mini-dress over her thighs and waited for Danni to pay the cab driver.

If the events company were any good they would have

sent VIP guests a stretch limo, she thought, rather self-satis-fied that their rivals evidently didn't have Blue Moon's class. And the red carpet thing was naff.

Whoever this lot were, they were clearly amateurs, and if the club's promoters thought they could attract celebrities to Purple Grapefruit on this dismal showing, they really had their work cut out.

But if all else failed and this launch failed to attract the big stars, the reality TV lot could always be relied upon to pick up the slack, Natalie thought, spying a well-worn regular standing on the sidelines gleefully waving at cameras despite the fact that they were pointed the other way. If she'd been handling this she wouldn't let those bottom-feeders near the place.

But she thought, as she and Danni entered and accepted a glass of champagne – *cheap* champagne, she discovered grimacing (she would have insisted on Laurent Perrier at the very least) – this wasn't her gig, so tonight she could just sit back, relax and if photographs from the event didn't make the papers the next day, some other poor sod could take the rap.

Barely an hour into the event, Natalie was bored sense-less. There wasn't a sniff of celebrity, even Cassandra hadn't bothered showing up and the atmosphere at a chess convention would have been more exciting.

Although Danni seemed to be enjoying herself, she thought wryly, spotting her assistant chatting with a group of men at the bar. Then again, she rarely got to attend one of these events outside work and she wouldn't be here at all if Natalie hadn't strong-armed her into accompanying her.

She sighed. She was definitely getting too old for this. A

few years ago she would have been the life and soul, flitting here there and charming everyone – no matter how tedious the company might be.

But these days, she just couldn't be bothered. While she still thrived on the cut and thrust of the day-to-day stuff, dealing with media contacts and managing client accounts, she was beginning to find the social aspect of it all so samey.

Fourteen-odd years working the London scene did that to you, she supposed, and it was inevitable that she'd eventually tire of it all. And once again she sorely wished, she had a warm house and welcoming partner to come home to.

Realising that lately she seemed worryingly prone to gloominess, Natalie took a gulp from her glass of cheaper-than-cheap fizz and strode resolutely across to Danni. She'd better snap out of this and start working the room – otherwise, word would get round that Natalie Webb had lost her edge and she'd be on the scrapheap in more ways than one.

"There you are!" Danni beamed at her, a smile that would have looked warm and welcoming to anyone else, but which she knew meant 'save me!'. "Everyone, this is my boss, Natalie."

As Danni didn't offer any further introductions, Natalie just smiled and said hello to the three men who all looked to be in their mid-to-late thirties, and dressed in a mixture of Hugo Boss and Paul Smith. The bald one, despite his thick gold wedding ring, was flirting unashamedly with Danni, while the others alongside him looked on, mildly amused.

City types, Natalie decided instantly. The kind who often got invited to these things to make up the numbers.

"You work in PR too?" One, also sporting a wedding

ring asked her, as the bald man renewed his onslaught on Danni.

"Yes."

"Sounds like an exciting job."

"It can be."

"Bet you get invited to parties like this all the time."

"Yes, but to be honest, most of them are a little more exciting than this," she couldn't resist saying. She shouldn't bitch but she was in a foul mood, and she'd wasted her first outing in her new Pucci dress on this poor showing.

"Really?" a third man turned in her direction. "You're not having a good time?"

"Not exactly." She wrinkled her nose. "Are you?"

"Well, we've got excellent food, champagne and a great atmosphere – what more do you want?"

Deciding instantly that she didn't like this guy with his haughty eyes, aquiline nose and slightly weird accent, she made a face. "A little bit of imagination be nice. Champagne and foie gras are so bloody nineties."

"I know what you mean," he agreed, much to Natalie's surprise, while one of his companions gave him an odd glance. "I suppose they could have tried something different."

"Something different – they could have made an effort to start with. This is supposed be a club, not a reception for the Queen. Now if I were organising a party like this, I'd give it a theme," she went on, warming to her subject. "This whole thing is crying out for a theme."

"Such as?"

"Purple, obviously," she rolled her eyes. "A purple entrance carpet to start with - the obvious choice, and something to really get the cameras clicking. And while we've got a theme going, why not serve Kir Royale instead of cheap sparkling Cava?"

"Purple drinks for Purple Grapefruit," he said, nodding solemnly.

"I know – and there's this fab Lebanese lemonade you can get that would be perfect too." She shrugged. "Of course it's all so tacky but tacky's in these days and celebs love it."

"I see. So tacky's the way forward?"

"For a place like this – definitely."

"Right, next time the company arrange an event of this size I must call on you for advice, Ms ... what was it again?"

She stared at him warily, for the first time wondering if she'd said too much. "Webb, Natalie Webb from Blue Moon PR. And you are?"

"Jay Murray," he replied, shaking her hand. "Labyrinth Event Management."

She closed her eyes. *Shit.*

At that moment she understood why Tara, the Irish girl she'd met on holiday, had taken the decision not to drink. If she'd put her foot in it like Natalie just had, then who could blame her.

She gulped and swallowed hard as she realised she had just insulted the work of one of London's most prolific event management companies.

How could she have been so stupid - not to mention unprofessional - as to openly criticise the party in front of the organisers? Or automatically presume that Jay Murray, with his Hugo Boss suit and stuffy, buttoned-up appearance, was simply a hanger-on?

Though given that he wasn't racing around the venue like a headless chicken, it was unlikely Murray was one of the planners. Which meant he had to be Labyrinth management.

Even worse.

"So I take it you're not a big fan of plain old canapés and champagne?" he asked, his dark eyes mocking her.

"It's Natalie," she said, with a nervous laugh. "I just thought that a place like this could ... could do better, that's all ..." she trailed off, too embarrassed to elaborate. Thanks to the aforementioned Cava, she'd already said way too much. "Look, I'm sorry if I insulted you – I had no idea – "

"No idea that we'd spent weeks organising this ... wait a second ... what was it you called it again? Ah yes ... 'a reception for the Queen'."

She bit her lip, mortified.

"But it's OK," he went on. "As it happens, I agree with you, and it's good to get the feedback. I like to get a feel for what people really think of our events, which is why I try to blend in at these things."

"Blend in, or go in disguise? When we were introduced, I had you pegged as a city trader."

He glanced down at his attire. "Really? I thought all the party people dressed like this," he joked, before adding, "But as I remember it, Ms Webb, or should I say Natalie, we weren't actually introduced before you so eloquently voiced your opinion."

Yikes! She'd walked into that one. Saying nothing more, she took another gulp of champagne, wishing that she were anywhere else but here. She hadn't really wanted to come to this sodding party in the first place – fitting that like everything else in her life these days, it should end up in disaster.

"In any case, I think you're right," Murray conceded. "We had some great ideas for this, but management wouldn't go for any of it. Although to be honest, nobody had come up with your purple carpet suggestion and you're right – it *is* the obvious choice. You could have a future in this kind of thing, Natalie – your talents are obviously wasted in PR."

By his tone, she knew he was teasing her. Thank goodness he hadn't taken serious umbrage. Jack Moon would kill her if he found out she'd managed to alienate one of the city's top people.

"Yes, well, it was just a suggestion," she said, cringing as she realised how stupid her tacky ideas must have sounded to someone of his expertise. "I see a lot of this kind of thing and well, it would be good for once to experience something different."

"You work with Blue Moon, you said?"

"Yes, I'm an account manager there."

"Great company – Jack's a good man."

Damn, this guy and her boss obviously knew each other. The last thing she needed was her work life going to pot too. If only she hadn't opened her big fat mouth.

Murray was now leaning casually against the bar, and Natalie realised that they had gradually moved away from the others.

"So, do you think the place has any chance of being the next Ivy? And this time, give me your honest opinion – I wouldn't want you to hold back or anything." His mouth curled up into a not altogether unattractive smile and yet again she tried to place that accent. It was London, but with a faint tinge of something more ... Scottish maybe?

She smiled back, thankful that the tension had finally been relieved. "Well no offence – but with a damp squib like this for a launch, I doubt it." She shook her head from side to side. "Never mind celebrities, it's not even the kind of place I'd hang out."

"I see, and where would that kind of place be?" he asked, looking her squarely in the eye, and with a jolt she realised he was flirting with her.

She took a second or two to study him properly. He was tall, so tall he towered above her five-foot-five frame by a good six or seven inches. And he seemed well built, although it was difficult to tell what lay underneath that banker's suit. But while he had a nice face, he wasn't conventionally attractive, save for his dark, almost black eyes, and now that she thought about it, rather arresting presence.

Natalie only wished she'd taken notice of that presence long before she'd started shooting her mouth off. Yes, she decided as Jay Murray's dark eyes stared back at her own, he wasn't half bad.

Almost instinctively she straightened, thrust forward her boobs and flashed him her most alluring smile.

"A million miles away from where supposed city-types like you hang out," she replied, her smile widening.

Freya had been right, Natalie thought happily, there *were* plenty more fish in the sea.

And she'd just decided she might like to land this one.

SIXTEEN

"You would have loved Natalie – she was an absolute scream," Tara told her friend, as the two of them sat in Liz's kitchen having coffee. "We had a such a laugh the day we went to Cairo. I've never known anyone to be so frank and open about what they really wanted in life. She's beautiful, successful, has the most amazing glamorous life and," she told Liz enviously, "from what I've seen, a better wardrobe than Kate Middleton. Yet all Natalie wants is to get married. Mad, isn't it?"

Liz said nothing.

"To be honest, she reminded me a little bit of you in a way," Tara went on. "You know, the way you were so excited about marrying Eric and having a family of your own."

"Maybe she should be careful what she wishes for," Liz said, her tone uncharacteristically sullen.

"Liz? What's the matter?" Tara asked, setting down her coffee mug. "Has something happened?"

"I don't know ..."

For the first time, she noticed how drawn and anxious Liz looked today. She hadn't really noticed anything untoward but come to think of it, *she* had been doing most of the talking about her holiday, whereas Liz had just sat there quietly listening and saying little more than a brief 'really?' and 'that sounds nice'.

She sat forward in her chair. "What do you mean you don't know?"

"I ... I'm not sure. I could be just imagining it, but I think Eric might be ... well, as I said I'm not sure."

"You think he might be what, Liz?"

Then Liz quietly told her about Eric's strange behaviour and the longer and more unusual hours he seemed to be working.

"But what makes you automatically think he's having an affair?" Tara asked, shocked.

Liz had always been one of the most rational people Tara had ever come across, so this was very disconcerting.

"I don't know how to explain it, and maybe it sounds silly to you, but I just know. Call it what you want, female intuition, whatever. He's my husband, and lately he's been acting very strangely, staying in Dublin for long periods of time – things like that. And then, when he is home, instead of spending time with us he goes out with Colm . . . or sometimes he doesn't even tell me where he's going."

At this, something niggled in the back of Tara's mind, but she was so surprised by Liz's revelations that she couldn't think straight. "But wasn't that the plan? That he'd do all these extra hours so you could get the house finished?"

She shook her head. "Maybe it all sounds irrational to you, but you don't know what's been going on."

"So tell me. Tell me what makes you think your husband, who I know adores you, is cheating on you. Liz, it doesn't make any sense."

Her expression closed over. "Fine – I'm sorry I said anything."

"Oh, don't be like that. I'm merely trying to get to the bottom of this, maybe try and give you a different perspective – "

"Tara, don't use your psychobabble on me," Liz snapped. "I'm not one of your clients."

"No, but you are my friend, and I'm trying to help you." This was *very* worrying. Liz and Eric were as solid as any couple Tara had ever known. "Look, maybe the move down here has taken its toll on Eric a bit more than it has on you. It must be hard on him having to go back and forth to Dublin and leaving you and Toby so often, mustn't it?"

"He doesn't seem to have problems leaving us to go out with Colm," Liz said petulantly.

"But he and Colm are friends, and you said before that it's been difficult for you and Eric to get out together or find someone to look after Toby." Then she had a thought. "Look, why don't I ask my mum to pop over some night, and keep an eye on Toby? Or, even better – I could ask Emma. She isn't doing much these days, and it would do her good to get in some practice before – "

"No, thanks," Liz said sharply, and Tara looked up, surprised by the vehemence in her tone. "Seriously," she added, her voice softening a little, "I'm sure we'll be fine. And you're right – I probably am just imagining things."

For a few minutes, the two of them sat quietly at the table, neither of them sure what to say. Shortly afterwards, the phone ringing broke through the silence and Liz stood up to answer.

"Hey love," Phone to her ear, she returned to the table and sat back down across from Tara. "Oh," she replied then.

She looked up at the tone of her friend's voice.

"I'm sorry to hear that. Is your mam OK?"

By Liz's concerned expression, it seemed that Eric was passing on some bad news. Tara stood up from the kitchen table, and wandered into the living room, wanting to give them some privacy.

"I know that," she heard her say in the background, "but you two will just have to go yourselves. We can't very well drag Toby along with us. It's a long drive up to Belfast and anyway, what about the dogs?" There was a brief pause. "Yes, I know but there's not a whole lot I can do about that. I have Bruno coming again on Thursday, and there are another two booked in so ... look, we'll talk about it when you get home, OK? All right, love – I'll have a dinner ready for you. See you then."

"Trouble?" Tara enquired, coming back into the kitchen.

"Eric's uncle just died," Liz said sighing. "He was Maeve's only brother, and he's being buried on Saturday in Belfast, where the family's from. Thing is, as much as I want to go, I can't just drop everything– not with Toby and the dogs and – "

"I'll do it," Tara offered quickly.

"What? How?"

"Honestly, Liz, I'll do it. Go with Eric – and stay for the weekend if you like. It would give me an excuse to spend some time with my godson – I don't see enough of him as it is." She smiled. "Honestly, it would be no trouble. I have a couple of appointments, but I can arrange to do those over the phone or online from here – if that's OK with you. And I don't work weekends so – "

"You can do that? People won't mind?"

"Not at all." If her offering to baby-sit made things that bit easier for poor Liz, who seemed to be having a tough time at the moment, then it would be worth it.

"You're sure? But what about the animals?"

"You let me worry about that. Looking after my favourite godson should be no bother, and walking and feeding a few dogs couldn't be that difficult either." OK, so she wasn't the world's greatest dog lover, but it couldn't be *that* bad, could it?

"Tara, I really couldn't ask you to do that."

"You're not asking – I'm offering, actually I'm *insisting*. Go to Belfast with your husband for the funeral. I'm sure he'll need you."

"Well, I don't know if he and his uncle were *that* close, but Maeve would obviously like us to go so ..." Liz was finally coming round to the idea. "Are you sure you'll be OK with Toby? He can be a bit of a handful, you know."

"Me and Toby will be fine," Tara insisted. "We'll have a ball. And I'm well able to look after a few mangy dogs."

Liz grimaced. "Please, don't say that in front of their owners or I won't have a business when I get back," she said, raising a smile for the first time that day. Then she shrugged. "But, if you're sure."

Satisfied that Tara really wanted to do this, Liz flicked through her diary. "Like I thought, there are only three dogs and one cat booked in over the weekend, which isn't too bad. One dog is already here, and the others are due in on Thursday evening. Obviously, I won't take any more bookings in the meantime, and I'll make sure I'm back early on Sunday evening, so you won't have to deal with any of the owners."

"Grand," Tara replied briskly. "I'll be down Friday morning and you can show me what needs to be done."

"What about Glenn?" Liz enquired. "Won't he mind?"

"Are you mad? Glenn will think he's died and gone to heaven having the house to himself for a weekend. He'll be able to watch Sky Sports morning noon and night. Although now that I think of it, he's working Saturday morning anyway, so I'm sure he won't miss me."

"I suppose," Liz looked thoughtful. "Do you know, it will be really strange – I don't think me and Eric have had a single night to ourselves since Toby was born. I know Maeve will be there of course, but still."

"Maybe the time away from here will do you two a bit of good. Help you get to the bottom of whatever it is that's bothering you."

Liz coloured a little. "You're right, we might get the chance to have a proper chat in Belfast over the weekend. Maeve will want to stay at the family home, which means we'll have to get a hotel somewhere. The circumstances aren't ideal, but at least I might get the chance to find out why he's been acting so strange lately."

"Exactly," Tara said, pleased that her friend's spirits had lifted a little. "A little bit of time together and I guarantee you'll come home feeling silly for even thinking such things."

SEVENTEEN

THE FOLLOWING DAY, Liz approached the cafe, Toby in tow. She felt pathetic sneaking around, but she had to know. She had to know if her husband had been telling the truth about meeting Colm for a drink that time.

Yesterday's conversation with Tara had spurred her into action. She couldn't go off to Belfast with Eric until she knew for sure.

She pushed open the door and manoeuvred the buggy inside the cafe.

As she headed towards a vacant table, she smiled briefly at Ella the owner, busy serving coffee to other customers. But the person Liz had really come to see was nowhere in sight.

Having psyched herself up, she felt strangely disappointed that Colm wasn't around.

She positioned the buggy against the wall, sat down at the nearest table and picked up a menu, her heart going like a jackhammer. What had she thought she was going to say to Colm if he had been here? 'Hey I just wanted to ask if my husband was really meeting you for a drink, or if it was just a cover to see his mistress?'

He'd think she was some kind of psycho. Which she admitted ashamedly, was exactly how she'd been behaving.

"Liz, hello!" As if on cue, Colm came through from the kitchen. "How are things?"

She coloured, as if he could somehow read her thoughts. "Great thanks." Of course, now that he was here, she was totally tongue-tied.

"Can I get you something?" he asked, crossing the room to talk to her. "Coffee, cappuccino – something like that? Or we have these fabulous caramel and hazelnut lattes?"

Liz thought about her thickening waistline and non-existent exercise routine. "A black coffee would be great, thanks."

"And for the little fella?" Colm bent down and tickled the toddler's chin, Toby smiling happily up at him. "A cupcake maybe?"

"Thanks but he's fine – I gave him something before we came out. Anyway, I'd be worried about what he'd do with a cupcake – he's a nightmare with food and drink."

Colm laughed. "The apple obviously hasn't fallen far from the tree then because Daddy is a bit of nightmare with drink too. How was he after the other night?" He went to get Liz's coffee. "I swear – it's the last time I let him drag me out for 'a quiet drink'. I think it was about two by the time we left."

Immense relief immediately rushed through Liz. She didn't have to ask Colm anything; Eric had indeed met him for a drink that night. She smiled. "He *was* back very late."

"Late? You were lucky he went home at all! Himself

and Charlie Mellon were pleading with poor Paddy to keep serving. Only for boys in blue were out, I'd say the two of them would still be there propping up the bar." He shook his head. "It was a great night though, and we all had a good laugh – although to be honest, the next morning I was cursing Eric through my hangover. Crikey Liz, I'm just not able for drinking anymore – certainly not the way I was when we were teenagers."

Liz smiled. She'd heard from Tara that the two had been very fond of a few pints in their younger days. In fact, Tara had confessed that she worried Eric would turn out like his dad, who had apparently been a bit too fond of the black stuff, and died of liver failure. His uncle too, which she guessed was partly the reason they were heading to Belfast this weekend.

"Speaking of teenagers," Colm went on, putting a cup of coffee on the table in front of her, "I found those old photos I was telling you about – the ones of me, Eric and Tara from back in the day."

"Oh I'd love to see them sometime," Liz enthused, genuinely interested.

"Wait there, and I'll pop next door to get them." Colm lived next door in a restored Swiss-cottage, which like the café had wonderful views across the water.

While awaiting his return, Liz sat back and exhaled deeply, feeling as though a huge weight had been lifted from her shoulders. She had to snap out of this, this pathetic, unreasonable unwarranted insecurity. She was Eric's wife, and the mother of his child and he loved her. So what if he had a history with Emma? It was exactly that – history. So she really should cop onto herself and start giving her husband the trust and respect he deserved.

"Here we go ..."

She looked up as Colm returned with a small bundle of photographs. He sat down at the table and slid into the seat alongside her. "I'm glad I went looking for them actually, they're really very funny. I still can't believe how much hair I had back then."

"Are you sure you have the time?" Liz asked. "I don't want to keep you."

"Not at all, the place is dead at this hour of the day," he said, gesturing around the café. "Give it another half hour and they'll all be in for lunch."

Liz eagerly picked up the first photo, a cheerful shot of a youthful Colm and Eric standing on the bridge, arms across each other's shoulders. Eric hadn't changed much in the ensuing years, but Colm did indeed have lots more hair.

"Obviously he didn't know about me at that stage," he provided jokingly, "although in all honestly, I hardly knew it myself."

Liz smiled, knowing that growing up, he had gone through the usual period of confusion, before eventually coming to terms with his sexuality.

She went on to the next photo, again a picture of Eric, Colm and a couple of other boys around the same age, who according to him used to get up to 'all sorts of divilment' together.

"That's Dave McNamara, you know – the local councillor?" Colm said, pointing at one.

"Don't think I've met him yet," Liz said, shaking her head.

"Believe me, you'd remember him if you had. A right ladies' man is our Dave."

"The Lakeview Casanova?"

"Exactly. But where's Eric in his reindeer jumper? Ah, there you go." He pointed at another photo and guffawed. "State of it ..."

Liz's eyes widened.

"I reckon Mammy McGrath knitted those for him."

"Oh dear," she laughed, understanding why Colm had been so disparaging about her husband's teenage fashion sense. "I sincerely hope she doesn't start knitting them for Toby. That's a fashion disaster all right."

Colm flicked through some more photographs. "Oh, here's a good one of us all – taken the night of our debs, as you can probably tell. And speaking of disasters, look at the state of Tara."

Liz studied the photograph, unable to believe that the gawky-looking teen wearing a strapless, shapeless and utterly hideous pink dress could possibly be her stylish, confident good friend.

The cerise clashed massively with her auburn hair, although the blonde highlights Tara sported these days made her hair-colour more strawberry-blonde. Still, there was no mistaking those lively eyes and warm smile.

Colm and Eric were there too, smartly dressed in tuxedos and looking stiffly at the camera. Liz was pretty certain that the bow-ties they were wearing didn't stay on for very long after that photograph was taken.

"See that tall nerdy one with the braces?" Colm pointed to the girl alongside him, a mousy kid who'd evidently been the class geek. "*That's* Ruth Seymour."

"What?" Liz looked at him, shocked, and then peered closer. "Hollywood Ruth?"

"The very one." Colm was delighted with himself. "Hard to believe, isn't it? None of us had any idea the ugly duckling would turn out like that, no more than we knew I'd turn out – "

"And who's this?" Liz interjected, pointing to handsome teen beside Tara, though he looked a little older than the others. "He was Tara's date?" she urged when he didn't reply.

"Yes," Colm answered slowly. "He was Tara's date."

"Well, there was certainly nothing ugly about *him*," she laughed. "Lucky old Tara."

Colm forced a smile. "Listen, Liz, sorry about this, but I'd better go back to it." He stood up quickly. "Do you mind looking through the rest of those on your own?"

"Course not – go ahead. I'm enjoying myself actually – these are great. I can't wait to tease Tara about her horrible debs dress when I see her."

He visibly paled. "Ah don't – she'd murder me for showing you these – she hated that dress afterwards."

"Well I can certainly see why."

"Liz really, don't say anything. She can bit a bit touchy about it – honestly."

A little taken aback by the gravity in his tone, she nodded. "OK sure," she replied, picking up the remainder of the photographs.

Liz was so engrossed in the pictures that she failed to question why Colm had felt the need to rush off, when the café was the quietest it had been all morning.

EIGHTEEN

Tara was sorely regretting her generous offer. She didn't know how Liz did this for a living.

"Are you sure you don't mind looking after the place for us?" her friend had asked for the umpteenth time, before she and Eric left for Belfast that morning.

"We'll be fine," she'd told her, shooing her out to the car. "And if I get into any trouble – which I won't," Tara added quickly, when her friend looked worried, "I can always call on Dad."

"Right, well, ring me if there's any problems and - "

"I will. Now go!"

Glenn had offered to come down after work on Saturday to help with the dogs, but Tara wasn't convinced she'd need his help at all. In fact, she was looking forward to spending some time in her hometown; it might help her decide whether or not she wanted to move back for good.

But right then, she was kicking herself. As per Liz's instructions, she was taking the dogs for their afternoon walk, and one of them, a huge brute of a thing called Bruno (and the most hyper and unruly animal she had ever come across) was practically dragging her across the fields behind the house.

And these two little rats who hadn't a hope of keeping up with the bigger dog, kept getting their leads entwined around her feet and tripping her up. It was bloody annoying, and dangerous given that she was carrying Toby in his harness. But judging from his excited giggles, the little boy was thoroughly enjoying his outing.

Now out of nowhere, Bruno took off at a hare's pace, dragging Tara and the others behind him.

"Bruno, come back!" she called breathlessly, as the little rats yapped in annoying unison.

Toby squealed again and as Tara spotted a small rabbit hopping away in front of them, she understood why Bruno had taken off like one the hounds of hell.

By the time she and her motley crew returned an hour later – the dogs still hyper and excited and not in the least bit tired after her strenuous efforts, Tara never wanted to see another animal again.

At least Liz's two, Ben and Jerry, were able to run around the place of their own accord and she didn't have to walk them too. Thank goodness for small mercies and big backyards.

But it seemed there was no let-up with the boarders. Liz had instructed that Tara should take each dog out of their holding-pen to do their business an hour or so after feeding. And while the rats seemed perfectly happy to do her bidding, the huge mutt seemed to treat the whole thing as a big game, and instead of obediently doing his thing in Liz's prescribed 'area' in the yard, began to merrily lead

Tara in circles around the back garden. She swore the dog knew she hadn't a clue and was acting up on purpose.

Honest to goodness, Toby was a saint to look after compared to this fella, she thought, trying in vain to steer him towards the yard. But the savage somehow got it into his head that he'd rather drop his load in the garden next door.

At that stage, she was sick to the back teeth of his antics, it was late and beginning to get dark, and she didn't have the inclination or the energy to stop him from going outside the boundaries.

Not that there were actually any boundaries between Liz's garden and the adjoining grounds. The old cottage had been vacant for years and the 'garden' was overrun with weeds, so as far as she was concerned Bruno could do what he liked.

In fact, she might even suggest to Liz that she use the overgrown garden for this very purpose, rather than have to shovel up the stink from her own backyard.

Tara's stomach turned as she thought about cleaning up after the dogs – especially this one. It was just as well that Bruno had taken a fancy to this particular spot – at least that would be one less to deal with.

Holding Bruno by the lead, she turned away, as the dog squatted bang-slap in the middle of the garden.

"Hey, what the hell do you think you're doing?" cried an angry voice, and she nearly jumped ten foot in the air with fright.

Tara looked around to see an annoyed man coming out of the supposedly abandoned house. Yikes! Liz hadn't mentioned that the house had been sold.

Or that the Incredible Hulk had bought it.

"Oh, my goodness – I'm so sorry," Tara began breath-lessly, her cheeks reddening, as she quickly yanked Bruno towards her, the dog still in mid-effort. "I didn't realise anyone lived – "

"So it's OK for your bloody dog to mess up the place, just because there's nobody there?" the man retorted in disbelief.

"No ... I mean ... well, he's not my actually mine," Tara spluttered, mortified that she'd been caught out in such a manner. She'd *strangle* that dog when she got him home. "And no, I don't think it's OK, but he was determined to do it here, and I'm really sorry."

She watched in surprise as he bent down and rubbed Bruno behind the ears. She didn't think she had ever seen a man so huge. With his broad shoulders and thick muscled arms, he looked like a pro-wrestler.

"He's gorgeous, aren't you buddy?" he said. "Despite the fact that your mam is happy to let you make a mess of my lovely garden."

Despite herself, Tara bristled. "He's such a pain in the ass that I didn't have much choice in the matter," she growled, a hand on her hip. "And I'm not his bloody mammy."

"He's not yours?"

"Certainly not," she replied, thinking that she wouldn't wish Bruno on anyone, while slightly miffed that a complete stranger could so easily calm the errant mutt. "I'm looking after him for a friend, who usually looks after him for ..." she sighed. "Look, it's a long story and I'm sure you don't want to hear it. Let me just say that I'm really very sorry about your – um, garden," she gave the weeds a side-ways glance. "I'm sure you worked very hard on it."

"I quite like the natural look, actually," the man shot back. "And isn't she very bold, calling you a pain in the backside?" He said this to Bruno, who was now the picture of well-behaved innocence.

"If only you knew," Tara rolled her eyes. "But hey, I'd better get back – my friend's son is having a nap, and I don't want to leave him on his own."

"You're a friend of Liz's?"

So he did know Liz – which meant that she in turn must have known that the house had been recently sold but hadn't mentioned it. Pity that she hadn't – then Tara wouldn't have dreamed of allowing Bruno near the place.

"I bought it a few weeks back," he told Tara, "and I met her a couple of times. She was a little worried about the kennels being so close and hoped the barking wouldn't disturb me." He grinned widely. "But I grew up on a farm, so noisy animals are par for the course."

"Well, rather you than me. This fella has a bark that would break the sound barrier. But again, I am really sorry about your garden."

"Don't worry about it – if I'd known you were a friend of Liz's I wouldn't have shouted at you like that. I just thought you were some passer-by taking advantage."

Well, Tara thought, deciding that Liz McGrath was a very dark horse indeed. With all her worries about Eric, she had neglected to mention that she had a new and (if you liked the meat-head look) good-looking neighbour.

"You don't need to apologise," she replied, feeling slightly flustered. He was just so ... huge, almost intimidatingly so. "It was my own fault for letting him get the better of me. But I really should get back to Toby. It was nice meeting you."

"You too," he replied easily, "and say hello to Liz for me, won't you?"

"I will," Tara answered, but it was only after Bruno had dragged her back to Liz's house that she realised she didn't know his name.

NINETEEN

"Oh, that was Luke." Liz told her on the phone the following morning, when Tara mentioned the encounter. "He's gorgeous, isn't he?"

Well, she wouldn't say that exactly. Yes, she supposed there was something attractive about those muscled, outdoorsy types, but brawn had never been her thing. She had always been attracted to dark, brooding, creative types. Much to her own demise.

"I was too embarrassed to take any notice," she told Liz breezily. "I really wish you'd told me there was somebody living there, though. The place looks just as abandoned as ever, so I'd no idea – "

"To be honest, *I'd* no idea he'd be moving in so soon," her friend replied. "He's abroad a lot – I think he works out on oil rigs. Last time I bumped into him, he said he had a long stint coming up and wouldn't be back for months. That was just after he bought the house."

"Well, he's definitely here now," Tara said with a sigh, "and Bruno gave him a lovely welcome."

"Didn't I tell you to be firm with that fella? Otherwise he'd walk all over you."

"Tell me about it," Tara groaned.

"Listen, I'd better go – Eric and I are just heading over to the house. Will you give Toby my love, and tell him Mummy and Daddy were asking for him?"

"Of course, I will." Tara rolled her eyes good-naturedly. This was the *third* time Liz had asked her to pass on such a message to Toby.

"And thanks again – I really appreciate it."

"No problem. How's it all going there anyway? Did you two get any time on your own?" Then she added, "Or can't you say anything at the moment?"

"Not really," her friend replied quietly, and Tara understood that Eric must be in the room with her. She really hoped that despite the circumstances, some good might come out of their time away.

"Well, say hi to Eric and Maeve for me, and I'll talk to you tomorrow afternoon."

"You too. And tell Toby I – "

"Yes, Liz – I'll tell Toby you and his daddy were asking for him. Take care."

Smiling, Tara hung up and went back into the living room where Toby was playing happily on the floor with his toys.

She checked the clock on the mantelpiece and groaned. It was almost eleven – time to bring those mental-cases for another trek. She almost felt as though she were preparing herself for battle as she fetched their leads and went to let them out of their kennels, the dogs leaping about excitedly upon her approach.

An hour or so later, she, Toby and the dogs returned to the house. The animals had been much better behaved this morning, or perhaps she was getting better at handling them, she wasn't sure. Then, as soon as they were all safely inside their kennels, she went inside and began preparing Toby's lunch.

"This is quite good fun, isn't it?" Tara said, as she rummaged through the fridge for something to make, Toby sitting quietly in his highchair as he watched her move around. He was a dream to look after really, she thought, deciding that while he was the image of his father, he had definitely been blessed with Liz's temperament. Her friend was so calm, so docile and unassuming, which were mostly lovely traits, but could often work to her own detriment.

She had urged Liz to use this weekend to find out what exactly was going wrong in her marriage, but she doubted very much that her friend would confront Eric. Liz hated confrontation and –

Hearing a loud roar from outside, Tara stopped short. Blast it – was one of the dogs due to leave today? No, that couldn't be it and even if that was the case, it was highly unlikely the dog's owner would be shouting his head off outside the door.

Then, she thought of something. Oh crap, had one of the animals escaped from its pen – maybe got out and bit someone even?

She rushed to the back door. "Stay right there," she told Toby, although there was little chance of the baby going anywhere strapped like that into his high chair. "Aunty Tara has to go outside and check on the doggies, OK?"

Going outside, she headed straight for the kennels, Ben

and Jerry circling around her feet. As she drew closer, she saw that all were still in their holding pens and amazingly, fast asleep. Phew.

She was just about to go back inside the house when she heard someone curse loudly.

Following the direction of the sound, Tara went towards the adjoining house. As she did, she spotted muscleman Luke standing outside his own back door, face red and fists clenched.

"Is everything ... OK?" she called across hesitantly. "I heard someone shout."

"Everything's fine," he replied, through gritted teeth. "I just have a couple of unwelcome visitors."

"Oh." Someone must have dropped by unannounced, she decided. Her own mother hated that too, hated people calling to visit when the house was in a state, so in a way she understood how he felt. Still it seemed a bit rude of Luke to go running out of the house screaming about it.

"Do you think you could get rid of them?" she heard him ask then, his tone softer and a little hesitant.

"Excuse me?"

"I mean, do they bother you?"

"Well," Tara wasn't sure how to answer that. Why the hell would people visiting *his* house bother her? "I'm not sure if ..."

"I hate the little bastards, always have. It's embarrassing but ..."

Oh, now Tara got it. Whoever his guests were, they must have brought kids with them. Glenn could be a bit like that too and would run a mile whenever Liz or any of her other friends brought their offspring to their house.

Though if Glenn were to express himself in such a horribly violent way, she would have something to say about it. In such an *unbalanced* way too ...

Now she began to feel a bit nervous. Was Luke quite sane?

"I think they're under the sink," he added then, confirming that he really wasn't the full shilling.

Under the sink?

"I opened the door and two of them ran out," he informed her, grimacing. "Aww, I can still see their feckin' tails ..."

Right then it hit her and she tried to smother a laugh.

"Mice?" she clarified, her eyes widening in mirth. "You're afraid of mice?"

His expression paled at the mention of the word. "Rub it in, why don't you? I know the place is old, but I thought it was so old that the little bastards wouldn't be bothered with it." He shook his head. "There could be hundreds in there for all I know."

"Oh, for goodness' sake." Tara was still struggling to keep a straight face. "Imagine someone your size being afraid of a tiny, harmless little animal."

"Yeah yeah, I know. But I can't help it, OK?"

He said this in such a way that Tara knew it was killing him to have to admit it.

"So do you think you could ... you know ... go in and take a look around? See where they went?"

She felt almost guilty when she saw his petrified expression. "OK, then. But let me get Toby first – I left him inside on his own when I came out to investigate all the noise."

Luke looked sheepish and still smiling, Tara quickly went back inside to Toby, who was chattering happily away to himself and totally out of harm's way.

"Sorry about this, buddy," she told him as she lifted him out of the chair and strapped him into his buggy, "but the scaredy cat next door needs our help."

"Cat!" Toby pointed out happily, as the two of them passed the cattery on their way through the garden to Luke's house.

Leaving Luke to keep an eye on Toby (or indeed the other way round) Tara was in and out of the place within a few minutes, having opened and closed all the old cupboards, and checked in various nook and crannies, but there were no 'visitors' to be seen.

"I know you think this is hilarious," Luke said, when she eventually reappeared outside, "but I can't help it. My mother used to freak whenever one appeared in our house when I was younger, so I suppose I've carried the fear since then." He shrugged. "Stupid I know but ..."

She was sorely tempted to keep teasing, but another look at his mortified expression told her it was unfair to embarrass him any further. "Like you said, it's a learned phobia ..."

"It's stupid," he insisted and she suspected he was trying to convince himself more than she. "I know they're only tiny, but ..." he winced again, "those bloody tails ..."

"They seem to have gone into hiding now. But I doubt that's the last you'll see of them so you really should think about setting down traps."

"Ugh." Luke shuddered.

"Well, if you're not up to it, you'll have to get somebody

else in. This place has been vacant for so long, I'm surprised it isn't ten times worse," she added thoughtfully.

"You know the house?"

"Yep. I grew up in the village – and me and my friends used to come up here when we were teenagers to drink and chat and ... you know."

Luke smiled. "Right."

"That's why I got such a fright the other day. Nobody's lived here for so long that I just assumed –"

"I know. And I still feel bad for shouting at you. But to be honest, the renovation work is not going as well as I'd hoped." He rolled his eyes. "Those bloody TV shows make it all look so easy."

"True," Tara laughed. "Not quite the same when you get down and dirty with it, is it? I'd love to have a house of my own to decorate, though it'll be a long time before I can afford to get any house in Dublin, let alone one I can restore to its former glory."

"Oh, you don't live in the village?"

"No, I'm just looking after the place for Liz. And speaking of which, I'd better go – this little fella will be needing his lunch soon."

"Well hey, thanks a million ... um, sorry, I don't know your –"

"It's Tara."

"Tara. I owe you a cuppa, only I don't even have a kettle in there yet. Speaking of which, can you recommend anywhere in the village for food? I was in that cafe yesterday, but they do all this posh organic muck, and I'm not really into – "

"Why don't you come back next door?" The words

were out before she realised it. "I was just having lunch anyway. I could do a fry-up, or an omelette or something."

"Are you sure? I'd love that, but I really don't want to impose."

"Don't be silly. After the shock you've had, you need a strong mug of tea," she added mischievously.

"I won't argue with that," Luke said, his mood greatly improved as he closed the back door of his cottage behind him. "And I'd kill for a decent cuppa. Those choco-mocco things they serve in that café taste like dishwater."

TWENTY

So far the weekend was *not* going well.

Liz and Eric had left for Belfast (picking up Maeve on the way) and he had been largely uncommunicative throughout the drive north.

Understandably, he hadn't exactly been in high spirits since learning about his uncle's death, but at the same time he barely knew the man.

"It'll be nice to get some time on our own, just the two of us, won't it?" she'd said while packing a weekend bag for them to take to the hotel. "It's ages since we've been anywhere without Toby."

"It's my uncle's funeral," he'd replied shortly. "Hardly a romantic weekend away."

"Oh, I know that, love – that's not what I meant." She could have kicked herself for sounding so unfeeling. But she'd been thinking out loud more than anything else. "I was just saying that it will be strange the two of us being away from Toby for the first time, that's all."

In Belfast, after the removal that evening, they'd spent

much of the night at the family home, before eventually getting back to their hotel around midnight.

So there had been very little opportunity for Liz to get her husband on her own and have the chat she so badly wanted.

It was only the next day after the funeral, once they'd again left Maeve with her family, that she and Eric got any time on their own.

Liz suggested going for somewhere local for dinner.

"I don't know if I fancy it, love – I'm fairly whacked after today."

"I know but we haven't eaten anything other than salad sandwiches all weekend," she argued. "Let's just have something here in the hotel even."

Eric relented, and now for the first time since the birth of their son, Liz and her husband were alone. But now that they *were* finally alone – sitting across from one another in the hotel dining room, she had no idea what to say to him.

Tears prickled at her eyes as she realised how unhappy they both seemed. This was no way for a married couple to behave. Tara had been wrong; far from bringing them closer, the time on their own seemed to only highlight just how far apart they were.

Still, Liz had to try. Something was wrong and she needed to fix it.

"I spoke to Tara on the phone earlier," she said, trying to sound light-hearted. "She and Toby are having a great time, and he doesn't seem to be missing us at all. It was good of her to baby-sit, wasn't it?"

"Good old reliable Tara," Eric replied, and Liz thought she noticed an edge to his tone.

"The dogs are fine too, which is great," she babbled on, deciding to talk about things that made her feel comfortable, normal everyday things. "I must admit, I did wonder how Toby would get on without us. He's not used to being left with other people and I thought he'd be a bit teary."

"Well, if Tara says he's fine, then I'm sure he is," Eric replied in a rather bored voice.

"Still, he's been a bit troublesome lately," she said. "I hope he hasn't been getting up to mischief." When he didn't reply, she continued, "Tara also said that if ever we wanted to go away for a weekend break she'd love to do it again."

"Did she offer to pay for the bloody hotel too?"

This time there was no mistaking his tone and Liz frowned. "What do you mean by that?"

"Well, she seems to enjoy throwing her money around, doesn't she? The fancy clothes and fancy car. Next she'll be buying a mansion in Dalkey."

Liz was taken aback. She'd never heard Eric criticise his old friend like that. "Tara works very hard for her money. Same as you, me and everyone else. And I don't think anyone can begrudge her anything, considering." She looked away. "Look, she was just being kind, and all she did was offer to baby-sit in order to give us the opportunity to get away. We've barely had a second to ourselves since we moved to Lakeview. I'm always busy with Toby and the kennels, and if you're not working, you're out with ..." She let her voice trail off, afraid that if she mentioned his nights out with his work friends or with Colm that it would sound like she was nagging. And Liz didn't want that, not when she was trying to get their relationship back on track. "But if you don't think we should accept her generosity again, then we won't. But you know as well as I do that we have nobody else to ask."

It was a barely disguised jibe at the fact that Maeve had never offered to baby-sit her grandson; in fact, she had never gone out of her way to spend any time with him at all.

"I know what you're getting at," Eric said. "And yes, maybe Mum should help out some more. But she's getting on now, Liz. She wouldn't be able to handle Toby."

In truth, when push came to shove, Liz knew she wouldn't be altogether happy with Maeve looking after her baby anyway.

But she didn't want this to spark off another disagreement, so she decided to change the subject. "How's your lamb?"

Eric had so far spent much of the meal simply picking at his food. "It's OK, nothing special."

"Here, have some of my sea bass then," she offered, pushing the plate towards him. It was pathetic the way she kept trying to ingratiate herself with him, but she didn't know what else to do. Tara wouldn't behave like this; no, if she were in this situation, she would just come right out and ask Eric what the problem was, instead of just sitting there, timid, pretending that all was well.

Liz cursed her own cowardice, cursed her inability to confront the situation head-on and ask her husband what the hell was wrong with him. Maybe she needed some life coaching from Tara - or *wife* coaching more like, she thought sadly.

The problem was that deep down, Liz really didn't

want to hear the truth. She didn't want to hear Eric admit out loud that something was indeed wrong. At least this way, she still had a hope that their marriage was OK, albeit a slim one, and could convince herself that they might get through it.

"I'm alright, thanks," he said, refusing her offer of the sea bass. "I'm not very hungry, to be honest."

"Eric, are you OK?" she blurted, deciding to just bite the bullet and ask him straight out what was wrong with him. "You seem very down in yourself lately."

"I'm fine," he replied and her heart plunged to her stomach when she realised that he wouldn't look her in the eye. "Just a little tired."

"Well, do you want to head back to the room after? I'm quite tired myself, actually." She pushed her plate away. "Now that I think of it, maybe we shouldn't go anywhere on our own – without Toby, we're both so tired we can hardly talk."

She got a brief smile in return. "I suppose it was nice of Tara to offer to take him again all the same," he said. "But don't you feel that sometimes she can overdo things?"

"What do you mean?"

"This whole 'look at me – I'm so successful' carry-on?"

"Well, she *is* successful, but no different to how she was when we first met. And you know as well as I do that Tara deserves every bit of success she has now."

"I suppose you're right," Eric conceded. "I know it's especially tough on Emma though when –" He stopped short, as if he'd spoken out of turn, and Liz's heart skipped a beat. "I mean, there's Tara with this great career, nice car and what have you, and on the other hand there's her sister, a soon-to-be single mother having to give up her job and move home."

'*Having* to give up her job' was a bit of an overstatement. According to Tara, Emma (after her first bout of morning sickness) had simply packed in the job and gone running home to Mammy and Daddy. But she didn't share her thoughts with Eric.

"Yes, but it's not as though she won't get plenty of support – much of it from Tara, I'd imagine," she added quietly. Then, she took a deep breath before adding, "Since the baby's father doesn't seem to want anything to do with it."

"And what makes you think that?"

"I'm only going on what Tara told me. I don't really know Emma, after all."

"Well, I do, and from what I can make out, things are hard enough on her as it is, without Tara gossiping to all and sundry."

"All and sundry? I'm one of her best friends." Hurt that he had so easily come to Emma's defence, Liz couldn't help her voice from rising. "And she's not *gossiping* about Emma, she's worried about her. Anyway, how do *you* know so much about it?" she added petulantly, and immediately wished she hadn't. Now, she sounded like a jealous nag.

"Oh for Chrissake, Liz, don't start. Emma's an old friend, you know that. OK, so we went out for a bit before I met you – big deal. I didn't marry her, did I?"

No, Liz replied silently, *but perhaps now you wish you had.*

Instead she said. "I know that, but to be honest, Eric,

since we moved, sometimes I can't help feeling a bit left out."

There she'd said it, she'd finally admitted that she felt an outsider in the village, that the idyllic life they'd envisaged in the country hadn't quite materialised. "You know so many people, which is of course understandable since you're from there. I don't know … people in the town are friendly, but I can't help feeling like an outsider."

"But that's only natural. These things take time."

"I know, but I just get the sense that it'll always be like that. I mean none of the locals have used the kennels yet – "

"That doesn't mean anything. Part of the problem is that everyone knows their neighbours so well that they don't need to put their dogs in kennels. They can just leave them with one another. Don't read too much into that, Liz. Anyway, what about Colm? Don't you get on with him?"

"I do, but I suppose he's still really your friend too. I don't really have any friends of my own." She hated the way this all sounded so whiny.

"Well, then you have to get out and about more. Bring Toby to one of those mother and toddler groups or something."

Liz had thought of that, but it was difficult to arrange it around the kennels. She had to be available in the mornings to take in and discharge the animals. Maybe when she was fully booked she needn't worry about it, but for the moment she needed to look after her customers' every whim, so she couldn't go gadding off to playgroups.

She sighed. "Maybe you're right. I suppose I just need to give it time."

"Of course you do," Eric soothed, but Liz suspected he

wasn't really taking her concerns seriously. "Now, will we get the bill? I think I'm ready for bed."

"Sure."

But much later, as she lay beside a heavily sleeping Eric, who had meant he was ready for sleep, and not for the lovemaking his wife had sorely hoped would bring them closer together, Liz wondered if giving it time would be enough.

TWENTY-ONE

Sunday lunchtime, Eric and Liz returned from Belfast.

While both were obviously excited to see Toby after the few days, Liz in particular seemed over the moon to be back, and upon arrival she practically swooped on the baby and covered him in kisses. Toby, in return, seemed just as pleased to see his mum and giggled with delight at her exuberance.

"Liz, leave him alone – you'd swear we'd been away for weeks," Eric admonished, but not in his usual, playful manner.

In fact, now that she'd observed him up close, he didn't seem himself at all. Funeral aside, he looked drawn and solemn and, Tara thought worriedly, a little uncomfortable and out of place with the cosy family reunion. She now understood why Liz had been concerned. Eric looked like a man who had the weight of the world on his shoulders.

"Thanks for looking after him," Liz said, coming over and giving her a hug, Toby still in her arms. "I hope he was OK."

"It was a pleasure – he wasn't a bit of bother."

"He wasn't?" Liz replied, looking oddly at her son. "Well, you're obviously much better at this than I am – I'm finding him very hard going lately."

"Liz thought the place would be in chaos without her," Eric drawled, and Tara could have kicked herself. The last thing her friend needed was to feel insecure, especially when she was feeling so anxious about everything else these days.

"Of course, it's always a novelty to have someone else looking after you, isn't it?" she added, tickling the little boy, who began to giggle. "But I'd say he can be a little terror when he sets his mind to it, can't you, Toby?"

"Or maybe you're simply much more of a natural at this than I am," Liz insisted tiredly.

Tara strained to think of something to change the subject.

"Oh I hope you don't mind," she said then, "but I had your new neighbour over for lunch yesterday."

"What new neighbour?" Eric asked, frowning.

"Your man who bought the place next door."

"That old rundown shack? I didn't know anyone had bought that."

"Well, I told you," Liz said with a jaded sigh.

Tara couldn't believe how sullen and distant she and Eric seemed around one another. For a couple that had always been so fun-filled and relaxed together, it was especially difficult to comprehend. She didn't have to wonder too much how their weekend had gone – she could see it all reflected in their faces. Liz was understandably delighted to get back to Toby, but the strain between Eric and her was evident.

"I'd better head home," she said, feeling again as though she should change the subject. "After a few nights surviving on takeaways, I need Glenn eating a decent meal."

"Oh, he didn't come down on Saturday then?" Liz asked.

"No, he got stuck at work till all hours. Apparently they're on the verge of cracking some incredibly important code – don't ask me." She rolled her eyes. "I wouldn't be surprised if he's still at Pixels in front of the PC surrounded by empty pizza boxes." Glenn was like a dog with a bone when on a project, so Tara wasn't at all surprised when he'd phoned to say he wouldn't be joining her.

And she had to admit she didn't mind either. She liked having a weekend to herself – well, she admitted guiltily, not quite to herself, as she'd shared most of the previous day with Liz's friendly new neighbour.

She'd really enjoyed their lunch yesterday. Contrary to first impressions Luke Cunningham was intelligent, talkative and very good company. Tara was surprised by how clued-in and sharp he seemed about everything, considering he spent months on end away from civilization and surrounded by what he laughingly called 'serious alpha-males'.

She didn't want to admit that she'd immediately dismissed Luke as one himself after their first meeting – although the incident with the mice had quickly dispelled that.

And (beefy biceps aside), he was also very attractive,

and from what she'd gathered, single, since he'd mentioned he was doing up the house himself. Not that she cared of course, Tara reminded herself quickly as she collected her belongings and went outside to put them in the car.

"Nice machine," Eric commented, joining Liz and Toby out front to say goodbye. "That must have cost a few quid."

"All Glenn's idea," Tara said, shaking her head as she struggled to cram everything into the convertible's tiny boot. "Never again will I take the advice of someone who reads *Max Power* magazine."

In truth, she was actually quite fond of the car now, but something in Eric's tone stopped her admitting it. For some reason, she got the impression that he begrudged her the little luxury.

With all the whispering that used to go on when they were younger about Eric going the way of his misfortunate father and turning into a no-hoper, she'd have expected better of him. What the hell was wrong with him?

Or more importantly, Tara wondered as she drove away, what was wrong with *them*?

Was Liz right – instead of making their lives easier, had the move to Lakeview driven them apart? Or was there another reason for Eric's odd behaviour lately?

Realising that his comment about the car sounded suspiciously like something Emma would say, Tara bit her lip, her unease about the situation growing by the second.

Over the course of the weekend, reflecting upon Liz's remarks about Eric going 'off somewhere in the evenings', her heart thudded as she'd remembered her mother recently mentioning Emma doing the same.

Tara's heart raced in her chest. Could it be... she thought panicking. *Could* Eric be Emma's mystery man? Surely not. Then again, given their history ...

With all her heart, Tara hoped this wasn't the case because she loved Liz like a sister.

Why couldn't Emma find a man of her own anyway? Why did she get such a kick out of wanting something she couldn't have?

If she put as much effort into building a life for herself instead of trying to wreck other people's, she'd be running the country by now. It was such a shame. Then again, Tara thought, who was she to pass judgement?

Maybe Emma thought *her* life was weird. Maybe *she* thought that Tara was mad for settling for a boring life with Glenn.

But as Liz was discovering now, married life didn't necessarily guarantee happiness, did it?

TWENTY-TWO

When Tara reached home, the house was strangely silent. On any typical Sunday afternoon, Glenn would be flaked in front of the TV watching the football and surrounded by a mountain of junk food. So she was surprised to see that the living room was not only unoccupied but, amazingly, free of clutter.

"Glenn?" she called out as she walked through the house looking for signs of life. Surely he wasn't still at Pixels?

Going through to the kitchen, Tara became even more puzzled. There were no dirty dishes piled in the sink, no sloshes of spilled coffee staining the worktop ... again it looked as though the kitchen hadn't been used all weekend.

Curiouser and curiouser ...

Trying not to read too much into it, she went back out to the car to unload her stuff, before going upstairs and dumping her bags in the bedroom.

"You're back early," Glenn's voice floated up from the hallway and in the distance, she heard the front door bang behind him. He must have been out at the shops or something.

"Yes," she called back, going back downstairs, "Liz and Eric were back at lunchtime, so I ... what are *you* doing here?" Her eyes widened at the sight of her sister standing in the hallway behind him.

"That's a nice way to greet your baby sister," Emma replied, her tone light. "I was in town for a scan on Friday and it was late by the time I got out of the hospital. So, I thought I'd pop over and maybe stay the night."

Tara bristled. Pure Emma to just decide to drop in unannounced whenever she pleased and expect everyone to run around after her.

"It's a pity you didn't phone first – then you would have known I wouldn't be here."

"Oh, it didn't matter," Emma replied nonchalantly. "Glenn told me you'd gone baby-sitting for the weekend."

"But didn't Mum mention it?"

Emma shrugged and walked into the kitchen. "She must have forgotten. Anyway, I was so tired that I couldn't face the bus journey home, so Glenn very kindly offered to let me stay."

He shrugged. "I had to go into work on Saturday morning anyway, so as long as she didn't mind being here on her own ..."

"Of course I didn't." she said cheerily. "Anyway, you kept me company on Saturday night."

"Strange you never said anything when I spoke to you on the phone," Tara commented.

"To be honest I was up to my eyes at work, and it went completely went out of my head."

That was understandable. When Glenn was in cyber-space Tara was lucky to get a word out of him.

Emma was helping herself to something from the fridge. "I'm starving. Glenn," she said, resting her hand lightly on his arm, "is there any chance you could make me another one of those yummy toasted sandwiches?"

"Sure." He looked at Tara. "I'll make one for you too, if you'd like. Or did you have lunch at Liz and Eric's?"

"No, a sandwich would be nice," she said, eyeing her little sister, who as usual was only too happy to have someone else dancing attendance.

"So, how did the scan go?" she asked as the two went into the living room, leaving Glenn to make lunch.

"Fine – everything seems fine." Then Emma sighed loudly. "I feel so tired all the time though. I hope you didn't mind Glenn staying here to look after me instead of helping you."

According to Glenn it had been work that had stopped him from coming down on Saturday evening, and he hadn't even remembered Emma was there. She chuckled inwardly.

"I quite enjoyed having the weekend to myself actually."

"Oh I just *had* to get out of the house," Emma went on, as she put her feet on the coffee table and waited patiently for lunch to be served up to her. "Mum is driving me demented with all her running around after me. She can be a bit of pain sometimes."

Tara held her tongue, keen to point out that their sixty-odd-year-old mother shouldn't have to be running around after her in first place, let alone be criticised for it.

"Well, I'm sure Mum just wants to make this as easy as possible for you," she said evenly. There was no point in having a row over it – especially not here. From experience she knew that Emma was more than likely to go home in a huff crying to their mother. So Tara couldn't win, no matter what she said. "So, are you planning to head back home this evening? It's just, I have a busy schedule in the morning ..."

"Oh – I'd thought we might go shopping or something," her sister said petulantly. "I've hardly seen you lately."

"Sorry. People are depending on me."

"Right," Emma replied in a disapproving tone that was remarkably reminiscent of Isobel's, and suggested that Tara was putting other people over her own family.

"But we'll do something else soon," Tara said, trying to appease her. Although she'd enjoyed spending time with Toby, she was tired and didn't have the energy for one of Emma's moods. "And maybe you could stay the night anyway."

"I think I might," she replied, smiling gratefully at Glenn, who'd just come in carrying a tray laden with tea, coffee and a plate of toasted sandwiches. Tara looked at him in shock, suspecting he must have been hit over the head or something.

"So," Emma asked then, unnerving Tara further as she took a bite of her sandwich, "how *are* Eric and Liz these days? Still love's young dream?"

TWENTY-THREE

Jay was the one, Natalie was sure of it.

They'd been inseparable for the rest of the night at the launch and when Danni had eventually made moves to leave around midnight, Natalie had ensured her assistant was safely ensconced in a taxi home, before she herself went back inside the club to continue chatting (and flirting) with Jay.

Though, unfortunately, and much to her disappointment, he hadn't been able to accompany her home that night, as he was still officially on duty with Labyrinth and needed to stay behind for a party post mortem with the club's management.

But that didn't matter. When Natalie eventually left the club sometime after two, he'd escorted to her cab and given her a highly satisfying kiss goodbye, having already asked for (and received) her number. And first thing the following morning he'd called and invited her to dinner this coming weekend.

She couldn't believe how quickly she had fallen for him

– well, she did tend to fall for most men pretty quickly - but this was different. Jay was mature, thoughtful, *very* attractive and absolutely the one for her.

Thinking of it now, Steve had been in totally a different league and Natalie didn't know why she'd been so upset that an thoughtless, immature footie fan was out of her life.

If anything, it was a blessing in disguise because if she'd still been with Steve, then she wouldn't have gone to the launch of Purple Grapefruit, and thus wouldn't have met the wonderful Jay, who really was everything her ex wasn't.

Successful, sophisticated - plus senior management in a dynamic and well-respected company, Jay Murray was the embodiment of the perfect catch. Also – and this was a first for Natalie – he was Irish. Well he'd been living in London for yonks, but had apparently grown up in Dublin, which is why at first she hadn't been able to place the accent.

But, once Jay had confessed his heritage, it made perfect sense as to why she'd warmed to him so quickly. He was funny, charming and had that lovely down-to-earth quality that most Irish people seemed to possess.

Still, however much she liked him, this time Natalie wasn't going to mess it up. She wasn't going to rush into things like she had before, and make a complete shambles of the relationship before it had even begun.

This time, she was going to play it to perfection, and since her track record in this regard had proven so hopelessly inept, this time she was going to call in the experts.

Natalie sank back onto her comfy office chair, and hummed to herself as she dialled the number.

"Hello?" A groggy male answered after the fifth or sixth ring.

At the sound of the voice, Natalie instinctively looked at her watch. She hadn't called too early, had she? It was after eleven on Monday morning, and she was pretty certain that Dublin operated in the same time zone.

"Hello, is that ... Glenn?"

"Yeah, who's this?" he replied testily, and she gulped. She'd obviously called at a bad time, or else he was in what Tara had referred to in Egypt, as one of his 'quare moods'.

"Glenn, hi – you might not remember me, but we met on holidays a couple of weeks back. In Egypt? I went to Cairo with – "

Almost instantly, he seemed to perk up. "Oh right, Natalie? How are you?"

"I'm good, thanks," she replied cheerily. "I hope I didn't wake you – you sounded a bit sleepy there."

He yawned again. "Well, I was on a late shift last night, but not to – "

"Oh, silly me, I'm very sorry."

"Not to worry." Then, when she didn't say anything else, he said, "Erm, did you want to speak to Tara?"

"Oh goodness, yes, sorry – that's why I was calling the landline in the first place. I didn't have her mobile, so I looked her up online. Would she be free?"

"I'm not sure – she could be with a client. No – hold on – she's just come in. Hey," he said then, and Natalie knew he was talking to Tara, "it's for you – that hot English girl we met on holidays."

Natalie raised an eyebrow at this, but quickly lowered it when she heard Tara on the other end of the line.

"Hi, how are you?" She seemed pleased, but also a little perplexed to hear from her.

"I'm good – and you?" Natalie replied. "How was your flight home? Great trip, wasn't it?"

"Brilliant – I'm still telling people about our Cairo jaunt," Tara said warmly. "And the flight was fine – *long*, but fine. How are things with you? It's so good to hear from you."

"Well, it's great to talk to you too, although I must admit that I have an ulterior motive."

"Oh?"

"Tara, I wanted to ask for your help."

"My help with what?"

"With my love life," Natalie blurted, dying to tell her everything. She hadn't bothered telling Freya about Jay – no doubt her friend would be too wrapped up in her own life to care. "I've just met the most *amazing* man, who I think could really be the One, and I don't want to – "

"Whoah, hold on a minute," Tara interjected. "What about Steve – who you told me was the love of your life, the one who was just about to propose?" Then she paused for a moment. "Or did you decide to dump him after he'd bowed out of the holiday?"

"Well, no, not exactly." Natalie wasn't about to go into the shameful details of her multiple texts or indeed Steve's 'psycho bunny-boiler' comments – not when she'd already convinced Tara that he was the man of her dreams. "I think we both realised that it just wasn't meant to be, in the end," she said with a deep sigh. "So I told him it would be better to move on."

"That's a shame."

"But it doesn't matter because I'm over it now, and the

other night I met the most amazing guy and he's taking me out to dinner."

"Well, that's wonderful, Natalie. I'm delighted you and Steve sorted things out so amicably. If you don't mind my saying so, I had a feeling from what you were telling me that he might not have been the right man for you."

"Did you?" Natalie wrinkled her forehead. She didn't know where Tara had got that idea. Maybe she wasn't all that good at this relationship counselling lark after all, she realised, her heart sinking.

No, that was being stupid. Tara was a professional, and from what Natalie could tell, a very good one at that. She remembered how she'd so admired the other woman for the calm, controlled and serene way she seemed to live her life. And in the end Tara was right; Steve obviously *wasn't* the man for her and she had spotted that way before Natalie did.

So yes, of course she had made the right decision in getting Tara on board. Although she wasn't actually on board yet because she'd yet to persuade her ...

"I didn't want to say anything but it did seem as though you and Steve wanted ... different things," Tara went on. "Anyway, I'm pleased you found someone else so quickly. I never doubted that you would."

"Thanks, Tara. Oh ... can you hold on for a sec? I've a call coming through on the other line."

Hoping it might be Jay, Natalie decided to take the call, but was sorry she did when it turned out to be one of the brats from Blast whining about the lack of press interest in their latest release. After listening to his rants for a minute or two, she eventually fobbed him off and returned to Tara.

"Hi – sorry about that – just some spotty boy band member I handle, who thinks he should be treated like a rock god just because he's got his nose pierced. Ozzie Osborne, he isn't," she added wryly. "Anyway ... oh, are you still there?"

There was a smile in Tara's voice. "Yes, I'm here."

"Good. Now where was I? Oh yes, as I was saying, I've met this new guy now – an Irish guy, believe it or not. So *obviously* I immediately thought of you and decided you'd be the *perfect* person to help."

"Help with what?"

"Well, with making this relationship work," Natalie replied, as if it were the most obvious thing in the world."

"But how can I help with – "

"Because you're an expert, and Irish! You know how their minds work."

"Natalie, I really don't think –"

"Please, Tara," she interjected before the other girl could say any more, "I *really* want this relationship to work – I *need* this relationship to work. I can't mess it up." Then suspecting that she might as well come clean, she sighed. "Look I haven't exactly been honest with you. I didn't ditch Steve – it was the other way round."

"Oh, I'm very sorry to hear that."

"He told me I was needy and stifling. Goodness knows where he got that idea," she said huffily. "And, Tara, he called me a sodding bunny-boiler." There it was out, and surprisingly, she felt liberated.

If this was going to work, Tara needed to know the truth, the whole truth and nothing but. She needed to know *exactly* what kind of raw material she had to work with if she was to help Natalie get this dating lark right. So she might have been full-on and stifling when it came to Steve, but she was trying to change, wasn't she?

"Gobshite," Tara replied in that lovely brogue of hers. "No wonder he didn't get in touch on holiday then."

Then, for a split second Natalie wondered whether Tara meant that she and not Steve was the 'gobshite' in question.

"Well, maybe I overdid it on the text messages," she said quickly.

"How? You sent him what – two or three in an entire week?"

"Um, thirteen actually," Natalie clarified meekly.

"Oh."

"It was a bit much, I suppose."

Tara seemed at a loss what to say.

"So, this is why I'm phoning you now. I don't want to make the same mistakes with Jay as with Steve, or indeed any of my old boyfriends. I don't want to frighten him away, nor do I want to act too cool and distant either. It's like in that Goldilocks story, I want to get this one 'just right'. And I want you to coach me how to do it."

"You want *me* to coach you? But Natalie, there are hundreds of relationship experts in London that you could use and – "

"I want you, Tara. You're perfect for this. And," she added quickly, "I suppose I don't want everyone in London knowing that I'm taking dating advice either. I know it's silly, but – "

"Well, I can understand that, but still – "

"Please," Natalie interjected plaintively, "I really need

you to help me do this. My love life has been a disaster for so long, and no matter what I do, I always seem to get it wrong. I'm thirty-two years old and evidently I haven't learnt *anything*. I need help - professional help."

"I know but, the thing is, I'm not convinced that what I do exactly suits your needs. I usually help people work through emotional issues and – "

"But this *is* an emotional issue!" Natalie interjected, now decidedly harried. "I'm getting quite emotional as we speak. I want this to work."

There was a brief silence at the other end and now she worried that she'd said too much.

"Look," she said, softening her tone, "there's no point in my muddling along forever and messing things up over and over again, is there? That would be foolish. I need to get this sorted."

"Yes, but it's not that simple."

"Tara, if I'm carrying a few pounds, I get them lipo'ed, if I spot a few wrinkles I get them botoxed, so why should this be any different? At our age, I'm sure you know as well as I do that holding onto our looks can be as much a battle as holding on to a relationship. And as one mostly depends on the other, I have to do *something*."

Tara laughed. "I've never heard it put quite like that, but you sound very sure."

"I'm sure, Tara. I've never been more sure of anything in my life."

She seemed to be thinking about it. "It's not usually the way I operate, Natalie. Life coaching's a very defined mode of operation and just because he's Irish doesn't automatically mean –"

"Tara, I just need help," Natalie cried. "I just need some guidelines as to how the hell I should handle this. And if you don't help me, I don't know who can."

"Well, what about your girlfriends?"

"They don't care," Natalie groaned. "They're all too busy with their own lives and their own relationships. None of them have been on the scene for years, and they're bored with me and my relationship problems." She was silent for the moment. "Will you help me?" she then asked, her voice plaintive. "Because I really can't afford to mess this up. For once, I'd like to give it a fighting chance. I've been trying to get it right for so long and failing, that I don't know what right *is* anymore. I'm either too full-on or too indifferent or – "

"I should tell you that I'm no expert either, and I can only go by what you tell me – "

"You'd be fantastic – I know it. And obviously I'd pay whatever rates you charge like any normal customer – "

"Well, we can work all that out some other time," Tara interjected, "but –

"So you *will* help me then?" Natalie cried gleefully. "You'll help me with this, coach me on how to properly handle Jay?"

"Well, if you're sure you really want this, then I'll certainly try," Tara finished, with the resigned tone of someone who was seriously wondering what on earth she'd let herself in for.

TWENTY-FOUR

A few days after their return from Belfast, Eric announced yet again that he was 'popping out'.

"Where to?" Liz asked, her heart dropping like a stone.

"Just down to Mum's," he replied, as he got up from the kitchen table.

Couldn't he go at least a few days without seeing *her*, whoever she might be?

You know damn well it's Emma Harrington, Liz admonished herself, her heart twisting as unbidden images of them together filled her brain.

But she couldn't do that, not just yet, she decided, trying to get a grip on things. Because as soon as Liz admitted to herself that Eric really was having an affair, then her life as she knew it was over.

She couldn't carry on like this – *they* couldn't carry on like this, pretending that everything was OK on the outside, when inwardly they were both falling apart. Well, Liz was anyway. Maybe Eric was finding this all very straightforward and *she* was the one feeling the strain.

"I know, but I promised Mum I'd call over," he told her. "She's still feeling a bit down after the funeral."

"OK then, why don't we all go?" Liz suggested, trying to keep her voice casual. "I'm sure she'd like to see Toby too."

At this, she could clearly see his facial muscles twitch. "Well, yeah, good idea, but won't one of us have to stay behind and keep an eye on the dogs?"

"Oh right, I'd almost forgotten." Liz *had* forgotten all about the dogs and the fact that one of them was being collected this evening.

"You don't mind me taking Toby, then?" Eric seemed thoughtful. "You're right, I'm sure Mum *would* like to see him."

She sat back, her mind racing. He wouldn't dream of involving their son in one of his trysts, would he?

No, she was being over-sensitive now. If Eric was taking Toby with him, then evidently he *was* planning to visit his mother and her mind was simply running away with her.

He wouldn't stoop so low as to bring his son, *their* son to a meeting with with a mistress. Because if so, then Eric really was no longer the man she'd fallen in love with, and a million miles away from the one she'd married.

When he had settled the toddler in his pushchair, and the two were ready to leave, Liz bent down and lightly kissed the top of Toby's head.

"OK, then," she told the two people she loved most in the world as they readied themselves to leave. "Have fun."

·   ·   ·

"HE LOOKS LIKE YOU."

"Do you think so? Everyone else says he looks like Liz."

"Naw, he smiles."

"That's not very nice."

"Oh, you know I'm only kidding. Don't take it all so seriously."

Emma sat on the park bench, she and Eric once again convening at their preferred meeting place.

He shifted uncomfortably in his seat. He hadn't liked the idea of taking Toby to the park with him, but it would have looked odd if he hadn't wanted to bring him along. So, in order to avoid suspicion about his whereabouts, he had indeed gone to visit his mother.

But only briefly.

But he'd got even more of a fright when, within about five minutes of their arrival, they'd spotted someone walking along the pathway through the park, though the man carrying a fishing rod just bade them a friendly hello as he passed.

"Relax – it's nobody from around here – just some tourist." Emma commented easily. She was dressed in loose trousers and a patterned top, her bump still barely visible beneath it.

"So how are you feeling?" he asked.

She made a face. "Like death. Although at least the morning sickness seems to have calmed down a bit. But I've put on lots of weight and it's driving me mad. My face looks like somebody stuffed cotton wool in my cheeks and my breasts are getting bigger by the day. Although maybe that's not such a bad thing, eh?" she added jokingly and he looked away, embarrassed.

She rolled her eyes. "Plus Tara and my mum are still driving me mad." She looked at him. "How's everything with you?"

"Things are getting worse. You know Liz and I were away last weekend?"

"Sure, how did it go?"

"The usual. She spent the entire time talking about Toby and the house and the dogs – it's all she cares about now." He sat forward. "At one stage, I was almost tempted to come confess all."

"You can't. Not yet – not until it's all sorted. And I'm trying my best to hurry things up but it's not as easy as I thought."

"I know, and thanks for that. It's just I feel so guilty keeping secrets. After all, this affects her too."

Emma put a hand on his arm. "Now is not the right time. And if she finds out that *I'm* involved, all hell will break loose. She'll want to throttle me."

"Liz wouldn't dream of doing something like that." Despite his guilt or perhaps because of it, Eric felt obliged to defend his wife.

"Right," Emma snorted, "I'm sure she's a *very* understanding person."

"She is actually."

"OK then, how understanding would she be if she found out that you've brought your son to one of our meetings?"

He bowed his head. "It wasn't like that. I didn't bring him here on purpose, and we went to see Mum first."

"Liz might not see it that way."

"I know.

She reached across and patted his thigh. "Hey, try not to worry about it too much for the moment. It'll all work out for the best, I promise."

"Will it?" Eric asked, deciding that things certainly couldn't get much worse anyway.

TWENTY-FIVE

Tara settled herself comfortably on the couch and tucked her legs beneath her as she began Natalie's first session.

In all her years in the coaching field, she had never come across a client like Natalie, one who seemed to know *exactly* what they wanted.

Usually, people's main issues were that they *didn't* know what they wanted and this could only be uncovered by gently discussing the workings of their lives, and eventually coaxing out their ultimate ambitions.

Then, having come to this realisation, the coaching process could begin and once they'd achieved their aims, her clients generally went off and did their own thing.

Tara had never been approached by someone who already knew exactly what he or she wanted, and enlisting her help in achieving it. Which meant that her usual methods needed to go out the window.

She began by asking Natalie some background information about her relationship history thus far, and was taken aback by what she heard. It was pretty obvious from the outset that she had been incredibly (almost scarily) full-on with previous boyfriends. In fact, it was shocking how quickly she pushed on in order to achieve her ultimate aim – a ring on her finger.

"So you've already decided that this guy might be the one," Tara stated, keeping her voice neutral. "Do you feel you already know enough about him to make a judgement like that?"

"Probably not," Natalie replied sheepishly. "I'm just going on how he makes me feel."

"OK, so he makes you feel good – why do you think that is?"

"I don't know. I suppose it's because even though I know I like him and he likes me, I still don't know where it will all go from here."

"And that excites you?"

"Yes."

"More than Jay himself?"

"Well ... well, yes and no."

"Yes and no?"

"I mean, yes, of course Jay excites me, but the idea that this could really be the right man for me excites me just as much."

"Just as much – or more?"

"Oh, Tara, I bloody well wish you'd just come right out and say what you think," Natalie said irritably. "All these questions are getting us nowhere."

"That's how this works. You're the one with the answers – not me." But Tara decided to change tack and proceeded to tease out more about her relationship history.

"Tell me, why do *you* think your other relationships haven't lasted the course?" she asked. "That they haven't resulted in the proposal you wanted?"

"Well, I've been thinking about that," Natalie replied solemnly.

Tara couldn't help but smile at her earnestness. When faced with a question like that women often blamed themselves – their weight, their clothes, their attractiveness.

But not this woman.

"I suppose some guys might've been quite ... frightened of me. Now, not wanting to blow my own trumpet but, as you know, I'm very successful at what I do. I have my own place here in London, a fantastic social life, lots of good friends and a bloody great lifestyle. So when it comes to men, perhaps I'm not really giving off the right vibes – you know, the 'nicey-wifey' type stuff? I think I might be too self-sufficient, too independent for them to think seriously about marrying me. And that's what I've been trying to change."

Tara thought for a moment before speaking. "OK, so you treat the entire process like a piece of PR."

"What?"

"Well, you just admitted that you think that you, the real you, isn't doing the job. You think men are threatened by you. So you consciously try to put a spin on it."

"Well ... I suppose I do, yes."

"So if you try to control the way the man you're with thinks about you, you don't really behave like yourself, do you?"

"What? Of course I do."

"Maybe you think you do, but Natalie, from what

you're telling me, you don't. Don't you think that's a strange irony? That you're so focused on directing the relationship where you want it to go that you don't seem to focus on whether or not *you* actually want it – or if you're really enjoying it? You said that you went to a cricket game with some guy, even though you hate cricket?"

"Well, yes. But relationships are all about give and take, aren't they?"

"Of course, but didn't this also imply that you were prepared to sacrifice your own enjoyment simply to take the relationship to the next level?"

"I suppose that could be true. But it didn't matter – I had nothing else on so ..."

"Still, by doing this, you effectively compromised your own enjoyment in the hope of moving the relationship forward. How did you know that you even liked this man enough to want to settle down with him?"

"I suppose I didn't," Natalie said simply.

"OK, then," Tara clarified, "from what you've told me, you meet a man, start going out with him and then do your utmost to push the relationship to where you want to get it. You don't seem to believe in letting things just run their course and go where they will. Instead, you're determined to direct proceedings – yes?"

"But I can't afford to just wait around for things to happen," Natalie argued. "That's not in my nature."

"I know, but think about what you're really doing. Aren't you trying to control and manipulate your relationships in the same way you try to control and manipulate your clients? Don't get me wrong, I can completely understand why you do it, but the important thing is that it's not yielding the results you want."

On the other end of the line, Natalie was silent.

Tara went on softly. "Don't you think that you're so obsessed with your long-term goal – that is, the ring on your finger – that you haven't given much thought as to what will happen after that? Let's imagine that one day you do achieve that goal – how will you feel then?"

"I'll be the happiest woman alive!" Natalie joked, but Tara sensed there was truth behind her words.

"Happy that you've found a man you really love and that you want to spend the rest of your life with? Or happy because you've finally got the ring on your finger? Have you ever really thought about what might happen after that?"

"Not really," she admitted shamefully.

"Hey, I'm sorry if this sounds a bit harsh, but the point I'm trying to get across is that you need to think seriously about what happens after the ring and the big white wedding. You need to think long-term. My advice for when you meet Jay for your date would be to try your utmost to put any long-term aims out of your mind. First decide if you actually like him or enjoy spending time in his company. If all you focus on is whether or not he might be the one, you've pretty much lost the battle."

"All right then," Natalie replied gamely. "I promise I'll do just that." She paused for a second. "Thing is, he really *could* be the – "

"Natalie."

"OK, OK, I'll try to control myself."

"Speaking of control," Tara said, a smile in her voice, "I don't want you sleeping with him on the first date either."

She knew this piece of advice would *not* go down well.

"What?" Natalie's reaction was as she'd anticipated. "But, Tara, you should *see* him – he's so sexy!"

"Maybe, but if you do that then you're clouding the issue."

"But why not? It's going to happen anyway, so why delay the inevitable?"

"Haven't you ever heard of playing hard to get?"

"I tried that once, and the guy told me I was a prick-tease and never called me again."

Tara felt the need to speak frankly. Unlike most of her clients, she already knew enough about Natalie to get that she didn't respond to subtlety.

"I hate to say it but don't you think that by sleeping with guys too easily, you're killing off the chase? Taking away all the mystery?"

"Mystery? What mystery? If a guy asks me out on a date in the first place he obviously fancies me – if I go, I fancy him too. Where's the mystery?"

"But what about romance, seduction, delayed gratification?"

"That's just a female thing – men don't like that."

"Who told you that?"

"Another ex. He reckons that women's magazines have fried our brains. Men don't care about the mental stuff, they're led by their anatomy."

"Well, if that was the case, how do people stay married, stay with the one person for the rest of their lives? There has to be more to it, doesn't there?"

"Look, Tara, maybe things are different where you

come from, but here, women are more sexually liberated. We don't beat around the bush, as it were."

Tara's eyes widened, and she smiled. "Natalie, I really don't think this has anything to do with where you come from. The fact is that by going straight to sex, you're killing off the prospect of romance. What about fun too? Look, if this is going to work, you really will have to try and change your approach. The first piece of advice I'm going to give you – and please try to stick to it – is you are *not* to sleep with Jay on Saturday night."

"But he'll think I'm a prude or – "

"Get those stupid expressions out of your head. The guys who told you that are irrelevant. You need to change your approach, that's what you told me, isn't it?"

Tara had long since dispelled with the usual coaching principles. Rather than the softly, softly approach, some serious straight-talking was in order when it came to Natalie.

"Yes."

"Right then," Tara said determinedly. "We're changing your approach. Now, where's he taking you?"

"Some posh French place in Covent Garden."

"Nice."

"Not really – I'm not really into truffles and foie gras and all that. We do so much of that kind of entertaining during work that it gets rather boring after a while. To be honest, I'd much rather a nice Tex-Mex or something."

"Well, did he ask if the restaurant was OK with you?"

"Yes."

"And did you tell him you'd rather not go for fine dining?"

"No – if he wants to do that, fine by me."

"OK, we'll let it pass for a first date, but remember what I said before about you not being yourself. You must stop that, OK?"

"OK."

"So, when Jay arranges something for your next date – if there is one and I'm determined there will be – and you don't like where you're going, you'll have to speak up."

It amazed Tara how full of contradictions Natalie was. She'd happily swap bodily fluids with a guy, yet was afraid to be upfront in the simplest of ways. Unconvinced that Natalie truly understood the message she was trying to put across, Tara decided to put it across in another way.

"May I be blunt?" she asked her.

"Please do."

"Well, don't you think that if a guy wanted a wishy-washy, do-anything-to-please him girlfriend, that he'd be much better off just buying himself a blow-up doll?"

When there was no reply from Natalie for some time, Tara briefly wondered if she'd gone too far. Then, on the other end of the line there came a burst of laughter.

"Bloody hell," Natalie chuckled. "You don't pull any punches, do you?"

TWENTY-SIX

Natalie's first date went spectacularly well.

That night, she took Tara's advice and admitted from the outset to Jay that the restaurant was wonderful, but truthfully she'd prefer something a little less formal.

"I get so much of this kind of thing with work," she told him, her tone apologetic, but not too much. No simpering, Tara had warned her.

Jay laid down his leather-bound menu. "You know, you're right. I'm the very same. We entertain clients in places like this all the time and while the food is great, it's nice to be able to go somewhere where you get by with using just one bloody fork instead of four."

"Or maybe even eat with your fingers," Natalie added.

Jay picked up the wine menu and gave it a cursory glance "Or have a cold beer instead of a fifty-pound bottle of wine."

"Mmm, now you're talkin'," she said, cocking her head towards the corner of the dining room. "Or listen to rock music, instead of screaming accordions."

Jay laughed and followed her gaze to where the restaurant's resident musician was happily providing what had to be described as very much *foreground* music. While it stamped an air of French authenticity on the place, it was invasive and largely not conducive to cosy chat.

Although the restaurant was expensive and upmarket, it was also very much in demand, and private tables were at a premium here, so much so that Natalie and Jay were practically bumping elbows with the party seated at the table next to them. That particular evening, the place was full of self-important business types, all of whom were too busy trying their best to look sophisticated to enjoy themselves.

"I'm sorry," he said, evidently reading her thoughts. "I've made a mess of this already, haven't I? Here was I, thinking you'd be impressed by all this grandeur, when inwardly you're hankering for *TGI Friday's*."

She grinned. "Well, not quite, but somewhere a little more ... fun, maybe?" Then she realised something. With all her talk about purple carpets, purple cocktails and now TGIF's Jay would think she was a right chav.

When she said this to him, he laughed out loud.

"No, I just think you're someone who knows how to have fun," he replied cheerily.

"I suppose that's what it's all about though, isn't it?" she said, echoing Tara's earlier words. "Having fun."

And to Natalie's surprise, she believed them. For once, she wasn't concentrating on whether or not she looked good in the dress, or if her make-up had run, or when she'd get to meet Jay's mother – instead she was concentrating on just enjoying being with him. And she admitted to herself, she didn't have to try too hard to do that.

Also, knowing that the decision of whether or not to sleep with him had already been made, there was a certain freedom in just kicking back and relaxing.

All throughout dinner, she and Jay entertained themselves by trying to apply silly chain-restaurant names to the fine-food dishes they'd ordered, (Jay's truffles were 'Viagra Mushrooms' and Natalie's rare-cooked duck was 'Quacking Daffy'). They'd laughed so much that at one stage the resident musician had come over to their table in an attempt to drown out the noise.

"This is terrible," he joked. "We really should be giving these lovely truffles the respect they deserve."

Natalie looked down at her meal. If she was going to be honest, she might as well be honest about everything.

"Do you know something? I really don't know what all the fuss is about."

Jay raised an eyebrow. "About truffles?"

"Yes. At eight hundred quid a pound, I guess there has to be something to it, and I know the way they can only be found by a certain breed of animal is supposed to be very romantic and so on. But tell me, how on earth is the idea of pigs snuffling round dirt for wild bloody mushrooms romantic?"

Jay's lips were pursed, so she wasn't sure how he'd react to this. She knew how Freya would – she'd think that Natalie had taken leave of her senses. 'But truffles are simply fabulous, darling!' she'd purr. That truffles were considered a delicacy and so expensive only a certain 'type' could afford them – Freya's type – would be enough for her.

Personally Natalie had never understood the hype and by admitting this to Jay, she was, possibly for the first time in her dating life – using a subconscious test on him.

Jay looked at her. "Is it a case of Emperor's New Clothes, do you think?"

"Would it be so awful if I told you that's *exactly* what I think?" she replied, setting down her knife and fork.

Then to her surprise, he nodded. "Well, I do enjoy the taste, but I know what you mean about the hysteria. Everyone else raves so much about the blasted things, you'd wonder if they had magical properties."

"*Phew.* So I'm not the only one then."

"I doubt it very much," Jay told her, smiling. "You know as well as I do how the glitterati fall over themselves to appear exclusive, when all they're doing is following the horde." Then he smiled wickedly. "So if we're going to take the piss out of expensive delicacies, what are your thoughts on caviar? Horrible shite, isn't it?"

By the end of the evening, Natalie's sides ached from laughing, and for once she didn't worry about whether or not she'd impressed him enough to want to see her again. In fact, it was no longer an issue – during dinner Jay had already promised to take her to the Hard Rock Café the following weekend.

"Then we can do the reverse – their curly fries will be 'delicately sautéed potatoes' and their burgers 'ground-up fillet de boeuf with tomato jus'," he joked, as they went out to the street afterwards, Jay casually linking her arm in his as if it was the most natural thing in the world.

"I'll have to have a proper think about what to call

buffalo wings then," she replied, enjoying the unforced intimacy. He wanted to see her again and they'd had a great night tonight.

Tara was an absolute *genius*.

TWENTY-SEVEN

THE SECOND DATE was even better. They did go to *TGI Friday's* for Saturday lunch (apparently there was a waiting list for the Hard Rock Cafe, something Jay found hilarious), and again spent the entire time again taking the piss out of the menu, while trying to speak over *The Best of Bon Jovi* blasting out over the speakers.

"Lunch is good," Tara had declared approvingly, during their interim coaching session. "It means he wants to spend time getting to know you, instead of simply wanting to jump your bones."

"I don't know if that's a good or a bad thing," Natalie murmured. "He's gorgeous, successful, good fun – why hasn't anybody snapped him up yet?"

"You're gorgeous, successful and good fun too – why hasn't anyone snapped *you* up yet?" Tara retorted before launching into another diatribe on how Natalie really should think of herself as the prize catch, instead of the other way round.

She was unbelievably bossy when she wanted to be.

Now, sitting in TGIF's staring at the remains of her 'boeuf' burger, and listening to Jay recite funny anecdotes from Labyrinth's most recent event, she wondered why she had ever bothered with a loser like Steve, whose idea of interesting conversation was how Chelsea's latest signing had turned out to be the greatest load of bollocks.

When they'd finished, Jay once again insisting on paying the bill, Natalie wondered what on earth they were going to do next. It was the middle of the afternoon – it wasn't like they could spend the rest of the time wandering around the shops.

Still, she supposed they could go for one or two quiet drinks somewhere. No, on second thoughts, she'd better not suggest that. Tara would *not* be impressed if Natalie ended up getting sloshed in some pub and then launched herself on him, which is exactly what would happen if they went for 'a quiet drink'.

She looked across the table at Jay, who was busily signing his credit card slip.

"So, are you heading away somewhere now – back to the office, perhaps?" she asked, when they got up to leave.

He frowned. "Why on earth would I do that?"

Recalling how Steve often used to abandon her for the office at weekends, Natalie was just about to say something about him being very busy and all that, when she remembered Tara's words about being too simpering. She shouldn't let him think that she believed his work was more important than their time together – that was laying the groundwork for bad habits in the future, she reminded herself.

Instead she smiled. "Well, I'm glad to hear it. I'd no

intention of being brought out to lunch on a Saturday, and then dropped like a hot potato in the middle of the afternoon."

"Believe me, there will be no hot-potato-dropping today – with luck there won't be anything dropping," he said, raising a cryptic eyebrow at her.

"What?"

He smiled but ignored her question.

Outside, on the street, she watched, confused but intrigued, as he hailed a black cab. When they got in, she heard him ask for Jubilee Gardens on the South Bank.

"What's going on?" she asked, not too thrilled at the idea of having to duck and dive through one of London's busiest tourist spots. "Why are we going there?"

"I want to do something different," he said, his dark eyes twinkling. "Have you ever been on the London Eye?"

Natalie groaned inwardly, her initial anticipation rapidly deflating. This wasn't her ideal way of spending a Saturday afternoon. With the capacity to handle hundreds of visitors every hour, a trip on the London Eye wouldn't exactly be relaxing. For one thing, they'd be queuing for up to an hour just to get a ticket for the wheel, and then another queuing to get onto the bloody thing.

Not to mention eventually being packed inside a tiny capsule with fifty-odd other sardines of various nationalities.

"Well, no – I know it's strange, the thing has been there for years, but I've just never got round to it. Probably because of the bloody queues. Are you sure you want to do this? We'll be waiting a while."

Jay nodded. "So what – it'll be a laugh, won't it?"

Wonderful, Natalie thought, as she slunk back down in the backseat. Now, if Tara was here, she'd advise her to put her foot down and inform Jay that she had no intention of standing in the freezing cold for up to three hours in Prada heels waiting to get onto a bloody tourist attraction.

But she just couldn't bring herself to do it. Jay was almost childlike in his enthusiasm, and seemed to think it would be a great way to spend the afternoon. And because he had at least made the effort to do something fun and different, Natalie thought she shouldn't really complain. Wait until he realised just how bad the queues really were. Then he might change his mind pretty fast.

As she got out of the taxi, and stood on the bridge waiting for Jay, she looked down at the crowds gathered along the riverbank, and tried to establish how busy it was.

People were swarming around in their hundreds, all of them no doubt heading towards the London Eye. Almost instinctively, the soles of her feet began to throb, probably in protest at the notion of having to stand in impossibly high heels for a couple of hours. This was crazy – she'd have to say something. Effort or no effort ...

"Jay, are you really sure you want to do this today? It looks frightfully busy."

"It does, doesn't it?" he said, lightly holding her elbow as she tentatively negotiated the stone steps down to the pier. "But we're not in any rush, are we?"

"Well, no, not really, but ..." Natalie grimaced as he wandered on ahead of her towards the attraction's entrance, seemingly oblivious to the crowds, and the fact that he'd bypassed the ticket office and instead was heading directly to the boarding area. She shook her head. Evidently, he didn't even realise the extent of the wait and she figured he'd change his mind pretty smart when one of the security guys told him where to go.

"Natalie – over here."

But strangely enough, she noticed, as Jay beckoned her to follow him, the staff at the metal detectors hadn't told him off. Instead they were holding back the crowds to let them through.

"What's going on?" she asked, pink-cheeked with embarrassment as a couple of tourists who'd been just about to go through the gate muttered profanities. "Why are we skipping the queue?"

"If you could just wait until the next capsule comes round, Mr Murray," a security guy was saying, and Jay nodded his head politely, a self-satisfied look on his face.

"Jay?" she asked again.

"I knew you probably wouldn't want to wait around … especially in those shoes," he said with a grin. "So I made some alternative arrangements."

"Alternative … what?"

"Here you go, mate."

Natalie stared as an empty capsule stopped at the boarding gate and the security people ushered them inside.

No, she corrected herself as she stepped in, it wasn't quite empty. To one side stood a small table and perched upon it was a bottle of Cristal cooling alongside a pair of tall champagne flutes. She'd only just about managed to take in this surprising sight when she realised that the doors had closed behind them, leaving them on their own inside.

She looked at him, open-mouthed. "How did you … where did you?"

Jay looked sheepish. "I wanted to do something different. I know the guys here – we've booked for a number of private events over the last few years – so it wasn't too difficult. I thought it might be nicer with just the two of us, rather than being crammed into another one full of tourists."

"*Nicer* – it's fantastic."

As she looked around the empty capsule, at the champagne and everything else, Natalie didn't know what to say. And just then, she felt tears prick at the corner of her eyes. No one had *ever* done anything like this before – something so original and thoughtful and ... romantic.

It felt ... strange.

"Oh shit, have I messed up?" Jay asked, looking concerned. He reached across and cautiously laid a hand on her arm. "You're not afraid of heights, are you? Because if you are, I can try and get them to let us out before we move up any further and – "

"No," Natalie sniffed, and shook her head from side to side, unable to speak for a couple of seconds. Then she straightened up, telling herself that she must not make an idiot of herself over this. She looked at Jay. "It's such a lovely surprise. I ... never expected anything – "

"Well, thank goodness for that," he interjected, his shoulders visibly relaxing. Then walking over to the other side of the capsule, he took the uncorked champagne out of its cooler, and went to fill a glass. He glanced hesitantly at the bottle and then again at Natalie. "I wasn't sure what you'd like, so I went for – "

"Are you mad?" she cried, practically snatching the glass of bubbly from him. "Who *doesn't* like Cristal?"

"Well, since you seem to have such strong opinions on this stuff," Jay laughed, as he filled his own glass, "I'd hate to get it wrong."

"No chance of that today," she replied with a smile.

He joined her at the front of the capsule as the wheel moved slowly upwards.

Then, as they lightly clinked glasses and continued to stare at the panoramic view of the city of London beneath them, Natalie suspected that Jay Murray was a man who very rarely got things wrong.

TWENTY-EIGHT

"He's just too easy-going sometimes," Tara grumbled to Liz.

The two were in the village café, and Tara was grumbling about the way Glenn had run around looking after Emma when she'd stayed over the weekend previous.

"I mean – it's not that I mind Emma coming to stay, of course, but I hate the way she just drops in unannounced and expects to be entertained. And I wouldn't mind, but Glenn was nice as pie to her all weekend and then as soon as she's gone, he goes back to leaving dirty dishes all over the place for me to clean up. I mean, honestly."

Liz said nothing, and too late Tara realised that the last person she should be complaining to about Emma was Liz. But unfortunately, old habits died hard. And of course she couldn't let on to Liz that she had her suspicions about Eric and Emma too, could she?

She took a sip of her coffee. "So, you and Eric didn't get much of a chance to talk while in Belfast?" she queried. It was obvious by Liz's demeanour that nothing had changed.

"No, we didn't get much of a chance to talk about anything, other than Toby or the house or the dogs. He was just so distant, Tara." Tears prickled at Liz's eyes. "And I just wish I had the courage to ask him straight out if he was seeing someone. That's what any normal self-respecting woman would do, isn't it?"

"It's not always that straightforward," Tara replied, thanking her lucky stars once again that she didn't have to worry about that kind of thing. Between Liz and Natalie (although admittedly things were starting to look positive there) she wondered if men were really worth all the hassle.

Liz was still talking. "I'm praying that it's just my imagination going into overdrive, that I'm seeing things that aren't really there. But yet, deep down I know that something isn't right. Why else would he be spending so much time away from me and Toby? Why else does he go out in the evenings for no particular reason?" Then she looked at Tara and blurted quickly. "I think it might be someone from the village."

Tara held her breath.

Reading between the lines, she knew that Liz was trying to broach the subject of Emma, but she just couldn't bring herself to do it. And Tara couldn't do it either, because she knew that once it was out in the open, their friendship would be fractured forever. Even though Tara had no control over her sister's (or indeed Eric's) behaviour, whatever way you looked at it there was a horrible clash of loyalties.

"Tara," Liz said then, glancing sadly at Toby, who was sitting in his buggy alongside the table, "would you have any idea, any idea at all who it might be? Who Eric might be seeing?"

She could see that Liz was steeling herself for the worst, steeling herself for the fact that she could very well be the last to know what the rest of the village already did, and her heart bled for her friend.

"Do you honestly think, if I knew for definite that Eric was fooling around with someone here, that I wouldn't tell you? Of course I would. After I'd given him a punch in the nose," she added vehemently.

Liz gave a half-hearted smile.

"Who's punching who?" Colm magically appeared at the table, bearing a tray of freshly prepared cheesecake.

"No one," Tara said abruptly.

"Well, I hope it's not you punching poor 'ould Glenn," he joked as he unloaded the cheesecake, but by the look on her face he quickly wished he hadn't. "Jeez, aren't you two a couple of rays of sunshine?" he said, rolling his eyes at them both before sidling off in the other direction.

Liz raised a smile. "I think you might have been a bit hard on him there."

"Serves him right for listening to other people's conversations," Tara muttered and a brief silence fell upon the table as the two women made inroads into their respective plates of cheesecake.

"I hate this," Liz said eventually.

Tara looked up. "What?"

"This. The two of us sitting here depressed and miserable, and me moaning again about Eric. I feel bad you coming all the way down here to visit me and all I do is whinge, whinge, whinge."

Tara didn't mind at all, but the whinging (as she called it) certainly wasn't doing Liz any good. She took a deep breath. Maybe it was time for drastic action.

She set down her fork. "All right then. Let's do something fun – something that'll cheer us both up."

"What – now?" Liz said, taken aback.

"I don't mean now – I mean – soon. Can you even remember the last time the two of us went out on the town?"

Liz looked guilty. "I know, and I'd love to but –"

"But nothing. Eric is off nights this week, yes?"

Liz nodded.

"Well, you've put up with enough of his disappearances over the last while – let him put up with one of yours. Come out with me tonight and let Eric look after Toby and the dogs for a change."

Liz looked at her son doubtfully. "I don't know ..."

"Why not? Surely you deserve a night out too? Let Eric take the responsibility this time. I'm sure he'd jump at the chance to have a boy's night in. You said yourself he doesn't get enough time with Toby." Tara squeezed her friend's hand. "Come on, Liz, we'll have a ball."

TWENTY-NINE

"He sounds so sweet," Tara sighed on the other end of the telephone line when Natalie told her all about Jay's London Eye surprise.

"He is," she agreed. "It's weird – I've never had anyone do something like that for me – ever."

"Neither have most of us – but this guy certainly seems to know how to push all the right buttons. You're certain he's not married?"

Natalie could understand why she'd asked the question. She'd wondered the same thing herself, feeling that a man with money, good looks and a personality had to be too good to be true. But no, she and Jay had discussed their respective love lives at length that Saturday, when after their highly enjoyable trip on the Eye, they'd gone for drink in Momo, a cosy Moroccan-themed wine bar in Mayfair.

She'd discovered that Jay was thirty-six, lived near Finchley and had worked in events and promotions for twelve years.

"I'm at Labyrinth for almost six years now," he told her.

"I love it and we've got an amazing team, but I think I'd like to go out on my own someday."

"I sometimes feel like that," Natalie admitted, and with a start realised that she'd never verbalised this largely latent ambition. "But I just don't know if a one-man or *woman* outfit would attract the calibre of client that Blue Moon does."

"You've got an amazing reputation though – I'm sure that would count for something."

"Do I really?" Natalie teased. "I see someone's been checking up on me."

Jay gave her sheepish look. "Well, I mentioned your name to couple of people – all of whom had nothing but good things to say." He smiled. "They were especially complimentary about your arse."

"Sexist bastards," But Natalie smiled too. She'd never had an issue about using her sexuality in this line of work (within limits of course) and she was pleased to learn that the lipo sessions were paying off. Although, if she continued scoffing burgers at *TGI's*, that wouldn't be the case for too much longer.

But it was telling that Jay had asked around about her. It meant that he was interested enough to do so – although after what he'd arranged for their date that day, Natalie was no longer concerned about that. Even Tara would have to admit that any man who went to the trouble of arranging a private trip on the London Eye was interested.

"So you're heading close to the big four-oh then," Natalie stated, taking a sip from her wine glass.

"Yes, and with very little to show for it unfortunately."

Her eyes widened. "A house in Finchley, a career in the legendary Labyrinth – how's that nothing?"

"It's just material stuff though, isn't it? And money, success and all that doesn't count for a whole lot when you get down to it."

"So you never married, then?" Natalie asked, seeing as he'd steered the conversation towards the personal stuff.

He gave a faraway smile. "Never really found the right woman, to be honest. Don't get me wrong, I've had my fair share of long-term relationships and 'nearly' women."

"Nearly women?"

"Ones that might have made the cut, but didn't."

"'Made the cut'?" she repeated, raising an eyebrow.

"OK that sounds pompous," he jumped in quickly. "What I meant was that I could have married certain women – simply for the sake of getting married. But somehow, I knew deep down it wouldn't last and so I thought what's the bloody point?"

That's the difference between you and I then, Natalie thought suddenly. Because she'd been with lots of men she knew weren't quite right, but wanted to marry them anyway, because she just wanted to be married. Jay was right. It was crazy to mess around with something so important, for the sake of it.

Tara had of course told her the same thing, but it hadn't really hit her how stupid she'd been about it all until now. At this stage, she could barely remember the faces, let alone the names of some of the men she'd seriously considered as husband material. She'd been so desperate to settle down, she'd felt that any man at all would do. She'd been that pathetic.

Still, now that she'd come to that realisation, it made her all the more determined not to get it wrong this time. So, she wasn't going to get carried away into thinking that Jay might just be the one, but at the same time, she didn't want to let him slip through her fingers either.

"What do I do next?" she asked Tara now. "Do I phone his office and thank him for a lovely day, or do text in the hope of organising another one."

"Don't you even think about texting him …" Tara warned her. "We both know what you're like."

"OK." Recalling her behaviour with Steve, Natalie was duly convinced.

"He didn't say anything about going out again when he dropped you home?" Tara asked then.

"He didn't drop me home as such – he just came as far as my place with me in the cab and then went home to his own. Tara, I was dying to ask him in. Especially after the cocktails at Momo."

"Didn't I tell you not to drink too much?" Tara scolded although her tone was light. "Still, I'm proud that you resisted the temptation all the same."

"Well, I knew I wouldn't hear the end of it from you if I didn't," Natalie grunted. "Still, it leaves me in a bit of a pickle as to what to do next. Maybe he didn't say anything because he was miffed that I didn't ask him in."

"From what you've told me about him already, that doesn't seem his style."

"Yes, but he organised this amazing thing with the London Eye with champagne and all that, and gets nothing at the end of it?"

"Natalie, I've told you before – it's not about rewarding

someone. Just because a man does something nice for you doesn't mean that you have to automatically sleep with him. You have to get out of that mindset."

"Yes, yes, I know. But that still leaves me at a loss as to what to do now."

"You do nothing, my dear," Tara assured her confidently. "You just continue to play it cool, sit tight and let him come to you."

THIRTY

Liz was getting ready to go out and hit the hotspots of Lakeview village.

To her surprise, Eric had readily agreed to look after Toby and hadn't batted an eyelid when she'd informed him that she and Tara were going out for drinks.

Liz, who'd been expecting some kind of argument, or at least a barrage of questions about her plans, was relieved, but also a little uneasy. Eric didn't seem to give a damn about her life lately. It was almost as though they were beginning to live separate lives, with Toby as their one remaining connection. She wondered how much longer this could go on.

But she wasn't going to think about it now, she told herself, as she stood in her bedroom and tried to decide what to wear. Tara was right, there was no point in trying to second-guess what was going on in her husband's head; she'd drive herself crazy.

No, tonight was about having some long overdue fun with her best friend, and knowing Tara, it was bound to be a good night – never mind that the village wasn't exactly hot and happening, and the bars were more *The Quiet Man* than *Sex and The City*.

She searched through her wardrobe, trying to find something decent to wear, something that at least wouldn't make her look such an overweight frump alongside Tara.

To her dismay, she realised that all her clothes were dark, dowdy and downright depressing, and mostly consisted of shapeless tops and too-big jeans, a throwback from her post-pregnancy days.

Before she had Toby she wouldn't have been seen dead in block colours, and had a selection of vibrant, multicoloured tops and dresses that showed off a pair of legs that back then would have made Giselle jealous.

And of course in those days she'd also had the figure to wear them, whereas now she was still carrying the extra stone and a half she'd gained since.

Which was also the main reason she hadn't gone clothes shopping in ages – all those gorgeous flimsy tops and clingy dresses she loved, but now hadn't a hope of fitting into, mocking her into hiding. Hence the uninspiring wardrobe better suited to a convent.

Liz sighed. How had she so easily let herself go? Since she'd had the baby, moved here and started working with the dogs (who in fairness, couldn't care less what she wore as long as they were fed and watered), she hadn't given her appearance much thought.

Despite her energetic walks with the dogs, she'd made no real effort to shift the weight, and of course with Eric away most evenings it was all too easy to sit in front of the telly with a four-stone bag of Maltesers and a gallon of Coke.

No wonder Eric had gone off her, she thought as she examined herself in the mirror. She was turning into Jabba the Hutt.

"Liz, Tara's here," he called down the hallway, and she jumped. Tara – here – now? She was nowhere *near* ready.

"OK, I'll just be a second!" she called back, hoping that her friend wouldn't mind waiting a few more minutes.

She riffled through her wardrobe once again, and eventually chose an ancient pair of black straight-leg trousers and a black chiffon top. A nice, safe, but utterly boring option.

Was it a fun night out or a funeral she was dressing for? She hoped against hope that Tara wasn't sporting one of those up-to-the-minute outfits she wore for nights out in the city, and had toned down the glam a tad.

Just then there was a soft knock at the bedroom door. "Liz?" she heard Tara call from outside. "Can I come in?"

"Sure." Deciding that she'd just have to make do, Liz went to the dressing-table and quickly began to apply some make-up.

She had been right about Tara's outfit choice. Her friend entered the room wearing a flamboyant emerald and purple patterned top over skinny indigo jeans and metallic stiletto boots.

A shimmering purple headscarf held back her golden locks and with her chunky beaded necklace, and bohemian hoop earrings, she looked dazzling – an exotic butterfly to Liz's garden-variety housefly.

All of this must have been written on Liz's face because

the very first words out of Tara's mouth were: "What's wrong?" She quickly raised a hand to her face. "Did I over-shoot my lipstick?" she said jokingly. "Is my mascara running ... what?"

Liz had to laugh. "No, no, you look perfect, stunning in fact. And I look like such a frump beside you." She sighed and stared again at her reflection in the mirror. "Tara, when did I turn into a middle-aged woman? No, I take that back, most middle-aged women look a million times better than I do these days."

"Don't be silly, you look great! Although, you could probably do with a little more colour. Here," She quickly removed her sparkling headscarf and tied it jauntily around Liz's neck.

Instantly the outfit came to life and Tara's cheery optimism (and her nifty accessorising) had the effect of erasing some of Liz's insecurities and buoying her mood.

"Oh, I couldn't ..." she began, wishing that instead of whinging about her lack of colourful clothes, she'd thought about accessorising what she had. But that was Tara, full of great ideas.

"Of course you can – it's gorgeous on you," she replied, waving away her protests. "Now, do you have a thick bangle, or some dangly earrings perhaps? Something like that and a pair of silver strappy heels, and we're away."

"Will these do?" Liz held up a pair of drop diamante earrings and Tara nodded her approval. Then, quickly finishing her make-up, she checked her appearance once more before they headed back out to the living room and said goodbye to Eric and Toby.

"Have a good night," Eric said with a smile, and Toby,

who didn't seem in the least bit bothered that his mum was leaving him, waved half-heartedly as she went out the door.

So much for being indispensable, she thought wryly, as she and Tara went on their way. She'd thought that there'd be mighty histrionics when she went to leave. But, she supposed, this was even better – now she didn't have to feel guilty.

Feeling happier and more confident than she'd been in ages, Liz followed her best friend down the driveway, and prepared for a rip-roaring night out on the town.

THIRTY-ONE

As THE TWO made their way across the bridge to the centre of the village, Tara breathed an inward sigh of relief.

This girly night out had been a brainwave. During the short walk from her house, Liz had been chatty, animated and acting much more like her old self.

Her heart had gone out to her when she'd seen Liz standing in front of the mirror, her insecurities about her appearance written all over her face.

For this reason, she'd insisted that Liz borrow her sparkly headscarf and wear a pair of glam heels. When it came to boosting self-confidence, Tara was a firm believer in the power of fabulous shoes. Although perhaps some of the male clients she coached might not agree, she thought with a grin.

Now, if Liz were a client of hers, Tara would spend time helping her realise that she was feeling insecure because she was finding it hard to settle, and could very well be manifesting these feelings via anxiety about her marriage. But Liz *wasn't* a client, so it was doubly important for her to refrain.

Instead, she'd try to do what any decent friend would do, and just be there to cheer her up and make her feel better about her troubles, rather than try to solve them for her.

Tara looked at her watch. "I booked The Steakhouse for seven thirty, so we've still time to get in a quick drink in beforehand."

"Great, I'm absolutely starving, but I wouldn't mind a drink to kick things off."

"Now, now, take it easy, you," Tara scolded good-naturedly. "It's been a while since you've done this, remember?"

"I know and I think that's half the problem," Liz grinned. "It's been so long since I've been out, I can barely remember what the inside of a bar looks like." She pushed open the entrance of the The Bridge and Tara followed her inside. "No, hang on – I think it's coming back to me," she added with a delighted wink, and sounding much more like the old Liz.

The two took a seat at the bar and Tara promptly ordered a glass of champagne for Liz, and asked the barman to fill another glass with sparkling lemonade for herself.

Liz had been thrilled at this little luxury but the champagne flutes caused much consternation amongst some of the locals present, who thought it outrageous altogether that these two glamour-pusses should be drinking champagne like celebrities (despite the fact that Tara was having mere lemonade). Who did they think they were?

"Hello, Tara – isn't it well you're looking these days?" said a male voice from behind them.

She looked around to see Dave McNamara, yet another old school-mate, approach the bar.

"You too, Dave," she replied warmly. "How have you been? I haven't seen you in ages."

"Not too bad." He nodded a greeting at Liz.

"This is Liz," Tara said, remembering her manners. "Liz, meet Dave – he was in the same class as me and Eric. Dave – this is Eric McGrath's wife, Liz. She runs the boarding kennels across town." She was extra careful to give Liz's business a mention, seeing as Dave was not only the local councillor, but also head of the Heritage Committee. As a result he was hugely influential in the village and could possibly put some business her way.

"Pleased to meet you, Liz. How *is* Eric these days? Keeping well, I hope."

As Dave flashed Liz his best politician's smile, Tara hid a grin. A notorious womaniser when they were younger, it was no real surprise that he had ended up employing his legendary charm in politics.

"So can I get you two ladies a drink?" he asked, nodding at the barman.

"Thanks, but no, you work away," said Tara. "We're moving on soon."

Dave stood alongside them at the bar as he waited for his pint. "So, I hear that Emma's returned to the fold," he said conversationally to Tara. "Any sign of yourself doing the same?"

"No fear of that. Anyway, after all this time I don't think this town would be able for me. Oh, by the way, congratulations," she said, remembering. "I hear you got engaged recently?"

Dave nodded proudly. "I did indeed. I'll bet you're sorry now you missed the boat. I tried my best with this one a long time ago," he said to Liz, who looked perplexed, "but she didn't want to know, so eventually I had to look elsewhere."

"And look elsewhere you did – everywhere else." Tara joked, while Dave looked bashful.

"Better not let my other half hear that – she's from out of town and knows nothing about my sordid history."

"Well, she's probably better off." Tara was enjoying teasing him. "But I hear she's lovely, and rumour has it she's also the right one to keep you on your toes. Have you set a date for the wedding?"

"Sometime next year – after the next election anyway."

Tara smiled. "Of *course*."

Dave picked up his newly poured pint. "Well, I better head away now and let the two of you get back to your night out. It was nice seeing you, Tara – and you too, Liz."

"Good seeing you too."

When Dave was out of sight, Liz raised an amused eyebrow. "He's right," she said, eyes widening, "I think you did miss the boat where he's concerned. He's *very* cute."

"Not my type," Tara said, "but unfortunately it took him a very long time to get the message. Even up to a couple of years ago he was still trying it on and Glenn can't stand him."

"I can imagine."

Tara grinned. "I suppose I could view it as some form of weird victory that I'm about the only girl in the town he hasn't 'conquered' over the years. I think he even fancied his chances with Emma at one stage," she added, recalling her sister's recent disparaging remarks about Dave. "Anyway he's engaged now, so the women of Lakeview are finally safe – or sorry, depending on who you ask," she added wryly.

Soon after, they decamped to the Steakhouse where for close to two hours they enjoyed a thoroughly satisfying girly chat over steaks the size of Texas.

"This was a brilliant idea, Tara," Liz said, taking another sip from her wineglass. "I didn't realise how much I missed this kind of thing. I suppose I took it all for granted before I had Toby. Not that I'd change things for the world," she added quickly, "but sometimes it's nice to just be me again, not just somebody's mum."

"I know. You and Eric should try and do it more often too. I know it's hard, what with him working all hours and that, but you two spending time together as a couple is important too."

Liz's looked wistful. "You know, I can barely remember what it was like before we had Toby. How easy it was just to go out to dinner or the pub on the spur of the moment. Now, it's such a military operation that you think it's hardly worth it."

"It's always worth it."

"You're right. Eric and I should do more things like this. But he's been so wrapped up in work, and I've been so wrapped up in the dogs and Toby, that we can't raise the energy at weekends. Not to mention raise any baby-sitters – other than yourself of course," she added with a smile. "Maeve is no help and ..." Letting the rest of her sentence trail off, Liz suddenly set down her wineglass. "Do you know something?" she said, and Tara could hear her voice slur a little from the effects of the wine, which she had of course been drinking on her own.

"What?"

"I've been acting like such an idiot lately whinging about Eric and thinking that he would cheat on me. If I really thought about it properly, instead of just jumping to conclusions, then I'd realise that he would *never* do something like that to me. For goodness sake, it's not all that long since we had Toby."

Tara hoped with all her heart that her friend was right.

"I have to stop feeling sorry for myself like this," Liz went on, after taking another sip from her wineglass. "I have to stop worrying about things, and try and be more confident – like you. I think I might just talk to Eric about it when we get home and – "

"Liz, I don't know if that's such a good idea – not tonight anyway. Why not wait until both of you are sober, and have your wits about you?"

"I suppose, but I really want to clear the air, and find out what's *really* bothering him, instead of making up all these stupid scenarios in my head."

"Seriously, I would wait until tomorrow, at least," Tara persisted.

"Maybe you're right. But Tara, I have to get it out of my head. It's been driving me mad lately. I'm so miserable, and emotional and ..." Tears sprang to her eyes. "I thought this move would be a good thing for us. I thought getting out of Dublin and having a quiet life down the country would be brilliant. But it's not. And I don't know whether the problem lies with me, or with Eric or with both of us."

"I'm sure you two will get to the bottom of it but there's definitely no point in trying to solve anything tonight. And speaking of getting to the bottom, look at all the wine you've drunk," Tara said jokingly.

"You're right – who knows what kind of rubbish I'd start spouting," Liz replied, picking up the bottle and looking surprised at the amount of wine she'd taken.

"Here, have some of this," Tara said, pouring a glass of water for her. "We've still got a few hours of this night left, and I don't want you wimping out on me before time."

"Thanks, Tara, you're a pal," Liz grinned and took a huge gulp of the water. "But if anything, I'm glad I got that off my chest. Now that I did I can't believe how pathetic it sounds. Eric having an affair – imagine!" Liz gave an amused roll of her eyes and tucked into the remainder of her dessert.

THIRTY-TWO

After dinner, the girls moved on to Clancy's Hotel for one more before returning home.

Liz felt on top of the world. It was as though a huge weight had been lifted from her shoulders when she'd finally realised how stupid and paranoid she was being.

But Tara was right. There was no point in talking to Eric about it, especially not tonight and maybe not at all. Instead, she'd just try and get back to her normal self and try not to read something into his every move or utterance.

What had made her distrust him so much in the first place? A few nights out and a text? Big deal – that could happen to anyone. No, she'd talk to Eric about maybe downscaling their plans for the renovations, which would hopefully allow him to work less, and stay home more.

And she might bite the bullet and go to some group or club in order to meet some more people from the community – or network, as Tara might say. And if she ended up getting some more business from the locals, then the kennels might bring in the extra cash they needed.

Fully determined to put her worries behind her and her marriage back on track, Liz followed Tara into Clancy's hotel bar. It had already been a highly enjoyable night, and she was delighted Tara had made her agree to it.

"A white wine spritzer and a Coke, please," Tara told the barman.

While they were waiting for their drinks to be served, Liz looked up and spied a familiar face sitting alone at the opposite end.

"There's Luke," she cried excitedly to Tara. "And look, he must be here on his own. Let's go over and say hello."

"Ah no, Liz, let's leave it."

"Why?" It wasn't like Tara to be unsociable.

"It's ... well, maybe he wants to be on his own." Tara paid the barman and picked up their drinks.

"I doubt it. He's only new in town, so he probably doesn't know anyone. I'm going over to say hi, anyway. He's my next-door neighbour, and I don't want to be rude."

"Oh, all right then." Tara picked up her drink and grudgingly followed her over.

As they approached, Luke looked up. "Well, hello there," he said, his rugged, face lighting up at the sight of them.

"Mind if we join you?" Liz asked and oddly, she sensed Tara stiffen alongside her. What was the matter with her? It wasn't as though Luke was a stranger – in fact she probably knew him better than Liz did.

"I'd be delighted," he said, nodding a greeting at Tara who did the same in return. "Pull up a stool."

"So how come you're back?" Liz asked, settling herself alongside him. He was a lovely guy and since he would be her next-door neighbour, she was determined to help him settle in. "I thought you wouldn't be starting the move for ages."

"Well our last stint on the rig went better than we thought, and we hit our quota, so I thought I might as well make a start. There was no point in paying the mortgage on the cottage and rent on my old place."

"I wish you'd have told me. I could have turned the heat on, or opened the windows, or at least bought in some groceries – something to take the bare feel out of the place." As Tara had so far said nothing but a brief hello, Liz attempted to try and draw her into the conversation. "Although, I hear Tara gave you a bite to eat last time – you two got to know each other, didn't you?"

"We did," Luke replied, smiling. "She makes great a fry-up. And she's pretty handy when it comes to pest control too."

"Pest control?" Liz was lost.

"I thought I'd better bring the subject up first, just in case you decided to out me in public," he said, eyeing Tara mischievously.

"Pity, I was thinking of saving it for ammunition," she replied. "Just in case you decided to sue me and Bruno for pooping in your *lovely* garden."

"I told you – it took me ages to get it just like that."

"What?" Liz looked at Tara. What were they talking about? "What did Bruno do?"

"She might be good with mice, but she's not so good with dogs," Luke told Liz. "Or am I allowed to say that?" he added, winking.

"I mightn't be so good at handling big strong animals,

but at least I don't start screaming like a baby at the sight of one the size of my thumb."

"I didn't scream, I shouted – once."

"No, you screamed – a big girlie, Ned-Flanders-type scream."

"I did not – "

"Um, sorry to interrupt but could one of you please tell me what the hell you're talking about?" Liz asked, wide-eyed. "And who is Ned Flanders?"

"Liz doesn't watch *The Simpsons*," Tara informed Luke.

"You don't watch *The Simpsons*?" he repeated in mock horror. "What planet are you on?"

"Well, I don't have time to watch TV," Liz said, getting frustrated. "Anyway, what's all this got to do with pooping in gardens and screaming like a girl?"

Tara and Luke's eyes met.

"You tell her," Tara challenged. "I swore I wouldn't say a thing."

"Pity you didn't keep your word, then," Luke countered, before turning to Liz. "I suppose I'd better come clean. I'm afraid of – no, strike that – I don't particularly like mice."

"Nope, he's terrified of them," Tara interjected, laughing.

Luke silenced her with a look. "I don't *like* mice, but unfortunately they like me, or at least they like the inside of my house."

"Ah," Liz said, understanding. They had that problem in their house too – especially around this time of the year. But she used one of those electronic plug-in things, the ones with the high-pitched sound that scared them out of the house. She wouldn't dream of using one of those horrible mousetraps or anything inhumane.

"So, the last weekend I was here, I was going about my business and cleaning out the cupboards, when two of the little feckers leapt out at me. Naturally, I got a bit of a fright – "

"And ran screaming from the house like a girl," Tara finished.

Luke feigned a glare. "Excuse me, I thought *I* was telling the story."

"Sorry."

"And your friend here, suspecting that I might have been in a bit of bother, came running to my rescue."

"What can I say? For a big strong man, he's a bit of a wimp really."

Luke and Tara were now smiling at one another like there was nobody else in the room, and just then, Liz understood why Tara had been initially so hesitant to join him. The sparks were flying in all directions between these two.

She studied her friend who was still in mid-banter with Luke. Tara was radiant. Her eyes were sparkling with amusement and her face glowed as she and Luke continued to banter.

Now, looking these two together, it was clear that they only had eyes for one another and if Liz decided to slip away without saying anything, they'd hardly notice.

She knew Luke was single; he'd told her a while back that his last relationship had finished some time ago, so there was no barrier on his side anyway.

"I don't know how you sleep at night," Tara was saying now, and Liz tried to tune into their conversation once more.

"Are the mice that bad?" she asked Luke. "You really should invest in one of those plug-in things then they wouldn't be keeping you awake."

Tara and Luke looked at one another and grinned – *again*. OK, Liz thought, it was starting to get a bit annoying now.

"We stopped talking about the mice ages ago," Tara said. "I was just asking Luke how he can justify what he does for a living."

"Why should I have to justify it?" He gave a nonchalant shrug. "It's what I do."

"Are you joking? Drilling for oil? You're raping the earth's resources."

Liz groaned and reached for her drink. "Oh *please* don't get her started on the environment."

"Ah, so you're a tree-hugger eh? You reuse and recycle and you've got your own compost heap, and all that stuff?"

"Of course." Tara nodded proudly. "We all have to take responsibility for the environment, one that the likes of you and your oil companies are destroying."

"I see. So you regularly use recycling centres and all that ..."

"Yep. I take my bottles and cans there every week."

"Every week?" Luke raised an eyebrow. "Well done, you."

"It's not that much of an effort. It's only a few minutes away in the car."

As soon as she had said the words, Liz realised that she was blindly falling into the trap Luke was setting.

"Oh. So you *drive* there, do you?"

Tara hesitated slightly. "Well, I have to – it's a mile away from our house."

"I see. So, it's OK to send all that carbon monoxide into the atmosphere because you're going to the recycling centre, is it?"

"Well, no, but ..."

"Take any holidays recently?"

Liz smiled. An almighty battle was about to commence and by the sounds of things, she'd be much better off staying out of it. Tara had met her match.

"Yes," Tara replied hesitantly.

"Oh, where'd you go?"

Her mouth set in a hard line. "Egypt."

"I see. And did you happen to get on your bike and cycle all the way to Egypt, sleep under the stars with the Bedouins, before cycling all the way back home again?"

Tara was silent.

"Well?" he prompted.

She rolled her eyes. "No, I flew."

"What? You flew?" He pretended to be aghast. "A conscientious environmentalist like yourself got into one of those machines that uses jet fuel, and pumps out gallons of pollution into the atmosphere? That same atmosphere you're so obsessed with saving?"

Liz wanted to laugh, but one look at Tara's expression made her think better of it.

"And you have the nerve to criticise me."

"Look, I never said anything about going overboard!"

Tara cried, totally wrong-footed. "I just think that all of us should do our bit. I mean, what about global warming and the melting icecaps and all that?"

"A myth," Luke said, reaching for his pint. "The atmosphere's been heating up and recooling for centuries. It's nothing new."

"But it is!" Tara retorted. "The icecaps are melting, there are floods and weird weather and droughts and it's all because of – "

"You think you can solve all that by bringing a few bottles to the bottle bin? Get real. The earth's been around for millions – billions of years. Why is it that the likes of us – who have only been around for half a second in the scheme of things – are so bloody egotistical as to think that *we* get to control the environment? The earth survived without human intervention for billions of years, and I'm sure it will do just fine without us."

Liz looked at Tara for a reaction to this, but none was forthcoming. For the first time as long as she'd known her, her best friend had been rendered utterly speechless.

Yep she thought, smiling, these two really were perfect for one another.

THIRTY-THREE

YET AGAIN, Tara called it right. To Natalie's delight, Jay phoned to arrange another date for the following weekend. She was amazed at how much the other girl knew about handling the opposite sex.

"I've got Glenn, haven't I?" Tara laughed, when Natalie told her this. "I've learned all there is to know about handling men."

"But you're so good at it. You're just a natural, Tara. I can't understand why you don't become a *wife* coach altogether."

"Maybe I will after this," Tara quipped, "and if all else fails, I suppose I could always fall back on a career in pest control."

"Sorry?"

"Oh, never mind," she replied with a little laugh. "It's just some guy that lives next door to Liz was afraid of mice and since they don't bother me, I helped chase them out of his house."

Natalie grinned. "Does anything *at all* bother you?"

"What do you mean?"

"Well, you just seem so calm and in control. I thought the same when I met you in Egypt. Nothing seems to faze you."

"Things faze me," Tara replied simply, "but I've learnt over the years not to let anything *really* get to me. What's the point?"

Natalie shook her head. "I really admire you, you know. You've really got it all under control – you and Glenn, your career, family, friends."

"Under control? I wish!" Tara laughed easily. "Natalie, my youngest sister is pregnant by a mystery man, which means the whole family is up in arms, my best friend is going through a marriage crisis and these days Glenn and I are so busy with work that we barely see one another. It's not *half* as calm and controlled as you make it sound."

"And then you've got me whining on about my relationship problems too," Natalie said, feeling guilty. "Oh, I'm frightfully sorry, Tara – I really didn't mean to take up so much of your time."

"No, don't be silly, that's not at all what I meant. To be honest, I'm enjoying this – and I think we're making very good progress."

"We certainly are!" Natalie laughed, relieved. "But are you sure you've got time to deal with me and my stupid problems too? It sounds as though you've got a lot going on at the moment."

"Honestly –I'm actually having fun, honestly."

"Well, as long as you're sure."

"Believe me – I'm sure. So back to Jay? What did he sound like when he phoned earlier?"

"Well," she said, "apparently, this time, he's cooking dinner for us at his place."

"I'm beginning to get a teeny bit concerned about this guy," Tara chuckled. "He's gorgeous, successful, single – and he can cook too? Are you absolutely sure he's an Irishman?"

Natalie laughed. "I know – I'm beginning to wonder if he's really a man at all. But, Tara, you know this will be a serious test, don't you? Me being with him on my own – in private?"

"Let me have a think about this for a second. This will be what - the third date?"

"Yes." Natalie was beginning to get excited. Would Tara give her permission to sleep with him this time? If so, she was going straight to Selfridges after work to pick up some decent Agent Provocateur underwear and –

"No, it's still too early. I think you should definitely hold off for one more date."

"What?" Natalie wailed. "But I'll be at his place, near his *bedroom* and –"

"I'm serious, Natalie, not just yet. Anyway, he hasn't been pushy about that, has he?"

"Well, no."

That was a good point. Jay hadn't tried anything – at all. They'd kissed of course, nice but brief goodbye kisses in cabs at the end of the evening, but nothing major or spine-tingly.

Goodness, he'd better not swing the other way, she thought, horrified. Maybe that's why he seemed too good to be true.

Tara was right. Forget the new underwear. She'd go to

his place on Saturday night for dinner and just wait and see what happened. And if Jay *didn't* make any sort of move on her, well, there was no bloody point in her jumping on him, was there? If he were the other way inclined, which she now thought was a bloody good possibility, then no amount of push-up basques and silk stockings would do it for him anyway.

"So," Tara asked the all-important question, "on a scale of one to ten, ten being totally committed, how committed are you to not sleeping with Jay on your next date?"

"Ten, definitely ten," Natalie replied with feeling.

"Good woman. It'll be worth it in the end, you know that, don't you? And this upcoming date will be a very good test."

Yes, Friday night would certainly be a bit of a test, Natalie agreed.

And she hoped to goodness that Jay would pass it with flying colours.

THIRTY-FOUR

Dinner at his place had sounded straightforward enough, but as Natalie discovered while the train they were on zipped forward to its destination, there was nothing at all straightforward about Jay.

She supposed she should have realised something was up when they spoke on the phone earlier in the week to arrange it, and he had insisted on sending a cab to collect her at her flat, instead of just giving her his address.

Then, when the cab did collect her, the driver had eventually dropped her off at Waterloo station, where a smiling Jay greeted her at the entrance.

"What's going on?" Natalie asked, bewildered, as they walked inside the train station. "Why are we here?"

"I told you – we're having dinner at my place."

"Yes, but I thought you lived in – "

"I do, but I have another place elsewhere, so I thought I'd cook for you there if that's OK."

"Another place? Where?" Natalie was in no mood nor in the right state of dress to go trekking down to Dorset or wherever it was that well-off London executives had second homes these days.

She'd chosen a deliberately provocative yet understated outfit this evening: a red low-cut v-neck cashmere sweater worn over a slim-fitting black satin pencil skirt and the obligatory five-inch heels. She didn't want to look too dressed up for a quiet night in, yet she wanted to be sure she looked good enough for Jay to at least *want* to tear her clothes off!

Now that the idea he might be gay had inveigled itself into her thoughts, Natalie couldn't think of anything else. It had to be the reason he hadn't yet been snapped up by some woman, didn't it?

"Why don't you go and get a coffee while you wait?"

Wait for what? Natalie wanted to scream with frustration at him, but just as quickly he answered her unspoken question.

"I'll just go and get our tickets."

Natalie ordered a latte for herself and another for Jay before sinking gratefully into one of the coffee bar's oversized armchairs, her mind racing as she tried to figure out what on earth was going on. Why was he being so mysterious? And what idiot thought that taking a girl on a train on a busy Friday evening was a nice idea for a date?

A few minutes later, Jay appeared alongside her table. "Ready to go? Sorry to rush you, but our train is just about to leave."

"Where are we going, Jay?"

"Oh, didn't I tell you?" he said, his tone cool as a cucumber. "On the Eurostar."

Natalie's mouth dropped open as the penny dropped. "To Paris? You have a house in *Paris*?"

Jay smiled insouciantly at her. "Well, it's an apartment actually. Is that OK with you?"

"But – but what about a quiet night in sampling your cooking?" Natalie was so overwhelmed she could hardly take it in. Paris! Thank goodness she hadn't decided to dress down in a pair of jeans or something like that. At least the Audrey Hepburn-style outfit she was wearing would look fine alongside Parisian haute couture. But Paris – wow! Natalie grinned delightedly.

"Well, that's still the plan," Jay told her. "I thought it might be a nice idea to go and cook up something nice there instead of Finchley."

"But ... don't I need a passport or ... oh no it's at the office. Danni needed it to arrange some visa for a trip I'm taking to the States soon."

Jay smiled knowingly. "That's what she told you."

Natalie looked at him shocked, as all at once she realised that he had arranged all this behind her back with her assistant as a willing accomplice. She'd kill Danni for making her give up her passport under false pretences. Well, no, she wouldn't really, because this was just wonderful – a truly wonderful surprise.

Here she was expecting a straightforward night in at some townhouse in North London and instead the man was whisking her off to Paris! Funny, she thought absently as she and Jay took their (first-class) seats on the Eurostar, how people always used that word 'whisk' when speaking about being brought to Paris.

But in this case it was certainly true, Natalie thought

now, as the train zoomed towards the most romantic city in the world – a city she'd always wanted to see, but would never dream of visiting on her own.

Paris wasn't the kind of place a girl visited other than with someone special, and none of the men in her life would have ever dreamed of taking her there. But it was becoming all too clear that Jay was different to any man Natalie had ever been involved with before.

She found the idea thrilling but also a little bit terrifying, the idea that there must be something wrong with him becoming all too sharply ingrained in her mind.

Yet, something Tara had mentioned before now came to the forefront of her mind. Why *shouldn't* she be treated like this? Why shouldn't a man like Jay want to impress or do something special for someone like her, Natalie Webb, who (according to Tara anyway) was just as attractive and as good a 'catch' as he was?

And there was nothing wrong with *her*, was there? Well, she thought grimacing, apart from the fact that she had a tendency to come over a little on the 'strong' side whenever a man paid her some attention. But she was over all that now.

And, speaking of Tara, she would be totally *gobsmacked* when she heard about this.

"You're very quiet," Jay remarked from alongside her. "Is all this OK with you? I hope I didn't overwhelm you too much or make you uncomfortable – it's just I wanted to do something special."

"Are you mad? This is amazing. No, I'm just thinking about how jealous everyone will be when I tell them all about this."

"Phew," he said in mock-relief. "I was thinking I might have made a serious cock-up. It's just ... Natalie, I know you're used to being wined and dined in the best places in London, and you admitted yourself that you're bored with all of that. I suppose I'm deliberately trying to up the ante by trying to be a little bit imaginative."

He sounded so sincere that Natalie wanted to hug him. Imagine doing all this just for her ...

"Please don't think that because I've overdosed a bit on foie gras you have to do all this. I'm just happy spending time with you, and it doesn't matter if it's afternoon tea at the Ritz, or greasy burgers at TGI Friday. Now, don't get me wrong – I'm loving all this, and visiting this city has been a dream of mine for as long as I can remember, but you really shouldn't feel you have to do something extravagant all the time." She grinned broadly. "Paris, I can't wait!"

"You're going to love it," Jay assured her, taking her hand in his.

THIRTY-FIVE

His 'place' was an amazing Haussmann-style apartment not far from the 4th Arrondissement, which considering property prices in Paris were some of the highest in Europe, must have cost him an absolute fortune.

"It's a leaseback," he told her, when Natalie remarked how expensive it must have been. "I get to use it for only a couple of weeks a year, and I have to book them well in advance, no matter whether I use it or not. So this wasn't as spontaneous as it might look," he added wryly, pouring her a glass of wine, while she sat at the counter and watched him prepare dinner. "I knew I'd booked it free this week, and again for a couple of weeks at the end of the year, so I thought why not make the most of it? And of course," he said with a wink, "it gave me the perfect opportunity to impress you."

"Great investment," Natalie agreed. "I wish I'd thought of doing something like this ages ago, but I suppose I'm still hanging onto my dream of affording something in Belgravia." She sighed dreamily.

Jay laughed. "You publicists are obviously earning much more than I thought."

"I *did* say it was a dream," she replied, making a face at him. "But honestly, I really adore this place – your own little piece of Paris, it's heavenly."

"I'm glad you like it and, to be truthful, it's nice to have someone to enjoy it with."

Natalie raised an eyebrow. "You didn't bring any of your previous girlfriends here?" *Or boyfriends*, a wicked voice piped up inside her, and she gulped.

"I've only had it a year, and since I broke up with my last girlfriend over a year ago ..." The rest of his sentence trailed off, as he went to check the food in the oven.

Behind his back, Natalie smiled, pleased that he'd taken the bait, and even more that his reply had put to rest the idea that he might be the other way inclined.

From what she could make out, he was preparing some kind of casserole, which in a way was a little bit of a letdown. There was a side of her that was sorry they weren't going out to some cosy Parisian restaurant on the Left Bank – despite her protestations that she'd tired of fine food – but no doubt whatever Jay had in mind, it would be gorgeous.

It was. When they eventually sat down to eat not two hours after their arrival in the capital, Natalie realised that, along with all his other attributes, he was a seriously good cook.

"What's the catch?" she asked him, as she tucked into the most fantastic beef bourguignon she had ever tasted. "What am I missing here?"

"Catch – what do you mean?" Jay said, looking a little worried.

"Well, this is clearly the nicest beef thingamajig I've ever tasted, and most men I know can barely boil a kettle, so what gives?"

"The best you've ever tasted? Wow, that's a hell of compliment. I'll be sure to pass it on."

"Oh, let me guess, you've got an army of bloody servants dancing attendance on you too, have you? Bloody hell, Jay, who *are* you?" she said, dropping her fork. "I'm sorry that I haven't had time to Google you before now. When I do, I'll probably find that you're a descendant of the Queen."

"Do people really do that?" Jay said, laughing. "Look people up on the internet?"

"Of course. Don't you?"

"Um – no," he said as if the thought had never, ever crossed his mind.

"Well, you should – you never know who you're dealing with these days."

Jay chuckled. "Now I know why you're so successful in your work. You know everyone's deepest darkest secrets."

"Don't change the subject," Natalie said, taking another forkful of food. "*Do* you have an army of servants dancing attendance on you, and making delicious beef thingamajigs for your lady friends?"

"I told you – I don't know who all these lady friends are that you're talking about," he insisted, before adding casually, "And this is M&S."

For a long moment, Natalie just stared at her plate.

"Bloody hell! I *definitely* eat out too much," she laughed, before launching straight back into her food.

They chatted for ages over dinner, finding out more about one another's likes and dislikes, where they'd travelled, where they'd like to travel in the future, and the more they talked the more Natalie found herself liking him. This – date or relationship or whatever it was, was so different to anything that had gone before. They had so much in common, and seemed to share so many similar values that it was quite frightening really.

Was this what Tara had been talking about? About finding out these things about the men she dated instead of just zooming onto the possibility of marriage like a radar missile? If so, she had to admit it was pretty good advice. Totally obvious of course, but sometimes these things needed to be pointed out; in her case they'd *certainly* needed pointing out.

So, by the time they'd finished their second bottle of wine, she decided she couldn't hold out if Jay made a move tonight, which he surely would, given that he'd brought her all the way to the most romantic city in the world – and to his own *place* in the most romantic city in the world – he was hardly going to have her sleep on the couch, was he?

As if reading her thoughts, Jay began to speak. "Natalie, we've had a great time this evening, but ... well, I didn't want to be presumptuous or anything, so I booked you a room at a small boutique hotel not far from here – just in case you thought I was pressurising you to spend the night," he added quickly, "with me."

Her heart sank to her stomach. What kind of man

would book a girl into a hotel in Paris when he had his own apartment?

"Of course," he added, twisting a strand of her hair around one of his fingers, his breath warm and tingly on her skin, "if you decide that you'd *like* to stay over, well, I won't argue with that either."

Then before she could think any more about it, Natalie threw her arms around Jay's neck and pulled him roughly towards her.

Sod Tara and her rules, she thought as he returned her kisses with a fervour that banished all doubt and pushed her back on the couch, his hands roaming freely over her body.

When it came to being committed to *not* sleeping with Jay, right then, on a count of one to ten, Natalie was minus one million.

THIRTY-SIX

Luke was out digging his garden when he spotted his next-door neighbour return from walking the dogs in the fields.

She was lovely, always so friendly and chatty. A good-looking woman too, he noticed, but what was most appealing about Liz was that she seemed to have a slight frailty about her.

In fact, with her dark hair and ladylike ways, she reminded him of his youngest sister, although Ingrid wouldn't go near a dog to save her life.

"How's it all going?" she called, giving him a friendly wave, while trying to herd the dogs back into their individual kennels. "Doing some work on the garden, I see?"

"I'm nearly sorry I started to be honest," he called back, standing up and leaning on his shovel. "It's bloody hard work. But I thought I'd better do something with it. Actually," he added, sticking the shovel into the dirt and coming across to chat to her, "your friend Tara shamed me into it with all her talk about it being a wilderness."

Liz smiled. "Yes, Tara can be a bit persuasive all right."

"Did you two enjoy your night out on the town? Apart from having to make conversation with me."

"Don't be silly – it was a great night, and once Tara got started there was no fear of us running out of things to say. But I'm sorry she went on at you like that about your job and everything."

"Yes, she speaks her mind all the same, doesn't she?" he laughed and Liz laughed too.

"Bit of an understatement," she said.

"I think she told me she grew up in the village?" Luke queried. "I take it you did too?

"Oh goodness, no. Can't you tell from the accent? I'm a true-blue Dub."

"I just assumed you two were childhood friends and your accent isn't particularly noticeable."

"No, we used to work together in Dublin. But my husband Eric is from here. That's how we met actually – he's a school-friend of Tara's and she introduced us."

"I see."

Luke hadn't met the husband yet, but he remembered Liz saying something about him working in Dublin. Lucky bastard, having a lovely wife and kid like that.

Having done the run of nightclubs and online-dating and what have you, Luke had just about given up on finding himself a decent prospect, let alone a half-decent woman. Until now.

"So," he began, trying to sound offhand, "does Tara get down to visit you all that much or ...?" He let the rest of the sentence trail off, as at this Liz smiled knowingly, a bit too knowingly, he thought, reddening a little. Damn, had he made it that obvious?

"She comes down to visit her parents a lot," said Liz, "so yes, we do see her quite a bit."

"Still, I suppose she's busy in Dublin with her job and everything – she told me all about it when you were away," he said casually, afraid that he was revealing too much interest.

"Well, she is busy, but as I said we do get to see her a lot." Liz met his eyes , her look, conveying to Luke that she was very much aware of his reasons for asking. "Why? Are you worried that you might bump into her again? And that she'll grill you about your job?"

"Well, if she does, I'll have an answer for her," Luke replied, feeling cheered by the fact that Liz hadn't mentioned anything about Tara having a boyfriend. With her good looks and seemingly fun-loving personality, he'd thought there might've been someone on the scene. But Liz, who clearly knew he was fishing for information about her, hadn't said a word about Tara being attached.

This was good news.

"Yes, you two seemed well able for one another that night," Liz laughed.

"Hello there."

Luke and Liz were so busy laughing together that they hadn't noticed the man come out of her house. Luke immediately twigged it was the husband, evidently wondering who it was that was making his wife laugh like that. And so he might.

"Oh – you're home!" Liz cried. "Come and meet Luke, our new next-door neighbour." She turned and looked questioningly at Luke. "You two haven't met yet, have you? Eric this is Luke."

"Nice to meet you – I hear you moved in recently. Sorry I haven't bumped into you before now," Eric said amiably, holding out his hand.

But as Luke went to shake the other man's hand and got a proper look at his face, he realised that Eric was correct in saying that they hadn't met, but wrong in his assumption that they hadn't bumped into one another.

They had, Luke thought, as he studied his new neighbour's husband, but at the time Eric had been sitting on a park bench by the lake, deep in conversation with a woman who was very definitely *not* his lovely wife.

THIRTY-SEVEN

"I just don't know how to thank you!" Natalie gushed down the telephone line to Tara.

Since her trip to Paris with Jay, the two had been inseparable.

"I'm still not happy that you broke your promise not to sleep with him," Tara reminded her briskly, "but I'll admit that had I been in your situation, I probably would've had problems keeping it too."

"Uber-calm and controlled you? I don't believe it for a second," Natalie joked.

"So things are still going well then?" Although any fool could tell from Natalie's elated tone that things were going very well indeed.

"He's wonderful, and we get on so well. We have the most amazing chats that last for hours, and at the end of it all, we can barely remember what we've talked about. I've never felt so ..." she seemed to be struggling for the right word, "so on a par with a man before. I'm not always worried about how I'm putting myself across or what'll happen next – I'm just being myself. And yes, I know it sounds corny, but it's true."

"I'm thrilled for you– I really am. Jay sounds terrific – almost too good to be true." He did sound wonderful – sensitive, thoughtful, romantic – and seemed to treat Natalie the way every girl would like to be treated.

Tara sorely hoped that the man was everything he seemed to be. Having genuinely fallen for someone this time, it would just be her luck for him to turn out to be married, or something.

"He is! Oh, Tara, you'd love him – you really would."

"I'm sure I would. So tell me, do you want to continue our sessions for a little while longer? Or are you happy enough to keep going on your own now? To be honest, I don't think there's a whole lot else I can help you with. You seem to be doing just fine on your own."

"Well, there is one more thing," Natalie said. "I'd really love for you to ... I don't know ... observe us together."

"Observe you?"

"Yes, I'd love to get your opinion – not only on Jay, but also on how the two of us interact. You know, just to be sure that it is as good as I'm making it all sound."

Tara smiled. "Don't be silly – you certainly don't need my blessing – not at this stage anyway."

"But I'd really love for you to meet him – I mean, it's all because of you that we're together in the first place."

"Um, I think your good looks and sparkling personality might have had something to do with it," Tara laughed.

"Nope, I was a disaster before you went to work on me, you know that. And if I didn't have you coaching me through our dates, I would have messed up this relationship just as easily as I'd messed up all the others. It was you, Tara – you made this happen."

"Maybe I *helped* make it happen, but all I did was give you a little push in the right direction. I certainly don't deserve all this praise."

"But you do! Will you come to London and see us? And let me thank you properly for the wonderful help you've given me. Don't worry – I'll take care of the flights and the hotel and all that kind of thing."

"Don't be silly – I wouldn't dream of letting you do anything like that."

"It's not a problem – it'll be my way of saying thank you, since you refused point blank to take any payment," she chided. "But will you come though? Besides meeting Jay, I'd love to see you again too. We could all go out for dinner somewhere, the four of us. I'm sure Jay would get on great with Glenn."

Whatever about her taking off to London to see Natalie, there wasn't a hope in hell of convincing Glenn to tag along. He was just way too busy with work at the moment and, in truth, she couldn't see him being the slightest bit interested in cosy dinners with Natalie and her new man. When she said this to her, the other girl sighed.

"I understand. But couldn't you come on your own then? I know it mightn't be as much fun, but you could stay with me and we could go shopping or ...no, wait – why don't you bring that friend you're always talking about?"

"Liz?" Tara sat back in her seat. *That* wasn't a bad idea. Although she seemed to have cheered up a little lately, Liz had been going through such a hard time with all this business with Eric, that it would be nice for her to get away and enjoy herself. Considering she'd got such enjoyment of their night out that time.

Liz would adore London actually. The two of them could go over on a cheapie weekend and stay in a nice hotel in town. They could go and meet Natalie (who Liz would love) and the famous Jay, and then they could use the rest of the weekend for shopping and maybe some beauty treatments. It sounded glorious now that she thought about it.

And it would be nice to see Natalie again.

"So what do you think? Will you come for a visit?"

"I think it might be fun," Tara replied, and instantly a high-pierced squeal was to be heard from the other end.

"It'll be brilliant," Natalie cried. "And hopefully it'll prove to you once and for all that Jay truly is as wonderful as he sounds."

THIRTY-EIGHT

LIZ WENT out the hallway to answer the ringing telephone, leaving Eric in the living room watching TV.

To her relief, things had improved somewhat in the McGrath household lately. His frequent disappearances had lessened and he seemed to be spending much more time at home. And although he still tended to be moody and pensive, he seemed to be taking more of an interest in Toby.

However, the majority of the changes were of Liz's own doing.

After her night out with Tara, she'd decided not to mention her suspicions to Eric about his having an affair, and had come to the conclusion that she'd been imagining the whole thing.

After all, had there been any concrete evidence to suggest that he was cheating on her? Emma's apparently 'blank' text message appearing on his mobile phone could have very well been as Eric had described it – an accident.

That time she'd suspected that he wasn't (as he'd told

her) going out for a drink with Colm, had turned out to be exactly that. As had his visits to his mother.

And the weird hours and late nights he'd been working in Dublin were for a very good reason – extra cash to renovate the house. And in fairness, she couldn't really have expected him to be chatting and laughing like a maniac in Belfast when they'd been there for a family funeral, could she?

So Liz had finally come to the conclusion that she'd imagined the whole lot of it, had spent the last while working herself into a frenzy about nothing.

All because of some stupid comment Emma had made that day in the village. So what if she had bumped into Eric? How, from that simple remark, had Liz made the giant leap to think that Eric was the mystery father of her baby? Eric was her husband and he loved her.

Insecurity was something Liz had lived with for most of her life and she couldn't help it. It was only natural that when she'd finally got the life she wanted, the life she'd dreamt about, a home and family to call her own, that she'd be terrified of it being taken away from her. She'd been that way all her life. When she was younger, it seemed that every time she'd begun to settle in with one of her brothers and his family that circumstances would change and she'd be uprooted and brought to live with another.

Since she lost her parents twenty years before, nothing, least of all family life had ever been stable in Liz's life and she supposed it was understandable that she'd worry about the stability of her own. Subconsciously, she'd often worried that the wonderful life she had with Eric and then

Toby seemed too good to be true and was probably only looking for something to go wrong.

But, she realised now, through her own insecurity, she could very well have ruined everything she had all by herself. So ever since she'd tried her utmost not to let things get to her, not to fret over Eric's distant moods and working hours, tried not to turn every molehill into a mountain.

She picked up the ringing phone to find Tara on the other end.

"Do you fancy coming to London with me next weekend?" her friend asked without preamble.

"London? What for?"

"Well, Natalie – you know, the girl I met in Egypt, and the one I've been coaching recently?"

"What about her?"

"She persuaded me to come over for a visit, to meet the man of her dreams and the reason she asked for my help in the first place. Apparently she needs my blessing," she added good-humouredly. "Anyway, you'd love her, Liz – she's a gas woman. And I'm sure she'd know how to show us a good time. She just emailed to tell me she's organised a gorgeous hotel and no doubt she'll take us somewhere swanky for dinner on Friday night so –"

"For *us* – she wouldn't mind me coming too?"

"Of course not, it was she who suggested it in the first place. So does that mean you will come?"

Liz bit her lip. It sounded wonderful. She hadn't been out of the country since her honeymoon in Portugal three years ago. And wouldn't it be great to get the chance to go shopping in London – especially with Tara. Her friend would know all the right places to go, and would ensure she had her wardrobe updated in no time.

"Oh I'd love to," she said, "but I suppose I'd better ask Eric if he's OK to look after Toby first. Can you hold on?"

She went back into the living room. "Didn't you say earlier that you're not working next weekend?" she asked her husband, unable to keep the excitement out of her tone.

Eric didn't look up from the TV. "Yeah – why do you ask?"

"How would you feel about looking after Toby and the kennels while I go to London with Tara?" Liz held her breath, waiting for him to make up some excuse not to do it. "We're hoping to go Friday and it'd just be for the weekend and – "

"No problem – go for it. I'll be coming off nights early Friday morning, and I'm not back in until the following Monday night. So it should be fine."

"But won't you be tired, having just finished your shift and everything?"

"Not at all! I'll get a few hours sleep in before you leave, and I'll be grand."

"Are you sure?" Liz couldn't believe he'd agreed so readily.

"Honestly – go. You'll enjoy it."

"I can go!" she laughed down the phone to Tara afterwards, feeling happier and more optimistic than she'd felt in ages.

"Fantastic, I'm about to sort the flights as we speak. How about a lunchtime flight on Friday, and a late one back on Sunday evening?"

"Sounds fine to me – just let me know how much I owe you."

"Don't worry about it," her friend insisted. "Natalie's insisted she'll look after it."

"Really? That's so generous of her. Oh, Tara, thanks for asking me. I really can't wait," Liz cried. "This will be great fun!"

"It certainly will," her friend laughed, "and I really think it'll do us both the world of good."

THIRTY-NINE

THE FOLLOWING THURSDAY AFTERNOON, Tara sighed with pleasure as she closed the office door behind her and raced upstairs to get changed.

That was it, she thought, as she cast off her work attire and changed into a pair of denims and a T-shirt – no more clients until the following Monday. In the meantime she and Liz were going to have a wonderful time visiting Natalie in London.

She couldn't wait.

She went downstairs and opened the fridge, wondering what to do for dinner. Glenn's shift ended at seven this evening, so for once he'd be home in time to eat with her.

She debated whether to go to the trouble of cooking or just order a takeaway. Blast it, she'd order in, she decided, closing the fridge door and rummaging in the drawer for a takeaway menu. Glenn certainly wouldn't mind – he preferred takeaways to her 'bland' cooking. Understand-able since she preferred using lots of fresh vegetables and lean meat, instead of fat-laden stuff.

But tonight Tara didn't care. The odd takeaway now and again wouldn't kill them. Still though, he would probably be living on them while she was in London, wouldn't he?

She bit her lip. Maybe she should prepare a few things in advance for him to reheat while she was gone – a few simple pasta dishes or something.

But blast it, she'd only be wasting her time. If Glenn had his way he'd live on pizza and Chinese, and it was unlikely he'd even go to the trouble of reheating something

Oh well, he was a big boy and she'd have to leave him to his own devices.

She was really looking forward to this trip and couldn't wait to meet up with Natalie again. The girl was so vivacious and fun-loving, Tara just knew she'd go all out to ensure she and Liz enjoyed their stay.

And it would also be nice to finally put a face to loverboy Jay, and suss out whether he really was as good as he seemed. She hoped so.

Natalie was a dote who, after so much disappointment, really deserved a good man in her life.

And apparently she was pulling out all the stops for their visit – despite Tara's protestations that she didn't owe her anything.

Instead of just meeting for a quiet dinner, Natalie had utilised all her connections and arranged a table for them in none other than The Ivy for tomorrow night.

Liz had nearly fainted with excitement when she'd heard this.

They were getting a lunchtime flight the following day,

so the plan was for Eric to drive Liz to here, and Tara would drive them both to the airport.

So they should get into Heathrow around early afternoon and then ... she frowned and set down the takeaway menu.

What would they do from there? She hadn't been in London in donkey's years. Was there a train they could get into Central London, or would it be quicker to just get a taxi?

She wasn't sure, but she supposed she'd better find out. Natalie had the restaurant booked for early evening, so by the time they got to the hotel and changed, there really wouldn't be a whole lot of leeway, and she couldn't take the chance on being late. Especially when Natalie had gone to so much trouble.

Deciding she'd better ask her advice, Tara picked up the phone and dialled her work number, but it went straight to voicemail. She was tempted to leave a message asking her friend what they should do upon arrival at the airport but then she realised how silly that sounded. Talk about Irish country bumpkins. There was no need to bother her – she could easily research some options herself.

Tara went into the living room and sat down in front of Glenn's laptop. Her office PC had been infected by some virus, and despite Glenn's best efforts was still off-limits. So in the meantime, she'd been using his for online coaching sessions and researching her trip.

She'd try the site she'd used just a few days before when looking up the location of the hotel that Natalie had arranged - that had loads of supporting tourist info.

But she couldn't for the life of her remember the web

address ... was it London *hotelbookings* ... *londonhotels* ... *hotelslondon*? Nope, obviously none of those, she thought frowning as the '*address not found*' page kept coming up on the screen.

Then she thought of something. Since she'd accessed it only recently, the site would still be saved in the history file, wouldn't it?

Tara clicked on the '*history*' button, feeling rather pleased with herself that she'd remembered to do it. Maybe Glenn wasn't the only dab hand at computers in this house.

A list of recently viewed pages appeared on the screen, and Tara scanned through them, hoping to spot the one she was looking for. But something else caught her eye instead; somewhere she'd find the answer in any case: *celticfemmes.com*.

The forum was a mine of information – its thousands of members exchanging information on everything from fake tan to failed relationships.

Tara had posted a request for information on Sharm El Sheikh there before eventually choosing it as a holiday destination, and she'd been inundated with lots of very helpful information and useful advice.

So why shouldn't she do the same for London? *Someone* would know how easy or otherwise it was to get from the airport into that part of the city, and how much it would cost.

She clicked onto the travel section, and posted a new topic, labelling it '*Weekend in London*'.

'*Hi everyone, heading to London for the weekend and wondered about the best way to get from Heathrow to Kensington. Is there a train I can get from the airport to this area, or should I get a cab directly? Prefer not to use the Tube if possible. Any info would be greatly appreciated. Thanks, Pixie.*

'Pixie' was Tara's username for the forum; preferring not to use her real name online. She then hit 'send' and waited for the page to reload, plus her query to appear at the top of the travel section. And within seconds, there it was.

Grand, she thought, standing up from the laptop. She'd come back after dinner to see what the femmes had to say and hopefully ... Tara's eyes widened as she realised she already had a reply; another member's nickname '*Obi-wan*' had appeared beside her topic. That was quick.

"Good woman," Tara muttered as she clicked into the topic once more to see what advice Obi-wan had given her. But when the page reloaded, she frowned. There was nothing there but her own query – no reply at all.

Perplexed, she refreshed the page, thinking that the post might not have properly registered yet, but then something caught her eye.

The topic she'd posted *was* there, but instead of registering under 'Pixie', it showed as originating via someone called 'Obi-wan'.

Flummoxed, she sat back in her seat and stared at the screen. How had that happened? Her username was the same one she used for all the various sites and forums she frequented. So how had her query been posted by 'Obi-wan'?

Of course. Tara grinned as the penny dropped. She was using Glenn's computer now, wasn't she? So clearly he had also visited this particular site previously, and logged on under his own username.

The moniker made sense if she'd thought about it for even half a second – he was such a *Star Wars* fan that she should have guessed immediately.

Then she thought of something. Why would *Glenn* be a member of a female-friendly site? She smiled. She shouldn't do it, but at the same time, this could be interesting.

Still grinning to herself, she clicked onto the *'View Member Profile'* section, revealing that 'Obi-wan' had only recently joined the forum and posted on only a handful of occasions.

Tara clicked into the *'View all Member Posts'* heading. She knew she shouldn't be so nosy, but she couldn't help it. She was *dying* to see what information Glenn might have wanted.

Knowing him, it was probably tech-related – though, considering his level of expertise, why he would seek out info from celticfemmes was beyond her. Though, more likely she thought then, could it be something to do with scuba diving?

Since the trip to Egypt, he'd been trying to arrange more dives here and thus could have come across the forum via a search for Irish scuba diving information. It seemed the most likely explanation anyway.

But the topic Glenn was active on was labelled: *'Serious shit – advice needed.'*

As she began to read through the thread, Tara soon began to wish she hadn't been so inquisitive. But once she'd started she just couldn't stop – couldn't tear her eyes away and her heart galloped as she read the words.

The query was initiated by another member, 'Mattie' who was asking for advice on some 'serious shit' all right.

'*Need some advice from a female perspective 'cos this is something I'm finding hard to deal with and can't exactly talk to my mates about it,*' Mattie wrote. '*My girlfriend's considering abortion. I don't want it – I'm totally against all that kind of stuff, but I also know that she's determined to go through with it. And the longer we fight about it, the more the baby will develop and the worse it'll be ...*'

The topic was hopping with responses, many members passing judgement, others giving genuine advice.

Heart pounding, Tara scrolled down through most of it until she found Obi-wan's reply. Evidently this topic interested Glenn enough for him to sign up, since non-members weren't allowed to post or reply.

Knowing well she shouldn't be doing it, and sensing that she wouldn't like what she found, Tara couldn't help but continue down the page until she found Glenn's contribution.

It was like a moth being drawn to flame.

Finally, she reached Obi-wan (Glenn)'s – reply.

'*I hear you. I'm in the same crazy boat. Because of our circumstances, we can't tell anyone and we've talked about the abortion thing too. I think she wants to, but I don't. We looked it up, and I think it's kosher up until twelve weeks, but after that ...*

Stunned by what she was seeing, Tara couldn't read any more. Was this some kind of sick joke?

Her heart pounded in her chest as she thought about it.

We can't tell anyone ... We talked about the abortion thing...

Glenn - *her* Glenn? But how ... and *who*?

Her mind struggled to comprehend the enormity of what she was reading, let alone the implications, while she stared at the screen as if in a trance.

Tara read back through it all again, her distress growing by the second, until eventually the words swam before her eyes and she could no longer focus.

Because of our circumstances, we can't tell anyone...

What in the hell had Glenn done?

FORTY

ONE LOOK at his expression told Tara everything she needed to know.

She'd sat stunned in front of the computer for what seemed like hours, but was actually just a few minutes. And was only woken from her trance when she heard his key in the front door.

"Are you here?" Glenn moved around the kitchen for a bit, before eventually finding her in the living room still-dazed in front of the laptop. "What are you doing? I thought you were finishing up early this evening, and ... hey, what's wrong?"

When she didn't answer - wouldn't look at him - he asked again. "Tara?" Then he looked past her face to the screen and his face paled.

It was then that she knew for sure that her worst fears had been realised.

"What the hell is going on?" she whispered, barely able to find her voice. "Is this ..." she turned to the computer screen, "all this ... really you? Or is it some kind of joke?"

But she knew deep down that it was no joke; Glenn's face had drained of colour and he wouldn't meet her gaze.

"What are you talking about?" he said, but his words held no conviction.

"I'm talking about *you* giving public advice on the some site about ... pregnancy and abortion. What the hell would you know about stuff like that, Glenn?"

"So you're checking up on me now – is that it?" he countered, but she knew it was just a delaying tactic.

"I wasn't checking up on you. You know I've had to use this while mine is out of action. I was looking for something totally different and I just happened to ... Anyway that's not the point," she went on, eyes flashing with anger. "What the hell is this all about? Tell me!"

He ran a hand through his hair and began to pace the room. "Look, I was going to tell you – "

"When?" she cried. "When were you going to tell me, Glenn? When this ... girl, whoever she is ... had the baby? Or were the two of you planning on keeping that a secret too?"

"I just didn't ... " He was lost for words.

Tara felt the room swim out of focus. She couldn't believe this. How could he? How on earth could this night-mare have happened?

"Tell me, Glenn."

"It wasn't going to be a secret much longer. I was going to tell you. Honestly I was going to tell you so many times," he repeated, "but I just couldn't bring myself to. You've been in such good form since we came back from the holiday – I didn't want to ruin things. And I know you're worried about this thing with Emma too and you've been up and down to Lakeview a lot – "

"Oh so while the cat's away, the mice will play?"

He shook his head. "No. I just couldn't ... *didn't* find the right time."

"Well, now is a good time," she said, her tone hardening. "Or should I just scroll through the rest of the forum?"

"I still can't believe you spied on me like that."

"It wasn't *spying*," she replied heatedly. "I was looking for something else and I came across the page. What were you doing publicly giving people advice like that? Were you not afraid of being found out? Glenn, of all people you should know enough to realise that everything's permanent online. Or was it that you just didn't you care whether or not you were found out... is that it?"

"Believe me, I didn't know that would happen. I was sure I'd logged out, but the cookies must've – "

"Spare me the technical stuff, and just tell me - *please* - what the hell is going on. Who is this girl?"

He sighed. "It's difficult to know where to start,"

"The beginning will be fine," Tara shot back, trying to keep her voice even.

He sighed deeply, and took a seat on the armchair across from her. "Her name is ... Abby," he began, his dark eyes studying the carpet. "We met a couple of months back ... in Egypt actually."

Tara couldn't believe what she was hearing. "In Egypt ... while you were supposed to be on holiday with me?" she croaked.

He nodded, ashamed. "She was taking the scuba-diving course too, and she's Irish – from Donnybrook – and over the few days going out on the boat, we sort of ... hit it off."

Now she understood why he'd been so unconcerned about her going off to the pyramids with Natalie. In fact, he'd practically insisted she go.

And why not – when it would free him up to go off and chase some girl he had his eye on. How could he? How could he deceive her like that? Glenn had *never* been the secretive type, they had always been straight up with one another.

Or so she'd thought.

"So, let me get this straight. All those times I stayed round the pool and you were supposed to be going out on the boat on a diving course, you were actually off with some girl?"

"No, I *was* going out on the boat. I did take the course. She was taking it too."

"I see – convenient, wasn't it?"

He wouldn't look at her. "I'm sorry – it wasn't intentional."

"And now she's pregnant," Tara stated acidly. "When did this happen? On some plastic sun-lounger in Egypt, or did you continue seeing her after we got home?"

Still, he wouldn't look at her. "We met up a couple of times after, yes," he said shamefully. "And then ... it happened. Look, we didn't mean for it to – "

"Oh, spare me! You know as well as I do that these things don't 'just happen'."

"I said I was sorry," he replied, his tone hardening somewhat. "This is tough enough as it is, without feeling guilty about you too."

"You selfish ... why shouldn't you feel guilty, going behind my back like that? And how else did you think I'd feel, considering? History repeating itself like this."

"I'm sorry ... I just ... I'm sorry - honestly," Glenn repeated ashamed, as she just stared into space, unable to believe this was truly happening. "Really, I had no idea what to do."

Eventually, she got up and walked out, unable to stay in the same room with him any longer. She went into the kitchen and put her head in her hands. In a few months' time, Glenn – her Glenn – was about to become a father.

Really I had no idea what to do, he'd said. While Tara could consider a variation of the same idea.

What on earth was *she* going to do?

FORTY-ONE

The following morning, a bubbly and energetic Liz arrived at the house.

Tara and Glenn had sat up for hours the previous night discussing everything, he apologising over and over, she trying in vain to come to terms with the implications.

She'd lain awake for hours afterwards, wondering what on earth would happen to them now. Glenn had insisted he was going to stick by this girl ... Abby.

"She needs my support," he told Tara, when she'd calmed down somewhat from the shock. "You must understand that I have to stand by her."

"Do you love her?"

He was hesitant and again wouldn't give her a straight answer.

"I ... I don't know. I think so," he said, while inside her heart shattered. Almost overnight, he'd become a completely different person.

It seemed he had it all worked out. He was standing by this girl – the soon-to-be mother of his child. He'd had weeks to come to terms with this, to think about what it meant to his future.

But what about her? What about what *she* thought? Didn't that matter to him at all? Did he think that Tara would just stand by, say nothing and just accept things as they were? That saying sorry would be enough?

She didn't know; and that morning she could barely see straight from lack of sleep, let alone get excited about the upcoming trip.

Earlier that morning, he had gone out to work as usual and hugged her goodbye, urging her apologetically to 'try and enjoy it' and that they'd talk some more on her return.

Tara hadn't returned the embrace and almost wanted to laugh out loud at the idea of her enjoying herself. A jaunt to London was the last thing she wanted or needed after the bombshell he'd landed on her, but yet she didn't want to let Natalie, or indeed Liz down.

"I'm so looking forward to this," her friend squealed, as she excitedly dropped her bags in the hallway, and followed Tara through to the kitchen. "And Eric was *fine* about my going – he actually told me I deserved the break – which was a turn-up for the books I can tell you, and ..." Her words trailed off as in the bright light of the kitchen, she properly caught sight of Tara's drawn and anxious face. "What's the matter?" she gasped. "Pet, what's wrong?"

"Oh, Liz – everything's such a mess." Unable to hide her distress, Tara sank into the kitchen chair, and put her head in her hands.

"What is it? What's happened?"

"It's Glenn," she cried. "He's made such a mess of everything."

And through her tears, she spilled out the whole sorry tale.

"I can only imagine what you're going through," Liz consoled, her voice gentle, "but on the bright side at least he admitted everything and was willing to talk about it with you. And no matter what, he's a decent guy. You'll work it out between you, I know you will."

Tara sniffed. She wasn't so sure whether or not she wanted to work it out.

It might be easier to just throw Glenn out on his ear, and let him and his new girlfriend go it alone. But deep down, she knew she wouldn't do that. They had been through too much over the years, and despite what had happened, she loved him like crazy.

"I just don't know how to deal with it," she told Liz sadly. "He's going to be a dad soon, he and some kid he barely knows. He's said he wants to stand by her, that he has to stand by her. And if he's so determined to do that; so determined to become involved in this girl and her baby's life, then Liz, where on earth does that leave me?"

THEY ARRIVED at Heathrow that same afternoon, and Tara resolved to try and take her mind off things for a while, at least until after they'd met up with Natalie and her boyfriend.

Then like Liz said, the two of them could spend the rest of the weekend 'locked in the hotel with chocolate and ice-cream' if Tara preferred.

She certainly knew she wouldn't be up for going shopping in Oxford Street or anything like that. She'd be lucky if she got through the day as it was.

"I'm so sorry for ruining your weekend," she told Liz, as they travelled towards their hotel in the taxi (which she mused sadly, had 'cost' her a lot more than she'd anticipated). "I know how much you were looking forward to this."

"Don't be stupid," Liz replied, horrified that she should think – let alone say –such a thing. "In fact, I think you're amazing for going through with this at all. If it were me, I know for a fact I'd be buried under the duvet with one of my four-stone bags of Maltesers."

Tara raised a smile. "Well, everything's arranged and to be honest, I don't think Natalie would hear of it if I told her we weren't coming. Let's just say she's a pretty determined lady."

Liz sat back and stared out at the London streets, which were today covered with mist and rain. "I'm looking forward to meeting her and this lovely man of hers all the same."

"Yes," Tara replied, hoping she'd be able to get through tonight without letting Natalie know she was off form. She knew how much she was looking forward to their visit and showing off Jay especially. She didn't want to ruin it for her. "I'm sure it'll be an interesting night."

FORTY-TWO

THAT EVENING, Liz checked her appearance in the mirror for what must have been the thousandth time.

Not that it mattered an iota what she looked like in the scheme of things, she thought guiltily. Here she was, idiotically concerned about clothes, when poor Tara, who was getting ready in the hotel room's en suite, was going through a terrible time.

Liz still couldn't believe Glenn had got some girl pregnant. Who'd have thought he had it in him? Especially when he'd always seemed such a nerdy type who never seemed interested in anything other than computers and bloody football. But as that old saying went, it was the quiet ones you had to watch.

And now poor Tara was devastated over it.

The more Liz thought about it, the more she decided that when she got home she was going to face up to the problems in her marriage once and for all. Even if it meant she had to face up to the fact that Eric had done the unthinkable, then she'd just have to do it.

After all, Tara had had to face worse and she'd come through it all, hadn't she?

Even now, at her lowest ebb, her friend was still putting a brave face on things – trying to overcome and put aside her hurt and disappointment, at least for the moment.

And although Tara looked wonderful in the black trousers and jade green velvet and lace cami-top she was wearing tonight, there was no mistaking the pain behind her eyes.

"Ready to go?" she asked tiredly.

"Are you sure you're OK to do this?" Liz asked again. "We could always call Natalie and cancel - say you've got a headache or something."

Tara managed a rueful laugh. "Believe me, Natalie would be over here with the cavalry and armed with a multi-pack of paracetamol. No, it's fine, honestly and in all fairness it might be the best thing – help me take my mind off it for a while."

"Well, as long as you're sure."

"I'm sure," Tara replied, and the two closed the hotel room door behind them and headed off to the West End to meet Natalie and man-of-the-moment, Jay.

AT FIRST, Liz didn't notice anything out of the ordinary. Anything that was, other than the restaurant's gorgeous décor and its welcoming and friendly maitre d' as he took their coats.

And of course she was too busy trying to spot celebs and well-known faces amongst the tables to concentrate that much on who they were meeting.

But as they approached their table, at which sat a woman so stunning she would make Jennifer Lopez feel like Quasimodo, she noticed Tara suddenly stiffen and then stop dead in her tracks.

"Are you OK?" she queried, as the gorgeous woman – evidently Natalie – smiled and waved in their direction. Liz put a hand on Tara's arm. "Because you know we don't have to be here if you don't want – "

"Mother of god," Tara whispered and when Liz glanced quickly at her friend, she realised that Tara was speaking, not to her, but almost to herself. "Please, don't do this to me – not now."

Confused, Liz followed her gaze to the table where Natalie and her companion, a tall and fittingly gorgeous man, watched their approach. Then properly catching sight of the guy, she blinked and looked again, wondering if her eyes were deceiving her.

Could it be? But how …?

Then as she and Tara drew closer, her friend moving alongside her as if in a daze, Liz took a better look.

No, it wasn't, but there was one a hell of a resemblance. Obviously Tara had noticed too, which was why she was acting so strangely.

But when he finally turned his face to the light, Liz realised she *did* in fact recognise this guy - albeit a much younger and less distinguished version of him, standing alongside Tara on her best friend's debs night.

"Tara," she muttered in hushed tones, almost stopping too as the image from the old photograph Colm had shown her flashed into her memory, "is that – ?"

"Yes," her friend replied shakily, before Liz had a chance to finish. "Yes, it is."

FORTY-THREE

Tara didn't think she could endure it for much longer.

Natalie was trying her best, and her heart went out to the girl, who she knew couldn't understand why the mood at dinner was so subdued. But mistakenly thinking it was Liz who was the source of discomfort, she'd spent much of the meal trying to entice her into conversation.

Liz of course, had figured things out immediately. How could she not?

Tara still didn't know how she'd found the strength to shake his hand when Natalie introduced them.

"Tara, this is Jay. Jay – Tara."

And as recognition finally dawned, she saw his expression turn from amiable to downright disbelieving until the shock and surprise in his eyes mirrored her own.

"It's ... nice to meet you," he stuttered, briefly shaking her hand, while Tara wished she could just race out the door and never come back. Out of the corner of her eye, she could see Liz watching her carefully as they shook hands, but luckily Natalie noticed nothing amiss.

"And this is Liz."

"Hello, very pleased to meet you." To her credit, and possibly so as to not to arouse Natalie's suspicion, Liz tried to make up for Tara's lack of enthusiasm as she in turn shook Jason's hand.

"And Liz, as you can probably guess –" Natalie went on, giving Tara a look of feigned disapproval for neglecting to introduce her friend, "I'm Natalie, and I'm *so* thrilled to meet you. Is this your first time in London?"

"Great to meet you too and no, this isn't my first time, but I haven't been here in years. Thanks for inviting me."

When they went to sit down, Natalie insisted Liz take a seat alongside her at the table, leaving Tara no choice but to sit beside Jason. She continued to chat to Liz about their flight over, if the hotel was OK, and what she thought of the restaurant while Tara, still reeling from the shock of seeing him again, just stared dumbstruck at the menu.

In truth, she was also shocked by how little he'd changed and how handsome he still looked after all these years.

In a way, seeing him face-to-face, and sitting in such close proximity to him almost reduced her to the naïve, love-struck teenager she'd been back then.

Almost, but not quite.

The ensuing years had made sure of that, had guaranteed that those carefree teenage years were long gone.

And so Tara sat there, within a couple of inches of the only man she'd ever truly loved; a man who'd broken her heart and trampled on her dreams, her silly pathetic teenage dreams of a great romance and a future together.

Despite Liz's and everyone else's insistence that she

should seek out real love and passion in her life, Tara knew that if passion led to such heartbreak and pain, she never wanted to experience it again.

And as for love, well, she'd thought Glenn would provide enough of that. But as she'd only recently discovered, maybe she had been wrong in thinking that her life was under control, that by not allowing herself to fall in love again she would be immune from sorrow and pain.

'Calm, controlled and serene,' she remembered Natalie describing her once, but what she didn't know was that Tara was that way for a very good reason.

And now, almost the instant she'd set eyes upon Jason (or Jay as Natalie called him – why had she never considered a connection since he was from Dublin?) the old Bryan Adams number, *Heaven,* began to play in her head. Their song – and one that always triggered a reflexive change of music station whenever it started up.

It was something that amused Glenn no end.

"Why do you hate that song so much?" he'd tease in the car, while Tara would nonchalantly declare that it was 'cheesy and pathetic' while inside she'd try desperately to banish the memories it triggered.

Memories of a time she wanted to forget, but wasn't allowed to.

"Whew, I'm stuffed after that," Natalie declared, pushing away the half-eaten plate of roast duck. "How was yours, Tara? Was it any good? Tara?"

"What?"

"How was your food? You've hardly eaten anything."

"Oh, it's great," she said, trying to raise a smile as she felt Jason's gaze on her.

"Are you sure? You haven't eaten much – we can send it back if –"

"Honestly, it's great, thanks a million. I just don't have much of an appetite this evening. Sorry."

"With all the travelling and everything," Liz inserted by way of explanation, even though their plane had been in the air barely forty-five minutes.

But Natalie didn't seem to notice. "I know, air travel can be sooo tiring," she agreed, turning once again to Liz. "I suffer from terrible jet-lag at times, do you?" she asked chattily. "Jay, you love flying though, don't you?"

"Yes."

He was being just as uncommunicative as she, Tara noticed, resolving to try and buck herself up before Natalie noticed that something was seriously wrong. It wouldn't be fair of her to ruin this dinner, not when she was making such an effort – especially with Liz.

At that moment, Natalie's eyes widened and she elbowed Liz's arm. "Do you know, I think I just saw that actress from EastEnders go into the Ladies'!" she declared, and despite herself, Liz's eyes went wide as saucers.

"Are you serious? Who?" her friend gushed, unable to help herself, and Tara smiled sadly. In normal circumstances this night would have been great fun.

"Come on," Natalie urged, putting her napkin on the table. "Let's do a little celeb-stalking."

Liz looked unsure. "Aren't you coming too, Tara?"

"No – you two go ahead."

Liz gave her a questioning look, as she followed Natalie away from the table, and she briefly nodded her assent.

When they'd left, Tara truly understood the expression

'you could cut the atmosphere with a knife' and she wondered why the gods had engineered this nightmare in the first place.

"Tara," he began softly in that familiar velvety voice of his, "this is very ... very misfortunate. I really had no idea."

Her voice was brittle, and as she spoke she really wasn't sure how she was getting the words out.

"Misfortunate is a bit of an understatement, Jason – or should I call you Jay?"

There was a slight pause. "It's a nickname that started in Uni, and it stuck. Everyone calls me that now."

"Really? So you went to university then, did you? How wonderful – I never got that chance."

"Tara ... believe me, I thought about contacting you many times after –"

"And why didn't you? What stopped you? Too worried that I might tie you down, cramp your style – all those stupid expressions that people use. But you wouldn't know anything about that would you? You got out quick, long before the trouble started."

"It wasn't like that – I ..." The rest of his sentence trailed off, and he shook his head.

For a couple of minutes there was silence, and right then she realised how surreal this was, the two of them meeting here, in a place like this, a place of wealth and opulence and celebrity, while their romance had taken place in an innocent, old-fashioned country hotel in Ireland.

Yet it was here they'd ended up.

"Tara, you must believe me when I tell you how sorry I am," he said again. "But I didn't think, I couldn't think ...

we were so young and I just didn't know how or what ... I was so scared – "

"You were two years older than I was. I was seventeen, barely seventeen, and I was bloody scared too. But then that didn't last long, because after that being scared was the least of my worries."

Yet again the two were silent, Tara twisting her cotton napkin so tightly in her hands she thought it might shred.

Eventually Jason turned to face her – the first time he'd looked at her properly all evening. "And how is ..." he began, before pausing to take a deep breath. When he spoke again, his voice shook a little. "How is – "

"How is *Glenn*?" she interjected breezily. "I'm delighted to say that he's grown up to be a mature, responsible, and utterly wonderful young man."

Finally, she looked Jason directly in the eye. "Nothing like his father."

FORTY-FOUR

IN THAT INSTANT, she was back on the dance-floor of Clancy's Hotel, barely seventeen years old, in the arms of the man she adored.

The dress was (in her opinion) the most magnificent ball-gown on earth. It had taken absolutely *ages* to find but was worth it, and as soon as Tara tried it on, she'd known it was the perfect dress for her. The colour was her absolute favourite – deep cerise pink - and a bodice and overskirt made of soft satin, and a lovely flowing skirt that shushed along when she walked.

When Jason called to pick her up, he'd told her she looked amazing. Tara was pretty certain that if she'd been going to the debs ball with any of the lads from the village they wouldn't have even noticed her dress, and *definitely* would not have referred to her as 'amazing'. More likely they'd have called to the door, fidgeted impatiently for the obligatory photographs and then hurried off so they could go and join 'the boys'.

But Jason Murray wasn't like any of the Lakeview lads

(thank goodness) and instead of trying to avoid the photographs like Deborah's Murphy's boyfriend Conor, he'd even offered to take a shot of her family; Tara standing in the middle between her mam and dad and a narky-looking Emma whinging about 'being swallowed up in a pink meringue'.

And he hadn't batted an eyelid when they'd reached the hotel and Colm had insisted on getting a group photo, even though Tara knew that he was a little uncomfortable around her friends, whom he didn't really know.

Now, as she and Jason danced slowly to Bryan Adam's *Heaven*, his arms wrapped around her waist and his cheek resting lightly against hers, Tara thought the lyrics had never seemed more appropriate. She truly *was* in heaven.

She still couldn't believe he'd agreed to go to the debs ball with her, this mature, sophisticated boy from Dublin who'd holidayed with his family in Lakeview every summer for as long as she could remember.

The two had struck up a close friendship over the years, and every time he came on holiday they'd spend ages just chatting about nothing in particular and enjoying each other's company.

She knew all of her fellow sixth years in Our Lady's Secondary School were pea-green with envy that the fine thing from Dublin had chosen Tara Harrington to go to the debs with. Even Emma, who was only a kid and didn't know much about fellas yet, was wide-eyed with awe when Tara told her who she was taking to the ball.

Her mam and dad hadn't been too happy about it though.

"He's a bit old for you, love," Isobel had pointed out.

"Why couldn't you go with one of the local lads, like Colm, or maybe Eric McGrath even?"

Tara had groaned inwardly at the notion. Colm was hyper - you wouldn't get a word in while he was around - and all Eric wanted to do was smoke fags and talk about boring football. Anyway, none of them were in the *least* bit good-looking, although this never seemed to stop them from getting girls – Colm in particular was meant to be a 'demon with the women', whatever that implied.

But what Tara's parents especially didn't realise was that age didn't matter when you had something special like she and Jason did. He didn't talk about Man United and stupid things like hurling; he talked about travel and was into astrology too. Jason was her soul mate; she was sure of it.

And tonight, as Bryan Adam's throaty voice and romantic lyrics filled the room, Tara closed her eyes and felt more certain than ever.

The only snag, she thought opening them just as quickly, was that the room was beginning to spin a bit, and it wasn't from dancing. She'd better slow down a bit on the gargle. Tara wasn't a big fan of alcohol, and had never been interested in going off down the park by the lake, drinking flagons of cider with the boys like some of her classmates did.

In all fairness, even Emma was better able to hold her drink. She knew her little sister thought she was a bit of a goody-two-shoes. Well, she supposed she was. But Tara couldn't help that she didn't like the taste, or the way it made people act the eejit and fall all over the place, like Eric McGrath.

No, drinking just wasn't Tara's thing, but the problem was, she couldn't very well refuse Jason's kindness, could she?

And they were expensive too – Southern Comfort, he'd told her – as if she should be impressed. Maybe this was the kind of sophisticated stuff they all drank up in Dublin so it would be rude (not to mention a little childish) to say no? Especially when he'd agreed to come along to her debs. So feck it, for tonight she'd let her hair down.

"Did I tell you, you look beautiful in that dress?" Jason murmured in her ear now, and as she pictured how they must look together, like Johnny and Baby in the film *Dirty Dancing*. That was a great film; sooo romantic. And just like her and Jason, weren't Baby and Johnny from different backgrounds too? Yet *they'd* fallen in love, and to hell with anyone who tried to stop them.

"Thanks – you look a bit funny in a suit, but it's nice," she giggled, then kicked herself when she realised how unsophisticated that sounded. Here he was complimenting her like a proper grown-up, and she giggles back at him like a schoolgirl.

Tara was no longer a schoolgirl; she was now a seventeen-year-old woman with the world at her feet. Not that she had much of a clue what to do with that world, she thought ruefully. At least not until she got her exam results.

She might like to go to college, she wasn't really sure. Some of the other girls in her class, like Deborah, couldn't wait to go to college and 'finally get out of this kip', whereas Tara didn't think she ever wanted to leave. She loved her hometown and its yearly influx of summer tourists (like Jason).

So at the moment, she didn't want to leave Lakeview - ever.

What would be perfect would be if he and his family moved here from Dublin or something, and then she could see him all the time, and their great romance would last forever.

As if reading her thoughts, Jason bent his head and kissed her gently on the lips. As she kissed him back, Tara's brain swam with the romance of it all, the softness of his lips, the taste of him on her tongue, as Bryan Adams was just about to finish the song with that amazing guitar solo.

Then, the wonderful slow set ended and a noisy Madonna number broke the spell. Tara loved Madonna as much as the next girl, but at that moment she really wished that the DJ would play some more romantic numbers, so she could stay wrapped in Jason's arms forever.

Although, she thought as he smiled and led her away from the dance floor and back to their table, *Heaven* would be *their* song, from now on – hers and Jason's.

"Let's go outside for a while, will we?" he suggested, interrupting her musings. "It's baking in here."

She loved his Dublin accent and the funny expressions he came out with sometimes. Lakeview people would *never* say 'baking'. It made Jason seem all the more special.

"Out to the garden?" she said, as he picked up her drink – another icky Southern Comfort.

"We could go for a walk down by the lake?" he suggested with a smile that made Tara's heart turn over in her chest. "It's always nice down there. And if it gets cold, you can take my jacket."

Her heart soared. The lakeside park had always been a

popular spot for couples in love – couples like her and Jason. She couldn't wait to spend time alone with him in one of the romantic places she could think of – especially tonight, and with a full moon out in all its glory too.

This truly was turning out to be the best night of her life.

FORTY-FIVE

IT WAS SHE SUPPOSED, every teenage girl's nightmare, discovering she was pregnant after making love for the very first time.

And she'd been stupid, she and Jason had been idiots that night, when drunk on romance (and liquor) they'd gone down to the romantic, moonlit park by the lake, and made love for the first time amidst the long grass.

It wasn't even all horrible and fumbling like Deborah had said – for Tara it was the perfect expression of their love for one another. OK, so it was a bit uncomfortable at first, lying on the ground with his coat beneath them, but eventually she gave herself up to the pleasure of just being with him and enjoying what they were doing.

Afterwards as they lay sleepily in one another's arms, she thought about how wonderful it had been and how this had to be true love. She knew they had some problems to surmount, certainly – what with Jason living in Dublin – and she knew her parents already disapproved of the fact that he was that bit older. But this was meant to be, and they'd get through those problems wouldn't they? They were soul mates.

Tara's euphoria was short-lived though, when Jason – who'd dozed off for a short while afterwards – woke up and began fretting over the realisation that they hadn't used protection.

Her heart sank to her stomach, as the dreamlike state she'd been in all evening began to wear off, and his anxious behaviour brought her right back to reality. He wasn't having second thoughts about their night together, was he?

"I don't make a habit of this kind of thing," he told her, obviously horrified that she might think he slept with girls without protection on a regular basis.

Shortly after that, they gathered their things and left the park, Tara still distressed and humiliated over what he'd said. But just before they parted, he kissed her goodbye and gently told her he'd see her soon.

Buoyed by this, she reassured herself on the way home that his behaviour earlier had more to do with not using contraception, than having regrets about what had happened. After all Jason was her soul mate, and he loved her, didn't he? All would be well and she was worrying for nothing.

But she'd been wrong.

Six weeks after Jason had returned to Dublin, Tara's worst fears were realised in more ways than one.

Upon discovering that she was late, she realised she had a much greater problem than a broken heart to contend with. She was barely seventeen and pregnant, and although she'd convinced herself it was a child conceived out of love, Tara wasn't naïve enough to think that this would make it any easier for her parents to accept.

"The little shit," her mother raved. "Isn't well for him taking off back to the city and leaving us to deal with his mess."

"It's not a mess, Mam," Tara insisted through her tears. "We love one another. Yes, we made a big mistake, but it'll be OK. Jason loves me – he'll come back and look after us. It'll be OK."

But it wasn't OK. When she finally plucked up the courage to tell him the news, his reaction wasn't quite what she'd expected.

"I ... I don't know what you want me to do," he'd said on the phone, after what seemed like an interminably long silence. "I'm starting college next week and –"

Naively, she'd hoped against hope that Jason would immediately rush to her side and proclaim that he was going to take care of her and the baby, that there was no need for her parents to worry, that he would face up to his responsibilities because he loved Tara and wanted to be with her forever.

Stupidly, she'd even allowed herself to pretend that the pregnancy might force his hand and get him to move here for good. But instead, he'd acted cold and uncaring, a million miles from the Jason she knew before their night in the park.

"What did I tell you?" her mother ranted. "Of *course* he's going to tell you it's your own tough luck. That's what happens in these situations. You're the one – or should I say *we're* the ones – who'll be left to shoulder the burden – so you might as well get used to it."

Looking back, the words seemed unnecessary cruel, but a teenage pregnancy in the family – a respectable family in a small Irish village – was every parent's worst nightmare.

But the words remained with Tara and, right then, she knew that if she stayed and tried to bring up the baby under her parent's roof, she'd regret it for the rest of her life.

So, when she'd eventually got over the devastation of his rejection she resolved to take the 'burden' and shame away from her family and deal with it all herself.

And when, many months later, an adorable bundle of dark hair and laughing brown eyes was born, Tara resolved to go it alone. She knew what to do; she'd thought about nothing else in the interim, and had already set the plans in motion, and spoken to the relevant authorities.

So, at barely eighteen, Tara got out of Lakeview and went to Dublin, taking three-month-old Glenn with her.

For the first few months of his life she'd ensured she learnt how to cope, how to feed him, respond to his cries and what-not - and while she had no illusions about how difficult it would be, she felt confident she could go it alone.

Much to her mother's protests.

"What do you think you're playing at?" Isobel had sniggered when Tara told her she wouldn't burden her any longer. "How are you going to raise a baby by yourself?"

"I'll get by," she said defiantly. "Other people do it."

Her mother shook her head. "Nonsense. You'll be back here within a week."

But Tara would not allow her son to be a burden on her

parents, and she knew that if she stayed she would become resentful and bitter, and that her mother would remind her every single day that she was beholden to them.

Granted, it wasn't exactly a bed of roses being beholden to the state services either. She couldn't go out to work just yet, so she'd had little option but to rely on 'handouts'.

They'd put her on the housing list, and in the meantime set her up in a tiny, airless bedsit on Dublin's Northside, in what could only be described as 'a troubled' area. But within the community Tara eventually made some good friends – especially amongst other mums, and while life was very tough for the first few weeks, as far as she was concerned it was only temporary. As soon as Glenn was old enough to go to play school, she'd come off benefits, get a job and make a life for them.

Still, in the first few weeks they'd barely coped, and many times Tara seriously considered going back home to her parents but her pride wouldn't let her. Then, almost two months after she first left Lakeview, her mother – grudgingly impressed by the strength and determination shown by her eldest daughter, and ashamed at her immediate response to her plight – had insisted she come home and raise the baby there.

"We can look after the baby for a couple of mornings a week if you want to go out to work," she'd offered. "Anything to make it easier on the two of you."

Initially, Isobel had been so consumed with anger and shame, that she'd been prepared to let her daughter go it alone and get it out of her system.

It wouldn't be long before she'd come crawling back to Lakeview begging for help. But when the weeks passed and that hadn't happened, Isobel had to admit that her daughter's tenacity surprised her. Still she had been horrified at the sight of roaming horses and burnt-out cars where Tara and the baby were living, and after that vowed that she'd look after them both properly.

But Tara didn't want to be 'looked after'; at that stage she didn't want anything from her mother that could be construed as charity. She didn't want to go back living under her parent's roof. So, she'd faced her mother down and told her that she didn't want to go home to be 'looked after' and that she was perfectly fine. If Isobel and her dad wanted to contribute to their grandchild's upbringing by giving her a hand to look after him now and again, they were most welcome.

That was a proud day. She hadn't asked, she hadn't begged, yet her mother was offering to help with the baby, not because she had to, but because she *wanted* to.

Once he started school, Tara kept them going by working in a telesales company, and took a correspondence course in Social Studies by night. And by the time she was twenty-five, she had a decent job, her own rented flat (not much bigger than the one the state provided but, most importantly, paid for out of her own wages), and a university diploma, all with an eight-year-old in tow.

Every day she thanked her lucky stars – Glenn was a wonderfully mild-mannered kid who loved nothing better than sitting quietly playing games. Initially, Tara had been concerned at his apparent contentment with his own company, but according to his teachers, he had lots of friends and was very outgoing at school so this wasn't an issue.

"Tara look what I can do," he'd say, hoping to impress her with his skills on some confusing game that would leave his mother dizzy trying to keep up with him.

"Why doesn't he call you 'Mammy'?" Isobel asked. "Strange that he calls you by your name."

Tara shrugged. "I don't really notice it anymore," she said truthfully. "Probably because he never heard me being called anything other than Tara by the other mums in the estate. I never really corrected him, so I suppose it stuck. And what does it matter?"

The ensuing years had been kind – even throughout the tricky teenage years they remained close, Glenn aware and evidently respectful of the sacrifices his mother had made on his behalf, and he'd never given her a bit of trouble or a night of worry.

And when Glenn had passed his state exams and gained enough university points for Computer Studies (what else?), she'd never felt so proud. It had been worth it; all the pain, heartache and poverty, and missed years. He was her life and everything she'd worked for had come good.

So Tara hadn't lied when she'd told Jason that he'd grown up to be a decent, respectable young man. Sometimes his level-headedness actually worried her. Immediately after finishing school and his exams, instead of taking it easy for the summer as most other seventeen-year-olds would, he'd taken the junior analyst's job at Pixels.

But Glenn's first love was and always had been

computers. It was only surprising he hadn't been born with a keyboard in his hands, she thought smiling.

Now in London, lying awake for the second night running, Liz sleeping soundly in the bed next to her, Tara worried again about Glenn and the situation he was facing.

She'd no right to criticise; after all, everything had turned out OK for her, but didn't he have any idea how hard parenthood was going to be?

She wanted more for him, of that there was no doubt. Yet she couldn't help but be impressed by his determination to shoulder his responsibilities. Whether or not this optimism would still be around by the time the child was born was another thing, but at least he was giving the girl the support she needed.

The kind of support that Tara had sorely craved from Jason.

The Murrays never again returned to Lakeview for the holidays, and after that initial phone call to tell him she was pregnant, Tara had never heard from him again either.

Back then, she had tried to convince herself that her reasons for moving to Dublin were purely for Glenn's good, but thinking about it, maybe there was a tiny part of her that subconsciously hoped she might bump into Jason in his home city, although apparently he lived in a big house south of the capital along the coast, a world apart from the run-down part of the city she'd had to settle for.

But he must have moved to England in the interim – Natalie had mentioned he'd gone to University in London.

Anyway, it was also likely he had forgotten all about Tara, and the baby he'd fathered, but had never seen. She smiled through her tears. It was strange, until tonight he wouldn't even have known if that child was a boy or a girl.

How sad for him, she thought now, her anger at his treatment of her long since dissipated, how sad that Jason had missed, and never could share the wonderful experience of being Glenn's parent.

There was a lot of his father in Glenn too though, so much so that even Liz had spotted the resemblance when she'd first seen tonight him at the restaurant.

They had the same dark colouring, strong jaw-line and proud Roman nose, the same chocolate-coloured eyes. And that same gentle way and restful personality that had made Tara fall for Jason in the first place.

And when tonight she saw how handsome he still looked, and how in the ensuing years life had evidently treated him well, she couldn't help but feel bereft once more. She'd loved him deeply – so deeply it hurt, and she didn't think she'd ever really got over that.

Of course, there hadn't been too many opportunities to meet other men, not in her situation and, in all honesty, she didn't care. Her priority had always been Glenn, and despite Liz's insistence that she should try and find someone special, someone for herself, she just didn't have the inclination.

Her son gave her all the love and companionship she needed, and although she knew deep down that the time would come when he would grow into adulthood and likely leave her to her own devices, Tara just hadn't imagined it would happen so soon.

This time next year, Glenn would have his own responsibilities, and a child of his own to look after.

Then Tara would no longer be the most important thing in his life – she'd be just his mam, there in the background, loved certainly, but no longer needed in quite the same way.

She'd have to face up to that now. Face up to the fact that for the first time in thirty-four years, Tara was facing life alone.

FORTY-SIX

"I REALLY HOPE you didn't mind my saying something," Liz said, the following morning over breakfast at the hotel. "I just thought a good excuse would make it easier for us to leave."

For her part, Liz still couldn't believe that the dream man Tara had been helping Natalie land, had turned out to be Glenn's *father*.

She'd seen the resemblance straight away in the restaurant of course; it was very difficult *not* to, when they looked so alike and she'd even gone so far as to think that it had been *Glenn* sitting at the table with Natalie.

But when she realised how tense and upset Tara was, the penny soon dropped. And she understood too why Colm had thought it strange at the time that she'd asked who the guy in Tara's debs photo was.

With the benefit of hindsight, it should have been obvious. But while she had of course known that her friend had given birth to Glenn at a young age, Liz had no idea he'd been conceived on Tara's debs night. No wonder Colm had been so insistent that Liz shouldn't mention the photograph.

Of course it was different now, and these days the event was more of an excuse for a big celebration, but back when she and Tara were teenagers, a girl's debs night was special – a Big Deal.

"Of course I don't mind you telling her about the Abby thing," Tara said now.

Natalie had been inconsolable. "Bloody hell, now I feel awful. If I'd known she was having family trouble, I'd never have insisted. Oh Liz, I feel so guilty."

"Don't - sure, you weren't to know," Liz had assured, wondering how poor Tara was getting on alone out there with Jay. Evidently, Natalie didn't know anything about Jason being a dad, to say nothing of his being Glenn's. "But I'm sure you can appreciate that she's worried about him, so she's not her usual self."

"I did wonder why she was being so quiet. Oh Liz, we'd better get back – I'd hate for her to feel that she has to make small talk with a complete stranger. Come on," And with that, the two of them returned to the table.

Later, Natalie had taken Tara aside.

"We'll head home soon– and you go back to the hotel with Liz and get a good night's sleep. I'll arrange for early flights home for the two of you tomorrow if you like. Please don't feel as though you have to stay in London any longer on my account. I'd much rather you went home and sorted it all out with Glenn. Liz didn't give me too much detail other than ... well, you know," she looked embarrassed, "but if you *do* need to talk sometime, let me know. I owe you one. It's the very least I can do." With that, she hugged

Tara tightly and after dinner she and Jay bade them goodnight.

Liz knew that the idea of returning home early was a godsend to Tara, who had got so many shocks in the last day or two it was a miracle she was still standing.

What with Glenn's impending fatherhood, and then bumping into her first love and father of her beloved son ... it was enough to make Liz thank her lucky stars for her relatively trouble-free life.

Tara was an incredible woman who had been through so much, and yet still managed to keep all the balls in the air, whereas Liz was a wimp who should be ashamed to call herself a woman.

If Tara could get by without a man for all these years, then so could Liz. If Eric had betrayed her, then he wasn't good enough for her, or indeed Toby.

"And how do you feel this morning? About everything?" she asked Tara now.

"I'm not sure. I suppose seeing Jason reminded me that Glenn's girlfriend ..." She grimaced, "is about the same age as me when I had him. So I'm not really in a position to judge. I wanted more for him but ..." she shrugged, "I have to admire the way he's dealing with it – well, the way he's *proposing* to deal with it anyway. Who knows how he'll cope when the baby is born and he has to support them? But honestly, Liz, the thing that bothers me the most is that he's all grown up now." There were tears in her eyes as she spoke, and her voice was full of regret. "He no longer needs me. And when someone has depended on you for half your lifetime, that takes some getting used to. I think I understand now why my mother and Emma have always had a much better relationship. With all her misfortunes, Emma's always needed her, and my mother likes to be needed. Whereas I made it clear that I didn't - that I could stand on my own two feet. I grew up too fast, and to this day I have never let her see anything other than the strong Tara, the one that can take on the world and whom nothing fazes. I think my mother doesn't know how to deal with that, she doesn't know what her role in my life has been for a very long time." She shook her head sadly. "Whereas Emma has always needed her – she was always in trouble with jobs, men ... and now this. And don't get me wrong, I don't resent the fact that single motherhood will be so much easier for Emma than it was for me; times have changed, and there will be none of the shame and disgrace that I experienced." She exhaled deeply. "And I have to be careful now not to do the same with Glenn. I have to let him know that I'll be there for him and Abby whatever they decide. And I'll do my best to help them out with my ..." she laughed as if unable to believe she was actually saying the words, "my grandchild. Imagine, Liz, a grandmother at my age ..." Then her face changed slightly. "Although make that an over-the-hill grandmother with no life of her own. Do you know, you were right all along. I should have thought some more about finding someone, someone just for me."

"It's not too late to do that," Liz told her gently. "You might be a granny soon, but you're still only in your thirties."

Tara shook her head. "I wouldn't even know where to start. I know nothing about men. The last time I had any sort of relationship was when I was seventeen and look where that led."

"You know more than most. Look at all the help and advice you gave Natalie ..." She winced, realising what she'd just said.

But Tara laughed. "Isn't it mad when you think about it? Here I was, coaching Natalie on how to land this so-called man of her dreams, when all along he was the man of my dreams too."

"And how do you feel about him now?"

Tara looked her straight in the eye. "To be honest, I feel ... sorry for him. Look at what he missed out on. Glenn is a wonderful gift, and I treasure every second I've spent with him. Yes, it was so tough at times, but wanting to do the best for him kept me going. Whereas Jason experienced none of that. He decided he didn't want to experience it. But I did OK. And to be frank, I could look Jason in the eye last night and honestly tell him that I did a good job. At least," she said, eyes dropping to the tablecloth, "at least I thought I did."

"You did a *fantastic* job," Liz assured her. "And you know better than most that teenage pregnancy isn't the end of the world."

FORTY-SEVEN

"Oh Jay, I felt so awful! I had no idea she was having problems of her own. Typical me - too self-obsessed to notice."

Natalie and Jay were having breakfast in her flat.

"Don't be silly, you weren't to know," he soothed, his voice soft and she thought, a bit weary too.

"Did you sleep OK last night? I know my bed isn't as comfy as yours but – "

"No, it was fine – I just have a couple of things on my mind at the moment, that's all."

"I can't believe she still flew over to see me – and you of course," Natalie prattled on. "When all the time she was worrying about Glenn." She spread some strawberry jam on her bagel. "I have to say, I'm surprised, he seemed like such a level-headed kid."

Jay's head snapped up. "You met her son?"

"Yes, on holidays in Egypt. Remember, I told you - that's where I met Tara in the first place?"

"What ... what was he like?"

"Like? Not too sure really – I didn't get to talk to him

much. Typical seventeen-year old, I suppose. Mad into sports – he did a scuba-diving course when we were over there. Although I will say I thought he was very good-looking. I told Tara that too and . . . what ...what's wrong?" It was weird, but if she didn't know better, she'd swear that Jay's eyes were glistening.

He mustn't have got a wink of sleep in her bed. Well, that was his own fault, for refusing to let her tire him out, she thought, still a little miffed that after their return from the restaurant he hadn't been in an amorous mood. "Jay? Are you all right?"

"Sorry, I was just thinking about something – what were you saying?"

"I was just saying I really am surprised at Tara's son. He seemed like such a gentle sort, the type who wouldn't look twice at a girl – let alone knock her up. And apparently he met her in Egypt too – "

"I'm sorry, what did you say?" Jason interjected.

"I really wish you'd wake up. I said he met some girl in Egypt and knocked her up - that's why Tara was upset. She only found out the day before yesterday. I thought I told you this. It was why she was so preoccupied last night."

"You told me she was having problems of some kind but you didn't tell me what."

Natalie shrugged and took a bite of her bagel. "Well, I suppose as a single mother herself, it's to be expected that she'd be apprehensive for his future. I must say I really admire her. Given what she's had to deal with, she's incredibly cool and in control. Course, I suppose she had to be considering Glenn's father - cowardly rat - ran out on her when she was just seventeen. Can you imagine it?" She shook her head. "Must have been a nightmare. And truly, what kind of man must he have been to just turn tail and run when the going got tough? Honestly," Natalie spat, shaking her head in disgust, "what kind of selfish dick would do that ..."

FORTY-EIGHT

As PROMISED, Natalie had organised flights to get them home late Saturday afternoon instead of Sunday as had been arranged.

When she and Liz arrived back in Dublin airport close to six pm, Tara insisted on driving her friend back to Lakeview.

"No, you head home," Liz said, dismissing the offer. "I'll give Eric a call. The traffic will be light and he'll be here in no time."

But Tara wouldn't hear of it and so, earlier than expected, Liz arrived back from her weekend away, tired but thankful she didn't have Tara's worries to deal with.

Waving her friend goodbye, and thanking her again for the lift, she made a quick check on the dogs before letting herself in the back door. There was no sign of life in the kitchen, so she threw her stuff on the kitchen table and went to look for Toby and Eric in the living room.

Expecting to witness a cosy tableau of her husband and young son sitting in front of the TV with perhaps the dogs at their feet, Liz couldn't believe what she was seeing instead.

"What the hell ...?" she hissed from the living-room doorway, as a shocked Eric, delighted Toby and a brazen Emma Harrington turned to look at her.

There she was sitting cosily in Liz's living room with her husband and son, and behaving as if she belonged there.

"Liz – what are you doing here?" Eric asked, the colour draining from his face.

"What am I doing here? I *live* here!" she raged. "I asked you a question, what the hell is going on? Do what you like behind my back Eric, but how dare you, how *dare* you bring that floozy into my house and flaunt her in front of my son. How dare you!"

Emma raised an eyebrow. "And here I was thinking you were the mousey type..."

"Keep your mouth shut, you little tramp," Liz spat. She couldn't help it; something inside her had snapped upon seeing that girl here, knowing she had the power to break up her life, mess up her family, in fact had probably done so already. So what was the point in holding back? Liz had no respect for Eric, and certainly none for that rap, but she owed it to her son at least to show some backbone, in the same way that Tara did for hers.

"Liz, what the hell is wrong with you?" Eric gasped. "Don't use language like that, especially not in front of Toby."

As if on cue, the baby started to cry and Liz immediately marched into the room, past a shellshocked Eric and took him in her arms.

"It's all right, pet, Mummy's here, now." She kissed her son gently on the head, swearing blindly that Eric could do what he liked but he would never, ever hurt this child. "Get the hell out of my sight, the two of you, and carry on with whatever you were doing somewhere else."

"Liz – "

"I don't want to hear your pathetic excuses, Eric. Be a man enough for once in your life to tell the truth."

"Wow, I *definitely* had you pegged wrong," Emma chuckled, and Eric silenced her with a look.

"I think you'd better go," he said gently.

For Liz, the way he spoke to her was like a red rag to a bull.

"Didn't you hear what I said?" she cried. "I want *both* of you out of my sight. This instant! I don't care where you go or what you're doing – to be honest, I really couldn't give a flying..." she caught herself just in time, "a damn about what's going on between you."

"Liz! What are you – ?"

"I don't want to hear it Eric," she raged. "Just leave us the hell alone, both of you." With that, she turned on her heel and marched into the kitchen.

Then, hands still shaking with anger, Liz rested Toby in his highchair, put her head in her hands and cried.

FORTY-NINE

"Liz, listen to me,"

"I don't want to hear it, I really don't. How dare you bring that floozy into our home."

When Emma had left and Eric followed her into the kitchen, evidently wanting to talk, Liz put on a Disney video for Toby who was now watching it happily in the living-room, and hopefully oblivious to his parents' 'discussion'.

"Why are you behaving like this? And as for calling Emma a floozy? What's all that about?"

"Oh, believe me I could think of plenty other names to call her," Liz said, lifting her chin.

"I don't understand, what's brought all of this on?"

"What?" She whirled round to face him, amazed at his brazenness. "What's brought all of this on? I come home early from a weekend away, away from worrying about our marriage to find you, your pregnant girlfriend and my son happily ensconced in my front living room – *that's* what's brought all of this on! How did you expect me to react,

Eric? Did you think that I would come in, pull up a table for Emma to put her feet on and offer her a cuppa or something? How can you be so callous, bringing her here, flaunting her in front of everyone and, worse, in front of Toby? What the hell is wrong with you?"

"Liz – "

" I said I don't want to hear it. I've seen and heard enough already. All I want now is for you to just get out of my sight – just pack your stuff and leave. Get out of the house. I'd go myself only I don't feel as though I should have to. This is my home, after all, my dream house, our dream house. Except it didn't exactly turn out like that, did it?" She bit her lip, willing the tears away.

"Liz, you have things totally wrong," Eric cried, white-faced. "I don't know why you think there's something going on between us – Emma is a friend and she just called over this afternoon to say hi. I didn't know she was coming, and I certainly didn't think it would be –"

"Oh for goodness sake, why can't you just come right out and admit it? All those secret meetings with her that you think I didn't know about, the texts and phone conversations, all the sneaking around behind my back. How long did you think it would be before I found out? This is a small town, Eric – as you should well know."

He blanched. "You seriously think I was having an affair with Emma?"

"Why not? She's the famous ex-girlfriend, isn't she? The one who supposedly broke your heart for some unexplained reason all those years ago. The one I've had to try and live up to ever since we moved to this godforsaken place."

"Liz – "

"So, you go and do what you like – go ahead, you're free. Free of me and Toby and the drudgery of married life. Though soon it won't be long before you're back in the same mindless boring existence you're in now."

"Mindless boring existence ... what the hell are you talking about? I love you and Toby, but you're too wrapped up in him to notice or care."

"Don't make this about me, Eric, don't you dare make it about me or try to blame *me*. You and Toby were all I ever wanted, a happy family is all I ever wanted, you know that."

"I do know that, which is why I've always done every-thing in my power to make that happen! I know how much it means to you, and it means everything to me too. But I did something stupid, Liz, something that could destroy all that and I couldn't tell you ...."

"Knocking up your ex is a funny way of keeping our family together, Eric," she spat bitterly.

"For heaven's sake, will you listen to me! I did *not*. I am not having an affair with Emma."

Something deep inside her began to flutter awake, but Liz didn't dare believe him, not just yet. "What about all those secret meetings? The texts ... the sneaking around?"

He slumped down alongside her at the kitchen table. "It wasn't like that. As you know, she and I used to be close and –"

"I think that's a bit of an understatement, don't you?"

"Liz, you have to understand that Emma and also Tara to a certain extent, understood what it was like for me, growing up here in this town. My family weren't respected, because of my dad's drinking – I wasn't respected ..." He shook his head. "But she and Tara were good friends to me back then. And when I moved back –"

"You remembered how good you and Emma were together, and decided to take up where you left off all those years ago?"

"That's not it. When we first moved here, things were going great. You said you'd never been so happy as in this house, with Toby and being able to run the kennels. I knew it was up to me to keep that going. I wanted you to be happy – for us to be happy. But recently it's seemed that Toby and the dogs are what's keeping you going."

"Oh, for goodness sake, Eric, spare me the 'my wife doesn't understand me so I was forced into another woman's arms' crap."

"It wasn't that. I just felt a bit ...remote from it all I suppose. And it was weird, because it had been my idea to move here in the first place, so I could hardly turn around and tell you that I wasn't enjoying it as much as you were."

"But you were commuting to the city. You weren't here often enough to enjoy it. You were too busy enjoying your-self in pubs in Dublin."

Eric looked right at her. "I wasn't enjoying myself in pubs. Liz, I was working in them."

"What? What are you talking about?"

"I got laid off from Securitex a couple of months ago, not long before Tara went on holiday. I couldn't tell you because you were so excited about getting the house reno-vations started, and I didn't want you to feel as though you had to succeed with the kennels to keep us going. I didn't want to put you under any pressure."

"But how could you not tell me you got laid off?" she gasped, stunned.

"I thought I'd find something soon enough, and again, I tried a couple of places here. But Liz, as you know, nobody needs security in a tiny place like this, I couldn't find anything different, and it wasn't easy getting somewhere in Dublin either. So I went back to bar work. I was doing days in a hotel and some nights – the nights I told you I was working overtime, in a place in Temple Bar. Anyway, one night, Emma happened to walk into the place I was working, and I was rumbled. So I had to tell her what had happened."

"You told *her* – but you couldn't tell me?"

"I couldn't tell you, Liz. I knew you'd be devastated."

"And you didn't think I'd be devastated even more to think that you were the father of her bloody child?"

"Liz, never in a million years did I imagine you'd think something like that. Why would you?"

"Because of all those secret meetings and texts, which I'm still not convinced were innocent by the way. What was going on? What else were you hiding from me? Because there had to be something else, Eric – losing your job is no big deal in the scheme of things. You'll easily get something else – and I'm sure if you sat it out long enough you'd get something here."

"You see, this is why I didn't want to tell you. I knew you'd try to convince me to get a job here. And when I didn't find anything – when I was sitting at home twiddling my thumbs while my wife had to look after other people's dogs to keep things going, then everyone would say that they'd been right all along, that I was Pat McGrath's son after all – a waster."

Liz was amazed at the pain in his voice. She'd never really understood why Eric felt he had to prove something to the people in the village. Tara had mentioned that his father had been troublesome and that she'd been afraid Eric would turn out the same, but she hadn't really understood what she meant.

But Liz couldn't let talk of all this distract her from what she really wanted to know, the real reason the two had been furtive.

When she said this to Eric, he sighed.

"Well, when I said Emma agreed to keep my secret, about working at the bar, it turned out to be quid pro quo. I eventually discovered that she had a secret too. When she came in that first night, she was with a few others and we started chatting. She seemed in really good form, and she eventually told me all about this guy she'd been with, though she wouldn't mention any names. Emma is a bit like that, a bit secretive."

"I'll say," Liz replied shortly.

"She started to come in to the pub a bit more after finding out I was working there. To be honest, I think she was a bit lonely in Dublin, despite this new man she'd found – at least that's what I thought at the time. And of course, when she came in, we used to chat a lot about harmless things like people we both knew and all that. And then one time, I made a casual, offhand comment about someone and her face crumpled. It *crumpled,* Liz – I've never seen Emma let her guard down like that. So, after a lot of persuading, she broke down and eventually told me what had been going on – that the person I'd so casually mentioned in conversation, meant something to her. Meant a lot to her. And she was heartbroken."

"Heartbroken over the mysterious father of her baby?"

Eric nodded. "But at this stage she hadn't revealed that bit. I only knew about that when you mentioned it here in this kitchen. So of course I put two and two together, and when I asked her about it, she'd no choice but to admit it."

"So, you knew who the baby's father was," Liz stated. "And Emma knew about you losing your job and helping you cover it up – "

"Yes, but things got worse shortly after that. Just when I thought I was getting back on track, and earning a decent crust, the pub in town began to cut my hours back. So I panicked, thinking that I was further away from getting things sorted than ever. I was desperate. And since Emma was the only one who understood – "

"Well, of course she was the only one who understood," Liz retorted, stung. "She was the only one you told."

"I know ... I know and that's not what I meant. I'm sorry ..." Eric shook his head. "Look, because she and I both knew what the other was ... going through I suppose, we began meeting up now and again, just to let off steam."

"While you kept secrets from everyone else – secrets from me."

"I know, and, Liz, you really don't know how hard it was to – "

"So who is it then?" she interjected, cutting him off. "Why all the mystery?"

Eric shook his head, his expression guarded. "Liz – she swore me to secrecy."

"Why – is it because it is someone from the village, someone I know?" she urged, her curiosity getting the better of her. She was *dying* to find out who this man might be, the mysterious Lothario who'd managed to melt Emma's ice-queen persona.

Eric sighed deeply. "I promised her I wouldn't tell anyone, but I'm going to tell you because you're my wife, and I don't want any more secrets between us. But you can't breathe of word, Liz – too many people could get hurt."

"Who is it, Eric?"

"You have to understand that Emma has always got what she wanted, all the way through life. She's been indulged, spoiled – she managed to get every man she ever set her sights on. Except one. I'm sure you know from Tara that when she doesn't get what she wants, it merely makes her want it all the more. And there's always been one person Emma could never have, and it's plagued her for a very long time."

"Eric, who the hell is it?" Liz demanded impatiently. "Just tell me."

He took another deep breath.

And when Eric finally did tell her, Liz's jaw dropped to the floor.

FIFTY

Emma hurried across the bridge towards Main Street, her cheeks burning with humiliation in anticipation of what she now had to do.

Eric would have told Liz by now. He'd need to in order to explain her presence in the house, particularly when Liz was so sure *he* was up to shenanigans. And that was her own fault for messing with Liz's head, wasn't it?

She was sorry for doing that now – if she hadn't sent the text and made that stupid comment, then Liz wouldn't be so paranoid.

And when she did find out, then no doubt she would be only too happy to gossip to all and sundry – Eric's wife certainly didn't owe her anything.

Damn Liz anyway. Emma had been looking forward to a quiet evening chatting with Eric at his house, although in truth he had seemed uncomfortable when she'd arrived at his doorstep unannounced.

She'd known of course that Liz was away for a weekend with Tara, so the coast was clear, so to speak.

THE WIFE COACH   309

But never mind trying to make Liz jealous, which she admitted to herself, had been good fun initially but quickly began to wear thin – she really did enjoy talking to Eric about everything.

Enjoyed getting her worries off her chest. And while he had initially been sympathetic, she lately got the feeling that he was reluctant to continue the charade.

He was clearly very much in love with Liz and worried for his family, and as time went on Emma did feel truly sorry for him that he couldn't find a proper job.

At first, it had been a bit funny, happening upon him working behind the bar in Dublin like that, and the poor guy obviously so embarrassed about it and desperate to keep it a secret. But when his hours were cut, and his worries multiplied, Emma realised that it was no joke at all.

And yes, maybe her own concerns were just as valid, but lately she got the impression that Eric was tired of listening.

"It can't stay hidden forever," he had insisted at his house earlier. "Surely he'll put two and two together? Maybe he already has."

"Too wrapped up in his own perfect little life to notice," she said bitterly. "And I'm not really showing enough yet."

"Yet," Eric repeated meaningfully. "He isn't stupid, though – he'll work things out for himself eventually."

"Being with me in the first place was stupid," Emma retorted quickly. "Why mess with my head?"

"I know, I know," Eric was soothing. "I wish I knew. But he's always been complicated – we both know that."

Now, as she made her way across the bridge, Emma

came to the conclusion that there was no point in keeping secrets any longer.

Eric was right. She had to come clean, and soon.

Before Liz McGrath did it for her.

STEELING herself for the confrontation to come, Emma tried to keep calm as she rang the doorbell. She stood back from the doorstep and subconsciously fastened her coat up to the neck.

The door swung open and there he stood in the doorway, handsome and wonderful as always, and again, her breath caught in her throat.

"Emma, hey." By the wariness in his tone, she knew immediately that (of course) there was someone else in the house with him. Well, she wasn't going to keep him very long.

"I'd like to say I'm fine, but that would be a lie," she said shortly, lapsing into defensive mode.

"Oh?" He looked confused. "What's up? And how can I help?"

"That night ..." she began, staring straight at him, her eyes cold and her chin upturned. "The night we – "

He visibly winced. "Hey I'm sorry ... but can we maybe talk some other time? It's been a busy day and now is not really a good time for me ... " He gave a surreptitious glance behind him.

The indifferent reaction and disinterested way he'd tried to brush her off lit a fire under her, and all thoughts of breaking the news softly went right out the window.

"It was a good time for you that night though, wasn't it, you two-faced prick," she blurted, her tone rising.

"Emma, please ... calm down." He glanced worriedly down the street.

"Afraid that everyone will find out? Afraid they'll all figure out the person they think is the salt-of-the-earth is nothing but a two-faced user?"

"Two-faced ... what's all that about?" he said, looking genuinely puzzled. "And how did I use you? It was just a bit of fun – for both of us no?"

She couldn't believe it. He had no idea. He'd really thought their night together was no big deal. *Just a bit of fun?* Having known deep down that she couldn't – *shouldn't* – put any faith in him, still she'd thought it meant something. But she'd been silly to think about trusting him, because most of the time the same guy couldn't trust himself.

"I'm sorry if you thought ...well, I didn't mean to ... as I said, we'd had a few drinks, and it was just a bit of a laugh, friends with benefits yeah?" He was talking as if it was all perfectly reasonable. "I mean, you know as well as anyone the story with me."

"Well, something did come of it, as it happens," Emma replied. "I'm pregnant."

"You're joking.| She watched his face drain of colour as his gaze quickly moved to her abdomen. "I don't believe you."

"Well, you'd better believe me, because it's sure as hell no joke."

"I don't ... know what to say," he managed eventually. "This is ... well, to be honest, I'm shocked."

The fact that he hadn't immediately closed the door in her face, the fact that he looked almost ... intrigued by the news, buoyed her a little.

"But why didn't you tell me before now?"

She looked quickly down at her feet. "I was going to, but then I heard from Eric that you'd ... well, that you'd found someone else – someone serious."

He coloured. "That's true. But you and me, that night ... well to be honest, after that I did feel a bit strange ... a bit confused, I suppose. But then I met Nicky, and right away I knew. It just felt right ..." His words trailed off, as the aforementioned appeared behind him in the doorway.

"Everything, OK, Colm?"

Emma looked from one man to the other and all of a sudden felt very foolish indeed.

Eric was right; she'd been stupid to think that she had a chance. Colm had struggled for years with his sexuality and she'd been stupid.

But you couldn't help who you fell in love with, and unfortunately for her, she had been in love with Colm for a very long time. And when, a few months ago, just before taking the new job in Dublin, Emma had worked her final shift alongside him in the cafe, and he'd taken her out for a farewell dinner and then back to his place to share a bottle of wine, she took her chances.

Colm was right, it had all been a laugh at first and in truth she had initiated everything, but at the time, he hadn't exactly refused. Still, she had been certain that their night together had made things clearer for him.

And she'd been right, albeit not in the way she'd anticipated. It had simply made Colm decide on his path once and for all.

Emma still recalled her devastation when Eric had mentioned in passing that he'd fallen for someone. And had nearly fallen off the bench when he'd told her Colm had begun openly seeing Nicky, some guy who'd recently moved to the village.

To complete her upset and embarrassment, not long after that she discovered she was pregnant. Pregnant by the town gay? Mortifying.

Strangely though, Emma thought now as she stood on the doorstep outside his house, Colm didn't seem all that upset.

Dazed, he looked from her to Nicky and then back again. "Come in for a coffee Em?" he urged. "Seems the three of us have a lot to talk about."

FIFTY-ONE

Back at the McGrath house, Liz was still trying to pick her jaw up off the floor. "Colm from the café?" she spluttered.

"I know," Eric said shrugging. "Believe me, I was as surprised as you are. Although, probably not as shocked," he added wryly. "Colm is an oddball – has been for a very long time."

"I'll say."

"Remember I told you before that he was a bit of a catch when we were younger?" Eric shook his head in exasperation. "To be honest, over the years I think he'd had some sort of fling with most of the girls around here."

Liz was still shaking her head. "Well, fair enough if he's confused – I've known guys like that myself, but what on earth was *Emma* thinking? Colm's in a relationship – with another guy. I mean, I know she's good-looking but she's not *that* – "

"He wasn't with Nicky when he and Emma ... got together," Eric explained. "And seems she really thought she was in with a chance. Turned out it was the complete opposite. I felt a bit sorry for her, to be honest. She always was mad about him."

"I can't believe this ..." Liz spluttered. "You're all mental cases in this town!"

Despite himself, Eric raised a smile. "I know it might sound a bit weird to you now, but you don't know what growing up in this place is like. It wouldn't have been easy for Colm to come out properly. But when Nicky came along ...." Eric shrugged, "I guess he finally thought; to hell with the begrudgers."

"And times have changed too."

"Yes, thank god. But Liz, Emma's terrified now. She hasn't been keeping the father a secret because she's afraid he'll find out about it, Liz; she's keeping it a secret because she's embarrassed."

Liz didn't know whether to laugh or cry. She believed her husband when he said he hadn't been cheating. But she was still hurt that he hadn't felt able to tell her about losing his job. She could imagine just how delighted the vindictive little witch would have been about helping him keep it all hidden.

And she was convinced that Emma had in the meantime been purposely trying to plant seeds of doubt in her mind about Eric too.

"Liz, I love you so much. All I've ever wanted was to make you and Toby happy, to look after the two of you like my dad never did for us. That's why I didn't want to tell you I'd lost my job – at least not until I'd had a chance to try and find another one – a decent one. I just didn't want to disappoint you." He shook his head and took her hands in

his. "You two are my life. I would never sacrifice that –
you've got to believe me."

She looked into her husband's face and knew instinctively that he was telling the truth. OK, so she still didn't
fully understand his need to keep the news about his job a
secret from her; after all it wasn't as though he was sitting
on his backside refusing to do anything else. But Liz knew
only too well that it was difficult to live up to other people's
expectations, and sometimes even more difficult not to.

She had to give him the benefit of the doubt.

"I do know that, love," she replied, squeezing his hand.
"But I think you and I have a lot to sort out. I'm hurt that
you didn't tell me, and doubly hurt that you felt able to
confide in someone else. And it's not a question of you
having to take care of me and Toby. We're a partnership
and we look after one *another*."

"As far as I was concerned we were just two old friends
discussing our troubles. Of course, Emma turned to me a
lot because she didn't have anybody else, and also because I
could understand better than most why it had happened.
But look, now that I've told you everything, including
Emma's private business, will you promise not to breathe a
word to anyone about it? Not even Tara?"

Liz sighed deeply as she thought about it. "I don't like
the girl, you probably know that by now, but at the same
time it's none of my business who's she with – thank goodness," she added, eyeing Eric who smiled ruefully. "So I
won't say a word." And despite all that had gone on these
last few months, she felt a stab of pity for Emma.

Colm had been the love of her life, but ultimately
rejected her. For once Emma Harrington didn't get what

she wanted. But by pursuing such a foolhardy and destructive course of action, the girl had eventually ensured that she'd got a hell of a lot more than she'd bargained for.

But thank the heavens, Liz thought now, thank the heavens that it wasn't Eric.

FIFTY-TWO

"Hey, it's Natalie."

By the other girl's tone, Tara realised that Natalie knew – that Jason had told her the whole sorry story.

"How are you?" she replied guardedly.

Natalie was solemn. "Tara, I can't tell you how sorry I am to have put you through all this. I had no idea. I knew there was something familiar about him when I met him – maybe it was because he reminded me a little bit of Glenn – although obviously I didn't know that at the time."

"How could you know? How could either of us have known we had that much in common?" Tara attempted a short laugh. "But please don't let this affect your relationship with Jay. It was a long time ago – a lifetime ago - and it shouldn't affect how you feel about him."

"It doesn't," Natalie said simply and for reasons she couldn't quite fathom, Tara felt a little wounded. "But that's not the reason I'm phoning. He's here with me now, and he'd like a word."

She stopped breathing. "That's not a good idea, I can't – "

"Please. He really wants to talk to you – to explain."

"There's nothing to explain – it was seventeen years ago. You and Jay should just get on with your lives and leave Glenn and I alone to get on with ours. I realise that you and I have been close this last while, but surely you realise now that our friendship can't exactly continue?"

"I understand, but if our friendship ever meant anything to you, then can I ask you to just talk to him, just hear him out? After that, I promise we'll leave you alone." Then she sniffed. "But I'll miss you, Tara – you've been such a rock for me."

Tara's heart went out to her. It wasn't fair of Jason to involve her, to use her as a go-between in an attempt to salve his conscience. "I'll miss you too, pet. But it's better for both of us."

"Will you talk to him though? For me?"

Tara sighed. She might as well get this over with. "Fine."

Then before she had a chance to prepare herself, Jay's achingly familiar voice appeared on the other end of the line.

"Hi," he said gently, and immediately she tensed.

"Pretty cowardly of you to get Natalie do your dirty work, isn't it?"

"It wasn't like that. I just knew it was the only way to get you on the line."

"We have nothing to say to one another, Jason. You said it all seventeen years ago."

"I didn't say anything," he countered softly. "You

wouldn't let me. You'd hung up before I even had a chance to think anything. Tara, that same day, I'd been out earlier picking up stuff for college. It was such a shock that I couldn't think straight."

"How nice for you," she said bitterly.

"Look, what I meant to say is ...that I wasn't in the proper frame of mind to tell you what you needed to hear – which was that I'd try to support you every way I could. But I couldn't say those words back then, Tara, because in truth I couldn't *be* sure that I could support you - at all. I had no job, no prospects, we didn't even live in the same vicinity for goodness' sake." When she said nothing, he continued. "I told my parents, who as you know were horrified, and embarrassed too. They'd friends in Lakeview and had visited for years, and then their son goes and gets a local girl into trouble. They wouldn't speak to me. I was confused, upset, I hadn't a clue what was going on."

"And how do you think I felt?"

"I know. I'll admit I tried at first to put it out of my head for a bit, tried to convince myself – as my parents did – that there was nothing I could do. I was too young to provide for you properly, they told me, better to let your family rally round and help you out. And I thought that was what would happen – you were barely out of school after all ... so I thought I was doing the right thing – they'd convinced me I was doing the right thing. Looking back, I know they were just trying to make sure I went to college and got my education. They didn't want me wasting my life on some girl I'd met on holiday. But they didn't realise how close we were, and how much... I cared about you."

At this Tara's heart twisted, and she closed her eyes.

"And I did care deeply about you, Tara, I never lied about that. The closeness we shared over all those summers was real, and it should have ... *I* should have stood up for that. But I didn't, and by the time I realised that of *course* I couldn't leave you to your own devices, it was too late. I phoned your house one day and your sister told me that you'd moved away somewhere since. And when I asked her for details she said she didn't know – said that you were somewhere in Dublin but she didn't know where. And when I asked to speak to your parents, she told me it was a bad idea because they'd want to kill me."

Upon hearing this, Tara's eyes narrowed. *Emma* had spoken to Jason - he'd phoned the house looking for her and she'd never said a word?

"I didn't know that."

"I'll admit that I was stupid at the beginning, that my reaction was naive and very hurtful. But you have to believe me when I tell you that I never meant for this to happen. I truly, honestly cared about you, and I don't know if we could have made it work, but now I really wish that I had tried. That I had tried to help you raise our ... raise Glenn. You don't know how much I regret everything that happened back then. I know it affected your life in an immense way, and I know you probably don't want to hear it but it affected me too. I've never forgotten you or the baby. I always wondered about you and every time I went back to Ireland I used to imagine I'd bump into the two of you on the street someday. Yet at the same time, I was afraid that I *would* come face to face with you again because I knew you'd hate me for what I'd done. But you were my first love, Tara and ... I've never forgotten you."

The lump in her throat was immense. He sounded the very same as all those years before, all those summers while they were falling in love.

She wanted so much to believe that he was being sincere, that he was telling the truth when he said he'd never forgotten them, that he'd regretted not trying harder to find them, that he'd wished he'd had the courage to try and make it right.

But no matter how convincing he might sound, Tara knew deep down that if Jason had really wanted to find them, he could have done so. While it was nice to know after all these years that he wasn't the heartless cad she'd believed him to be, this didn't change what had happened.

"Natalie asked one time why I'd never married," he continued, "and I told her it was because I'd never found the right woman. But the truth was, I'd never really got over how I'd made such a mess of it all with us. You know how close we were back then, how close we'd become during all those summers. And then I ruined it – and worse, by abandoning you, I know I ruined your future too. But we were young, and I was stupid and I didn't know what to ..." His voice trailed off then and he took a deep breath. "Remember when we used to talk about being soulmates, and how the universe must've conspired to bring us together?"

Tara nodded, but then remembering he couldn't see her, she croaked, "Yes."

"If you believed in that back then, don't you think that maybe the universe just might have conspired to do the same now?"

She swallowed as Jason continued, his tone gentle.

"That there was a reason you and Natalie met, so that she could be the conduit for this conversation right now. So that I could tell you how sorry I am about everything, and how I so wish things could've been different."

"Is she there with you now?" Tara asked, blinking through tears, worried that Natalie might be hurt by his words.

"No, she popped out to give us some privacy." There was a brief silence. "I know I said I never found anyone to live up to the closeness I had with you. But now, with Natalie, I think I have."

Tara closed her eyes, unsure how she was feeling about the whole thing. She didn't want Jason back, of course she didn't, but the emotions she was feeling just then were confusing and all-consuming.

"I'm ... pleased for you both," she forced out eventually. "Natalie is wonderful and I know you two will be very happy."

"Thank you – it means a lot to hear you say that."

"I appreciate you telling me all this. And maybe you do have your regrets. But Jason, it doesn't change the last seventeen years of my life, and it doesn't change the fact that Glenn has no idea who you are, nor does he want to."

"I know."

"And I'm not going to tell him about this either. He's got too much going on in his life right now."

"I understand that," he demurred politely. "And I don't blame you. I would hate to stir things up for either of you."

"But ..." Tara said then, and she could almost hear his breath catch, "one of these days I will tell him about you. To be honest, up until now he's never been inquisitive about anything like that. But this might change once he has a child of his own. And when I do fill him in, it'll be entirely up to Glenn what he wants to do. If he wants to see you, well and good but if he doesn't, I won't force the issue."

"Thank you," Jason breathed, relieved. "I know I don't deserve that much."

"No, you don't," she reiterated, but then she smiled. "Though I think I'd like you to meet him one day, all the same. He's a very special person."

"Then he most definitely takes after his mother," Jason replied in a gentle voice, and for a long time, the two just remained on the line saying nothing.

Because – Tara realised, tears slowly streaming down her cheeks – at this point there was simply nothing more to say.

FIFTY-THREE

ONE DAY, Glenn arrived home with a visitor in tow.

"This is Abby," he said, his cheeks colouring as he introduced a petite and timid-looking dark-haired girl.

"Pleased to meet you, em, Mrs Harrington," the pretty teen said, limply shaking Tara's hand.

"Call me Tara," she urged with a friendly smile, while inwardly wondering how on earth this harmless thing was going to deal with all that lay ahead. "Mrs Harrington sounds so old."

"Abby was asking why I always refer to you by name too,"Glenn mumbled, casually picking out pieces of vegetable from Tara's stir-fry, "but I've been doing it for so long I hardly notice. I don't think I've ever called you Mum, have I?"

"If you do – I know you've done something wrong," Tara teased with a playful wink at Abby, who blushed deeply. She turned back to the hob and smiled. He *had* indeed called her that very recently, when she'd returned from London and they'd talked some more.

"The last thing I ever wanted was to disappoint you, Mum," he'd said and tears pricked at the corner of her eyes. Hearing Glenn call her that for what must have been the first and only time made Tara understand how truly emotional he was - which made her doubly-resolved to help them in any way she could.

By the looks of this timid little creature, they'd need it.

But over dinner, Abby gradually began to come out of herself and judging by the calluses on her fingertips, it seemed she was as much a computer freak as Glenn.

"One of the best hackers ever," he enthused, his mouth open as he ate. "She's kicks my ass at Linux."

"Really," Tara smiled, trying to conceal her worries about the kind of offspring these two would produce.

It'd either be Bill Gates or Forrest Gump.

FIFTY-FOUR

"FOR THE LIFE OF ME, I can't understand how they ever got round to any funny business in the first place," Tara laughed later that evening, over a cup of tea at Liz's place, leaving Glenn and Abby alone in her house to 'discuss stuff.' "You should have seen the two of them plonked happily in front of the computer when I was leaving." She sighed. "They're such kids really."

"They'll be fine," Liz reassured her, "and if they run into any problems, they'll always have you to fall back on for a helping hand."

"Speaking of a helping hand, any word on a job for Eric?"

Since coming clean about his employment circumstances, Eric had asked around the village and currently keeping busy by doing some carpentry work locally. He was still working bar shifts in Dublin, but with any luck would soon be in a position to give those up for good.

"Not yet unfortunately, and I think he's finally

coming round to the fact that he might have to retrain. He doesn't want to stay working in the city, and I don't want him to either. We need to be together as a family. But lately he's been doing a lot of work for Luke next door."

"Really?" Tara looked up.

"Yep. He's trying to give him a hand with much of the heavy work that needs doing in the house. Can you believe it? And our place practically falling asunder? The two of them are next door putting in a new kitchen at the moment." She shook her head. "I'm pleased they're getting on so well, actually. For some reason, I got the impression that Luke didn't really take to Eric initially." She frowned. "But they certainly seem grand now."

"I'm so glad you two managed to work things out – and I'm especially glad that ..." the rest of her sentence trailed off. "Well, you know ... that it had nothing to do with anyone else."

"Thank you," Liz said, a guilty smile on her face.

"Thanks for what?"

"For not vocalising my own suspicions back to me. I wouldn't have been able to handle it if you'd told me you had the same idea – about Emma. Convincing myself that it was all in my own head was what kept me sane, so you really don't know how much I appreciate that."

Tara smiled back. "Well, at least the mystery has been solved. I was going mad trying to figure it out. I'd started to wonder only recently if she might have had a bit of thing with Dave McNamara, but wouldn't say anything because of him getting engaged. What with him being a councillor and a pillar of the community."

"Interesting theory all the same," Liz agreed nodding thoughtfully.

"I nearly fell down when she told us, though," Tara continued. "I knew she had a thing for unavailable men, but ... Though apparently he's determined to give her all the support she needs, which is great, so ..." She'd known that her sister had always had a bit of a soft spot for Colm – as had many women over the years – but had no idea that it had been anything more. "But can you imagine what'll it be like around here when the news finally gets out?" In the end, her poor sister had been right to keep it quiet for as long as possible. "The gossips will have a field day."

"I don't envy her to be fair. But Emma's a resilient girl – I'm sure she'll cope."

"Resilient?" Tara repeated wryly. "That's a slightly different description to the one you said you used the night she was here, isn't it?"

Liz grimaced. "I know – I feel awful now. But I was so angry I *had* to lash out."

"From what you were telling me, she was messing with your head anyway. She seems to like doing that." Tara had already told Liz all about Jason's call after Glenn was born, and how Emma hadn't mentioned anything. "I just hope that when she does have this baby, she'll stop all her silly games and start behaving like an adult."

"At least the child will have two other sensible parents to rely on if she isn't up to the task," Liz quipped, unable to resist a giggle.

"Less of the sneering at my family, Liz McGrath," Tara joked. "Now you're sounding like one of the natives."

"Yep, with all these secrets and lies, I think I've just

about qualified," her friend laughed. "And speaking of which, are you going to make the move?"

"Where? Back here?"

"Of course."

"Dunno. I've thought about it a lot lately – especially now after all this stuff with Glenn, but I just don't know."

"I know someone who'd be happy about it anyway," Liz said, her eyes dancing.

"Who?"

"Well, our favourite next-door neighbour for one. He's always asking for you. Every time I meet him he manages to bring the conversation round to you."

Tara snorted. "Probably just needs a pest controller."

Liz rolled her eyes. "Bloody hell woman, can you not see something when it's staring you plain in the face?"

"What do you mean?"

"Luke's mad about you. And I know you're a bit partial to him too – I saw you that night in the pub. So you'd want to do something about it before someone else snaps him up. I know I would, if I was single, which I'm not of course," she added primly. "In fact, I'm very happy with my man."

"You and Natalie both then," Tara said.

She had phoned again a couple of days after her conversation with Jason.

"I'd love us to stay friends," the other girl said, "but I know it's not ideal. Especially not since," then she added, almost apologetically, "Jay's asked me to move in with him."

"Natalie, I'm so happy for you, truly I am," Tara assured her, "but you don't need me to help you out with your love life. And don't apologise for that," she added quickly, before the other woman could speak. "You and

Jason ... Jay . . . are obviously well-suited and you deserve to be happy. You both do."

"Tara, I really don't know what to say," Natalie blubbed. "Never in a million years did I expect something like this."

"I'm sure we'll keep in touch."

But of course that wouldn't happen and they both knew it.

It was a shame, because she guessed in different circumstances, she and Natalie would remain great friends, but such was life.

Though she couldn't help but be reminded of Jason's comment about how the universe conspired. So maybe she shouldn't think too more about it and just leave it all up to the gods.

"I'm telling you – you'd better do something about Luke," Liz was saying. "The other day, I saw Nina Hughes flirting with him in the greengrocer's."

Although Tara thought, smiling to herself, as she thought about it, maybe this time, she should just bite the bullet and take destiny into her own hands.

FIFTY-FIVE

A WEEK LATER, Tara approached the front door and rang the bell.

What the hell was she doing here? And *why* had she let Liz talk her into this?

"Hi."

When he opened the door his eyes lit up, but when he looked down and noticed what she was holding, he quickly took a step backwards. "What ... what's that?"

"This? Oh nothing." She tried to sound nonchalant. "Hey the place is looking great." Tara looked past his bulky frame into the hallway. The walls were freshly painted, there was a new wooden floor and skirting in place of the old worn linoleum, and from her vantage point, she could see that he'd redone some of the kitchen too. "Well, aren't you going to invite me in? Or do I have to stand out here all day?"

"Erm, sure." Still trying to avert his eyes, he stood back to allow her entry.

"Well," she announced breezily. "You've certainly been busy."

"Yes ... erm what *is* that?" Luke urged again, his voice quivering a little.

"Oh, this?" Tara held up the cage as if she'd forgotten all about it. "A gerbil," she told him nonchalantly. "Isn't he cute?"

"Right. And what is it doing *here*?" he asked, backing away.

"Ah silly me – I forgot. It's a present," she said, thrusting it at him.

Immediately he recoiled. "A present?"

"Yep - a housewarming present."

"Erm, Tara, it's very nice of you to think of me but –"

"I thought it was perfect."

"Um – why?"

"Well, I get that this is more my territory than yours, but you do know the best way to overcome your fears is to face them head on, don't you?"

And by being here today, that was exactly what *she* was doing. Finally taking Liz's advice, Tara was opening herself up to the possibility of a relationship, friendship ... whatever, with Luke.

It may well come to nothing but wasn't it – as Liz always insisted – wasn't it worth taking the chance?

It's not as though she could use Glenn as an excuse anymore. He and Abby had since announced they were moving in together, and as much as it would kill her to let him go, Tara knew she had no choice.

She needed to allow her son to get on with his own life, and now she with hers.

Starting today.

"Hey, I appreciate the gesture but – "

"Just let me help, OK?"

"Help with what? I'm already overrun with feckin' mice, I don't need another rodent to add to my collection."

"I told you – it's not a mouse – it's a gerbil," she repeated, thrusting the cage at him. As he reached out to take it, their fingers touched and an unmistakeable spark of electricity passed between them.

For a long moment, the two remained still - gazes locked together - while in between, the gerbil innocently munched on a piece of lettuce.

"Tara," Luke said, gently resting the cage on the floor, "did it ever cross your mind that I might not *want* to make friends with rodents? That I'd much rather make friends with a more ... agreeable species?"

"Like what?"

That bright flash of attraction, the promise of more to come - she hadn't felt something like it in a very long time.

And all at once she realised how much she missed it.

"Like ... you," Luke admitted, folding her into his huge arms and making Tara feel - in more ways than one - that finally she'd come home.

Read more unputdownable novels by Melissa Hill, available now.

Read on for an excerpt of her latest pageturner,
ONE LAST THING.

ONE LAST THING

Just when everything is falling into place, fate has a habit of throwing curveballs ...

After a series of relationship disasters, life is finally good for Jenny. She's planning her wedding and looking forward to settling down with the perfect man. Until one fateful morning, her troubled past rears its head again in an unexpected way.

And the timing truly could not be worse.

Fiercely independent Karen is launching a legal challenge to help pick up the pieces of her own shattered life. And even though her battle seems doomed to fail, there's no way she's going down without a fight.

Over the years, the one thing both women could truly count on was their friendship. Or so it seemed.

But when a devastating truth is uncovered, can anything - including their bond - remain?

ONE

THE SCALES LAY MENACINGLY on the bathroom floor, daring Jenny to put herself out of her misery.

She stepped on and felt her throat go dry watching the needle come to a standstill after a long time bobbing back and forth. Then winced at the verdict.

Damnit, she really needed to get her act together.

Getting into the shower, she heard Mike whistle from downstairs in the kitchen. She couldn't understand how her fiancé could be so sprightly in the mornings. He never seemed to want to pull the bedcovers over his head and drift back to glorious sleep, shutting out the rest of the world. Whereas she was *definitely* not a morning person.

Pity this exam was so soon she sighed, rinsing the shampoo out of her hair. She would need to study like the clappers today, so the earlier she got started the better. No way she'd nab this promotion if she didn't pass.

Life was so chaotic lately she'd been finding it hard to concentrate, but needed to make up for lost time now and hope that today's cramming would be enough. To be fair,

Mike had gone out of his way to ensure that she had a quiet day to herself.

Jenny wrapped her wet hair in a towel before joining her fiancé downstairs in the kitchen.

He put a steaming mug and a plate of warm buttered toast on the table in front of her and kissed her lightly on the forehead.

"Morning sunshine."

She made a face.

He chuckled. "Now I know why I'm marrying you – your morning scowl always brightens up my day."

Biting back a grin, she took a bite of toast, grimaced and then spat it back out onto the plate. "Ugh. What's that?"

"What's what?"

"The toast - what did you put on the toast?"

"Kerrygold," he answered nonchalantly. "Why?"

"Kerrygold...." She trailed off in amazement. "I'm eating Low-Low these days, remember. I *can't* have real butter on my toast or anything else when I'm watching the scales."

"Low-Low, huh?" he said, his eyes twinkling with amusement. "So Leo Burdock's fry chips in Low-Low these days?"

"That's different. Chipper chips don't count..."

"Right," he said, struggling to keep a straight face. "Come on Jen, forget this dieting nonsense – you're perfect the way you are." He reached across the breakfast bar and planted another kiss on the top of her head.

"Nope, I'm determined, *really* determined to fit into that wedding dress in my wardrobe."

"Really determined, huh?"

"Absolutely."

"Right. So what about the Low-Low thing?"

"What?"

His eyes danced. "You're still eating that toast."

"But that's because – because I'm rushing, so I don't have time to wait for fresh stuff and – ah, stop it ..." Despite herself, Jenny chuckled, until remembering what lay ahead. "I dread hitting the books and look – it's such a nice day too." She looked wistfully out the window at the cloudless spring sky.

"You'll be fine once you get started." Mike pushed his plate away and refilled his teacup. "Anyway, it will be all over soon and then you can forget about it."

"That's the problem though," she mused. "It's *too* soon." She picked up one of the study manuals that lay on the table and stared at it as if willing the info to transport itself from the pages into her memory.

"You'll be grand," he soothed again. "You're already familiar with most of the material. Haven't you been working alongside the mortgage manager for months? You're bound to have picked up on the important stuff. Just use today's peace and quiet to cram and then tomorrow night we'll go out for a bite and a couple of drinks. What do you think?"

Jenny nodded and they shook on it. He was right. There was no point in fretting about the exam. She should just get stuck in.

"I was thinking," he added. "If you don't mind combining work and play, I might ask the new guy along. I haven't had a chance to get to know him socially yet."

Jenny helped herself to another piece of toast. "Cool,"

she said. "I'm eager to meet the new whizz kid too. What's he like?"

"I think he's going to be a real asset. He's had plenty of marketing experience and you know how useless I am at that."

She smiled. Mike was an excellent programmer and while his firm provided software for some of Ireland's biggest companies, he was no marketeer. His business needed the right person to promote their stuff within a rapidly saturated Irish market. He and his partners had been trying for some time to find someone who knew the industry from the inside out. Seemed this new guy was a rare breed: a highly proficient programmer and equally adept at sales and marketing.

"He's no fool either," Mike continued. "Took us a while to hammer out a decent contract. Fresh from the States, he didn't want to come in on ground level and commission bonuses like the rest of them. Stephen thought he was a cocky little git."

"Ha. I'll bet he was just disappointed that you weren't employing some ravishing redhead with a cleavage to die for."

He chuckled at her all too accurate assessment of his business partner. "The lads already had a few run-ins as it is. Poor Frank kept calling him Ronan last week – he couldn't get the hang of his name and your man wouldn't stand for it. It's Roan, not Ro-n-an,'" Mike mimicked exaggeratedly.

Jenny's toast stopped halfway to her mouth. "What did you say his name was?"

"I know. Unusual, isn't it? Roan – I've never come

across it before. I think he's originally from Kildare some-where, he said."

Her mouth went dry and for a second she didn't think she would be able to breathe.

It couldn't be *him*, could it?

"I knew a guy from Kildare a few years back when I lived with Karen," she said, trying to keep her voice even, although her hands were shaking. "Roan Williams – I wonder is it the same person?"

Mike didn't seem to notice her discomfort.

"Yeah, Williams, that's his surname all right. Crikey. It's true what they say about it being a small world. Did you know him well?"

Jenny tried to swallow. The toast felt like a lead weight in her mouth. "Not that well," she answered auto-matically, her mind racing, unable to get to grips with this.

Roan Williams of all people ... working with Mike. Should she just say something? No, not yet. She needed some time to think about this, to process it.

Her fiancé's voice interrupted her thoughts. "Jen, did you hear me? Maybe we should go into the city centre tomorrow night – what do you think?"

She looked at him blankly.

"OK." He held his hands up, chuckling. "You're miles away already so I'll leave you to it. I'm off to battle the traffic and when I get home this evening, I'll pretend to be a first-time buyer and you can tell me everything there is to know about securing a mortgage for the house of my dreams, OK?" He drained his cup and put it in the sink, then gave Jenny a light kiss on the nose.

She instantly felt like a heel. "Sorry, I don't know how you put up with me. I'm just a bit … distracted."

"Dunno either, but come August I'm stuck with you for good so I suppose I'd better get used to it." She swung at him as he ducked out the doorway, laughing as he went. "Oh, and don't forget," he added, popping his head back around the door. "I'll be back a bit later this evening so don't start on dinner too early."

"Are you sure you don't want me to go? I can always finish up early …"

"It's grand. I just wish my little sister would get herself a job south of the Liffey and save us the journey. See you later."

Jenny nodded and forced another smile but it was a relief to see him leave. She remained sitting at the kitchen table for a long time after she heard the front door close, her thoughts going a mile a minute.

She shook her head, unable to believe this was happening, to say nothing of the timing.

Just when everything was going so well, fate had to throw one last curveball.

TWO

Karen checked her watch and quickened her pace as she strode down Grafton Street, cursing under her breath when she read the time.

She was going to be late.

It was almost nine o'clock and she still had to find the place. Pushing her dark hair away from her face, she stopped suddenly when an outfit caught her eye in the window of Pamela Scott - a seventies-print halterneck dress that would be perfect for Jenny's wedding.

Pity she already had her outfit. Ah, she might buy it for herself anyway. With everything that was happening lately, she deserved a treat.

Karen continued quickly towards College Green, and just as she reached the pedestrian crossing at Trinity College, she heard her phone ring from inside her handbag. The lights went green and she struggled to find the device whilst crossing the road. Blasted things....

She'd only just stepped into the doorway of the Victorian bank building to take the call when the ringing promptly stopped. Typical.

"Shite," she exclaimed, glaring at a passer-by who was staring at her with undisguised interest. She was about to replace the phone in her handbag when it beeped loudly.

A text from Jenny: *CALL ME AS SOON AS YOU GET THIS.*

Sadly her friend would have to wait, Karen thought, rushing up the street. She was *definitely* late now. She raced along and eventually stopped in front of a building with Stevenson & Donnelly Solicitors inscribed on a brass plaque by the doorway. Then pushed the intercom buzzer to gain entry.

Inside, the receptionist smiled at her. "Miss Cassidy? Mr Donnelly is ready for you." She gestured to one of the doorways behind the reception area. "Would you like some coffee?"

"I'd love a cup, thanks." Karen smiled back as she removed her coat and knocked on the heavy wooden door.

"Come in, please."

She was duly greeted with a nod from a serious-looking older man seated behind a large oak desk with heavy books and sheets of paper strewn all over it.

Typical solicitor's practice.

"Karen, hello. It's nice to finally meet you face to face. Please – sit down." The solicitor gestured to the plush leather armchair in front of his desk.

"I'm very sorry I'm late, I couldn't find you at first."

"That's no trouble at all, dear. Did Linda offer you some coffee?"

At that very moment the aforementioned receptionist

appeared with a tray, and Karen gratefully accepted a mug of strong coffee and a Rich Tea biscuit.

"Thank you, Linda." The solicitor smiled and then sat back in his chair. "So, let's get down to brass tacks. We discussed the basics over the phone but I just want to run through the broader specifics with you again, to get a better sense of the issue. The property in question - it's located in Harold's Cross, you said?"

Karen nodded. "Yes, a two-bedroom townhouse jointly purchased a couple of years ago."

"And there's a mortgage remaining on the property?"

"Yes. Which is basically the root of the problem. I'm unsure of my rights – legally I mean, because the house was never in my name. I just didn't see any need at the time."

"I see. Both mortgage and property were solely in your partner's name?"

"That's right," she answered solemnly.

"But you contributed financially throughout."

"Oh, absolutely – Shane and I each had separate accounts but we keep – I mean we kept – a joint account for utility bills, heating and whatever."

"Well, that's a start certainly. I assume you have bank statements that verify same? And Mr Quinn does not dispute the fact that you made mortgage contributions?"

"Not as far as I know, he doesn't. It's just ..." Despite herself, Karen was nervous. "From what I've read, it seems that it was always Shane's house, wasn't it – legally I mean and what I paid means nothing?"

"Mr Quinn may have been registered as sole mortgage holder, but in truth, the building society holds full title until the mortgage is fully repaid. Though based on what you've just outlined, any courtroom is likely to rule in favour of the other party."

He was so dispassionate about it all. Didn't he realise how hard it was for her to come here and discuss all of this with a complete stranger? Still, it meant nothing to him, she supposed. He was just doing his job. Sympathy didn't come into it. Karen had sought his advice and here he was advising her. What did she expect; a big hug, soothing words and a box of Kleenex?

"You see," she told him, "I have nowhere else to go so I'm still living there. Mr Quinn has asked – " She frowned. *Asked? That was an understatement.* "that I move out so that it can be sold. But I don't see why I should move out. That's why I'm determined to bring this to court. That house is my home and it's just not fair that he can evict me after ... everything."

She noticed that Donnelly was writing all of this down on a notepad as she spoke. At least she *thought* he was. Maybe he was just doodling; bored by her predicament. Probably used to more exciting stuff.

The solicitor said nothing for a while until he asked, "I assume you've discussed all this with Mr Quinn at some point?"

Karen stiffened. "At this stage, we communicate purely through our solicitors. Mine – the one I had before you I mean – initially hoped we might be able to come to an arrangement. But Mr Quinn and I have quite an ... acrimonious relationship. He won't agree that I'm entitled to anything. Which is why I am here with you today."

She was amazed at how civil she made it all sound.

"I see," Donnelly stated. "Well, as things stand at the

moment you may indeed have no option but to take this to the courts. You are quite fortunate that Mr Quinn has let you stay on so far. However, I would imagine – if things are as you say – that he may well be keen to move on and bring matters to a satisfactory conclusion."

Karen was fuming. Why was he taking *his* side? Keen to move on indeed. He made it sound like she was nothing – just a temporary inconvenience. What about *her* feelings? She wanted this sorted out so she could begin to move on too. But she'd be damned if she was going to just roll over and play dead. There was no way anyone was going to throw her out on the street. She had paid her dues too; hadn't Donnelly himself admitted that?

The solicitor noticed her expression and smiled kindly.

"My dear, I know nothing about your personal relationship with Mr Quinn, which has no bearing on this situation regardless. I'm merely discussing legal options with you, but one thing you also need to consider is that the sooner this matter is resolved, the better for both parties."

Karen nodded. This was awful. At least with marriage, everything was pretty much black and white and you knew your rights.

How did it ever come to this? she wondered, her heart aching afresh. She and Shane had so much fun at the beginning, picking out bits and pieces in DIY and furniture stores, and making that house into a home together.

Stop it, she warned herself then. Don't get maudlin; just concentrate on the task at hand.

"I understand and I'm sorry if I seem a little ... emotional." Her head lowered and she looked up at him through dark eyelashes. "I suppose I just never considered that something like this could happen." She felt a lump form in her throat.

"I appreciate the personal difficulty," he said kindly, "but now you must try to be pragmatic. Please think some more about an agreement with Mr Quinn before you opt for the courts. Because you were never married and the house was never in your name I worry that your claim may be dismissed as frivolous. As for contents ... this is something you may well have to iron out between you. Unless you have retained receipts for each purchase, it is nigh on impossible to ascertain ownership of fixtures, furniture etc." The solicitor leaned forward and regarded her thoughtfully. "Are you absolutely sure that you want to follow through, my dear? I must tell you that I don't believe you can retain even part-ownership of the property. The law is pretty clear in this instance."

Karen wasn't fazed. "You're not the first person, or indeed the first professional to tell me that. But I owe it to myself to follow through, and I'm determined that nobody will take that house from me – not without a fight."

He set down his pen. "All right. I'll press ahead with Mr Quinn's solicitor and be in touch again with next steps."

Karen stood up and went to shake his hand. "Thank you. And thanks also for taking the case. This means a lot to me. I haven't had much luck over the last while."

"You're welcome and rest assured that I'll try my best for you." He smiled and shook her hand warmly. "You have my number– any further queries, please give me a call."

As she left, Donnelly noticed the steely determination in her dark eyes and shook his head as he sat back down behind his desk. It was a common occurrence these days.

So many couples buying property outside of marriage without giving a second thought to their legal rights should anything go awry.

Poor girl, she was determined to go as far as she could with this. And despite his intricate knowledge of the law and the futility of such a case, the solicitor hoped that somehow, this lady might emerge victorious.

She deserved to.

THREE

"Not much of a housekeeper, is she?"

Barbara Quinn looked around the small kitchen and wrinkled her nose in disgust, eyeing used teabags on the table, a smear of butter and scattering of crumbs on the worktop, dried spaghetti on the wall above the cooker and a pile of used dishes in the sink.

"No, tidiness was never Karen's forte," her brother agreed, opening the fridge and stepping back as a strong whiff of something unidentifiable filled his nostrils.

"I wish the estate agent would hurry up. What if she comes back?" Barbara didn't want to stay here any longer than necessary. She was sorry she had come actually; sorry that her curiosity had got the better of her. The place was an absolute dive.

"Relax, she's at work." He looked around the room and frowned. "It *is* an awful mess, isn't it? I suppose I'd better go upstairs and do a bit of tidying up in the bedrooms."

"Don't be long. It's nearly lunchtime and I fancy going into town for a bite once we're finished."

Barbara went into the living room and flopped onto the small two-seater couch among a couple of brightly coloured scatter cushions. This was a nice room. The bay window was a lovely feature and seemed to make the space feel a lot bigger than it was. Despite the mismatched furniture and that gaudy rug.

If she got her hands on it, she'd replace the cheap pine laminate flooring with solid oak, and have the walls repainted a more muted colour - anything but that vulgar terracotta. And purple cushions on a cornflower-yellow couch? That girl hadn't an ounce of taste.

Barbara picked up a magazine from the coffee table and began to flick idly through it. She was studying a page from the fashion section so intently that she didn't hear the key turn in the front door. She did, however, hear it shut and startled by the noise, leapt up from the couch.

"Hello," Jenny greeted, surprised. "I didn't realise there was anyone here. Karen's on her way – she just stopped off at the shop. She gave me the keys." She held them up apologetically.

"He's just upstairs. I'll get him," Barbara mumbled, quickly starting up the steps, but mercifully her brother was already on his way down.

"Jenny, how are you? I haven't seen you since –"

"Fine, thanks," she interjected shortly. "I didn't realise you'd be here today." Before adding pointedly, "I don't think Karen did either."

"Well, we just needed to check out a few things." He nodded at his companion. "You remember Barbara, don't you?"

Jenny turned and studied her with undisguised

surprise. Shane's sister – she hadn't recognised her at all. She was certain that her hair had been darker the last time she'd seen her.

"Can we go now, please?" Barbara asked, ignoring Jenny. "I don't think I can stand the stench in here any longer and now my skirt's ruined too. Those cushion covers have obviously never been washed."

Jenny examined the other woman's clothing for signs of spoilage but couldn't see a thing. The cheek of it – Karen would be livid. She was sure that her friend had no idea anyone was here. And if Jenny had known from the outset who was, she wouldn't have been so pleasant when she came in.

"I suppose we'd better go," he muttered. "Nice seeing you again, Jenny."

"No rush. I'm sure Karen would like to see you both before you go," she replied archly, enjoying the sight of the two of them squirming.

"Ah no, sure we'll head away – we have to be some-where else anyway. Tell her I said – "

The door slammed and they heard a voice call out angrily from the hallway. "You can tell me yourself!"

Karen bustled past, her arms laden down with groceries. She dropped the shopping bags and turned to him, furious. "What the hell is going on? How did you get in?"

"Now hang on just a minute. I have as much right to be here as you do – more actually."

"Well, I've got news for you, Quinn. According to my latest solicitor, I've paid my dues too. Which means," she added, eyes blazing, "that I have every right to tell you to get the hell out of here." She was pleased to see his eyes widen at the mention of a new solicitor. "Why did you have to go behind my back?" she continued. "But that's not your style, is it? You can't be straight up about anything; never could."

"Maybe you'd better leave," Jenny said quietly, feeling that she needed to say something to defuse the situation.

The sister rounded on Karen. "How dare you? You're lucky that he's let you stay here for as long he has. If it was up to me ... " Barbara trailed off, glaring at her. "Though at least it won't be long before we're all rid of you – finally."

"Barbs, there's no need to upset anyone – we're going now ..."

Just then, the doorbell rang, and the Quinns looked decidedly nervous as Karen went to answer.

"Hello, Patrick from Ryan Mitchell Auctioneers," said the affable-looking man standing in the doorway. "I'm here for the valuation."

"Valuation..." Karen whirled around to face them. "You organised a valuation on my house without my permission? How dare you. How *dare* you try to sell this house from under me, you gutless bastard..."

"Erm, maybe now's not a good time ..." the estate agent murmured, mortified.

"You're damn right it's not," Karen growled. "I'm very sorry but it seems that someone has wasted your time. There will be no valuation of this property today - and not for as long as I'm here."

"We'll see how much longer that will be," Barbara hissed, easing out the door past the white-faced agent, who stood back unsure of what to do next. Eventually, he retreated to the safety of his car parked a little way down the road.

When the siblings followed, Jenny closed the door behind them and went back into the living room.

Karen was sitting on the couch and hugging one of the purple and gold Sari cushions she was so fond of, her face red with anger.

"How *dare* he come here behind my back? And worse, I would never have known if I wasn't off today. It mightn't have been the first time either – he could have been here loads of times that I didn't know about." Enraged, she threw the cushion across the room. "Why did he have to go behind my back and why did he bring that botoxed, bleached-blonde bimbo with him?"

Then despite her tears, she grinned, seeing Jenny trying to hide a smile.

"Sure enough the place would have to be in an awful state. I was late for my appointment this morning, so I didn't get a chance to tidy up." She snorted. "Typical."

"*He* had a cheek coming in without telling you, don't forget," Jenny reminded her.

"I know that Jen, it's just that I don't want to give him any excuse to get me out." She sniffed. "But the solicitor I met with this morning reckons that he'll take the case for me."

"I'd forgotten that you were seeing him today. That's great news. What else did he say?"

"I'll tell you over a cuppa and a muffin." Karen stood up, gathered her shopping and went into the kitchen. She put the food in the cupboards and then filled the kettle, absently removing a piece of dried spaghetti that had somehow ended up on the wall above the cooker. Then turned back to Jenny. "First, you tell *me* why you sounded so anxious in that text earlier. And why you're here now, instead of at home studying?"

Jenny glanced down at the floor. "It's nothing really; you've enough on your plate. Tell me what the solicitor said about the case."

Karen picked a chocolate chip from one of the muffins and popped it into her mouth. "Forget that. I know there's something up. Did you and Mike have a fight?"

Jenny sat down at the untidy kitchen table and absently began playing with the sugar bowl. "No. But the thing ... the thing is ... I think Roan's back."

Her friend immediately stopped picking at the muffin.

"Roan Williams? Back here - in Ireland, you mean?"

Jenny nodded, her eyes firmly fixed on the table in front of her.

"But how do you know?" Karen asked. "Have you seen him, have you heard from him .... what do you mean you *think* he's back?"

"He's back in Dublin and he's taken a job at InTech." Catching her look of disbelief, Jenny continued. "Mike told me his name this morning – you know the way they've been looking for someone to take over the sales and marketing end? Apparently, the new guy is Roan."

"But are you sure? I mean, how do you know it's actually him? Oh," she said, as a thought crossed her mind. "Mike doesn't know, does he? Roan didn't say anything ...."

"I doubt he'd know that Mike had any connection to me. Anyway," she looked away, "it's unlikely he's given me a second thought since."

"Jenny, are you absolutely certain that it's the same Roan? I know it's an unusual name but ..."

"With the same surname and from Kildare too?"

Karen grimaced. She poured boiling water into the teapot and stirred it. Then she looked at Jenny and hesitated a second before speaking. "Look I don't mean to sound flippant, but ... well, that was years ago. His coming home shouldn't mean anything to you at this point."

Tears were streaming down Jenny's face now, and Karen noticed that she was shaking. Perplexed, she went to put a comforting arm around her friend's shoulders.

"You're not still carrying a torch for him, surely? You've got Mike now and he's one of the nicest guys you could meet. You're getting married soon and –"

"It's not that and ... hell, I *know* I should have told you already. To be honest I didn't know where to start..."

"Go on," Karen urged, somewhat perturbed.

Jenny took a mouthful of steaming tea and looked her friend squarely in the eye. The hot liquid burned her throat as she swallowed, but she didn't care.

"It's just ... it's just ... you know pretty much everything about that time. You were there for most of it, after all. But there's something you don't know, one last thing I was afraid to share that could ruin everything..."

CONTINUE READING *ONE LAST THING*, out now in print & ebook.

ABOUT THE AUTHOR

International #1 and USA Today bestselling author Melissa Hill lives in County Wicklow, Ireland.

Her page-turning emotional stories of family, friendship and romance have been translated into 25 different languages and are regular chart-toppers internationally.

A Reese Witherspoon x Hello Sunshine adaptation of her worldwide bestseller SOMETHING FROM TIFFANY'S is streaming now on Amazon Prime Video worldwide.

THE CHARM BRACELET aired in 2020 as a holiday movie A Little Christmas Charm. A GIFT TO REMEMBER (and a sequel) was also adapted for screen by Hallmark Channel and multiple other titles by Melissa are currently in development for film and TV.

Visit her website at
www.melissahill.info
Or get in touch via social media links below.

Printed in Dunstable, United Kingdom

67844215R00211